HAPPYISH

ALSO BY JEANETTE ESCUDERO

The Apology Project

HAPPYISH

A NOVEL

JEANETTE ESCUDERO

LAKE UNION
PUBLISHING

Text copyright © 2022 by Jeanette Escudero
All rights reserved.

Published by Lake Union Publishing, Seattle

www.apub.com

Amazon, the Amazon logo, and Lake Union Publishing are trademarks of Amazon.com, Inc., or its affiliates.

ISBN-13: 9781542032674
ISBN-10: 1542032679

Cover design by Philip Pascuzzo

Printed in the United States of America

Now that I have a daughter, all I can say is: Sorry, Mom, you were right all along!

PROLOGUE

I'm a feminist. A hard-ass, bra-burning feminist. I was raised by two mothers who instilled the belief in me that anything a man can do, a woman can do better. And I truly believe this to my core.

Or so I thought.

Apparently, my brain chose this moment to turn its back on my deep-rooted beliefs. Right now, staring me in the face, with its disgusting little moving antennae and segmented legs, there's a cockroach mocking me. When I was married, Michael killed all the roaches. That was his job: as a man, as my husband, but mostly as someone whose skin didn't crawl at the mere mention of a roach.

I've made it this last year without Michael, without falling apart, without needing anyone. Today, my divorceaversary, is all about perseverance and accomplishments. I will not let this flying insect best me, but the roach is standing between me and the elevator, and it won't move. We're at a standstill, and Michael isn't here to fix it.

"Shoo. Shoo. Go away!" I yell from afar, and then it inches up a bit, its wings expand, and I squeal like a little un-feminist girl and decide to take the stairs.

I haven't had any of these "Michael moments" in months, and today is not the day for it. I will not let such an insignificant thing like a roach ruin my day.

Just ten minutes ago, there was a spring in my step, a little orb of sunshine around me, an actual rush of joy in my soul that I'm going to channel back and forget the vermin that forced me to take the stairs.

Okay, okay. I'll try and tone it down. It's only nine in the morning, and most people will side-eye me or give me the finger if I start belting a show tune at this time of the day.

It's just that exactly a year ago today, I was at rock bottom. I didn't think I'd ever smile again, and not only am I smiling, but I'm also excited for what's ahead.

It didn't come suddenly. I didn't wake up and just snap my fingers and decide to be content. I wish it was that easy. It's been growing, like a tiny plant that you water and feed and love and then one day two leaves fall off and it starts to tilt sideways and wilt and you know it's going to die. You give up hope and ignore it. But then one day, you look across the room, and there's a flower bud. You didn't even know it would survive, let alone flower.

That was me: an almost-dead potted plant that woke up a year later and realized—holy crap, I'm blooming! I've survived. Things will be all right.

Why not celebrate all the small milestones of the last year—post-divorce? Last week, I put an offer on my very own condo, and it was accepted. That same afternoon, my boss put me in charge of a major project, which I'm now pitching this afternoon. I've even been able to save money, despite leaving my divorce with a total of six hundred and twenty-one measly dollars and seventy-nine miserable cents in my bank account and half a worthless home. Half, because I had to split the gains and losses (all losses) evenly with my ex, and it turns out we owed more than it was worth. And finally, I think I no longer want to hunt down my ex and kick him in the balls. So much growth!

Even my migraines are about to get resolved. I'm on my way to the doctor, and once he injects me with some of that magical migraine-killing Botox or gives me some other medicine, I'll be all set.

PART ONE

BOB

CHAPTER ONE

"Can you spell that, please?"

"Alexa, if you'd please take a seat—"

"My name is not Alexa. It's Alex. Just Alex," I say and tap my pen on the piece of paper I've taken out of my purse, waiting for him to spell the words that sound very scary and very foreign and very, very much like cancer.

The roach was absolutely a bad omen.

"C-e-r-e-b-r-a-l m-e-n-i-n-g-i-o-m-a," Dr. Devi says slowly as I write out the words. Later—could be tonight, could be next week— when I process this, I'll need to know what to type into WebMD.

"Cerebral meningioma," I repeat and then tuck the paper into my purse. The words are unfamiliar to my mouth.

"Alex, did you understand what I explained? Do you have any questions? I know it's a lot to take in."

Are you kidding me? I have *all* the questions! But I don't say that. Instead, I succumb to the fog and the tunnel vision and the headache I came in for—it's now a full drum line beating in my skull. "Nope. I'm good."

"Please sit. I think we need to discuss this further."

This is the second time I've met with Dr. Devi. The first time was three weeks ago, and that time he called me Alexandra. For someone who's giving me what feels like a death sentence, he should at least know my first name, right? Anyway, I came to see him because I fell at work. Okay, it wasn't exactly a fall. I'd been having a migraine for two solid days, and I got up too quickly from a meeting that lasted twenty-seven years, and my legs gave out on me. I was sure it was just a head rush or maybe my legs fell asleep from sitting so long.

Unfortunately, Bernard Rey, my boss, saw the entire humiliating spectacle and insisted I (strong-armed me to) schedule an appointment with the doctor. Consequently, I called my PCP, who recommended I see a neurologist who could prescribe something for the migraines. And here I am. With a cerebral meningioma—whatever the hell that is.

I thought going to the doctor was a waste of time and I hate—*hate*—people fussing over me. When I was sixteen, I fell off my bike and broke my arm in two places. I didn't tell anyone until the pain was so unbearable, I just couldn't hold it in any longer. My mothers drove me to the hospital, and when we got back home, Mima immediately took my bicycle to Goodwill. I didn't ride a bike again for ten years. *"Of course you didn't forget how to ride a bike,"* Michael had said with a giggle as he helped me on the shiny yellow cruiser he'd gifted me one Christmas. *"There's a saying for that exact thing!"* I exhale loudly. I don't know why that particular memory comes back into my mind when this is so much worse than any broken arm. Except that my arm had hurt like hell and my head . . . it doesn't hurt. At least not right now and not very often.

People get headaches all the time. I'm overworked and overstressed, but who am I to complain about that? I'm blessed to have a great job and to have pulled myself out of the hellish year I've had. Less than an hour ago, freaking rainbows were practically shooting out of my butt.

And now here I am, with a tumor. Who has time for a tumor? I certainly don't.

"Alex, please—" He again points to the chair.

"I can't." I wave him off. "I have a presentation in the office in an hour, and then I have my divorceaversary party. If I don't leave now,

I'll be late." Also, the walls seem to be closing in on me, and I need air. Fresh, outside, doctor-free air.

He looks bewildered for a split second, then reverts to that fake-friendly tone doctors use when delivering bad news. "Ms. Martinez—Alex—the tumor is large. It's pressing against important nerves in the part of the brain that controls your extremities. Without surgery, you—"

"Yep. Paralyzed. You said that already."

"Actually, no. I did not say paralyzed. I said trouble walking. Lack of muscle control and/or stability. It could also cause seizures and memory loss. It absolutely accounts for your headaches, as well. It's a very slow-growing tumor. You've likely had this for a long time. Unfortunately, it's reached a point where it must be removed." He's still pointing to the chair, but I just hoist my purse higher on my shoulder and take a step closer to the door. I need to get out of here. The walls are closing in on me.

"Can you give me a time frame? Are we looking at days or years?"

"It's hard to say. It's not days. I would say that based on its size, location, and the manifestations you're already exhibiting . . . four or five months before you start exhibiting major problems."

I've never had a panic attack before, but maybe . . . am I having a heart attack? I'm having something, that's for sure. My breathing is labored, and my palms are clammy, and I'm transported to the day we received the news that Annabel had leukemia. I wasn't at the doctor visit that day, but I vividly remember seeing my mothers' faces when they arrived home that afternoon. The level of stress, worry, and heartbreak reflected on both their faces was tangible. They didn't have to say the C-word to know that they'd been given the dreadful news.

My mothers . . . Mima, specifically. She can't know about this. Oh my God, what if they find out? I don't want to be the cause of that level of worry. Hell, I don't think a human being can be given that news twice in their lifetime and survive. I start really panicking now.

The doctor approaches me cautiously. Like a person approaching a skittish cat about to bolt or scratch his eyes out. I hold my hands up defensively and take half a step, my back hitting the door. I need space. I don't like being coddled or pitied. I just need to get out of here and think. Alone.

"Alex?" he begins.

"My sister, she died of leukemia."

He looks at me, frazzled. "You don't have leukemia."

"I know, but that was bad. She was on machines and radiation and chemo for a long time. When she was diagnosed, they told her it was not an aggressive form of leukemia and that they'd caught it early and she'd be okay, but she died anyway."

"That's not what is happening here, Alex," he tries to reassure me, but there's no reassurance. As a rational person, I am aware that I'm not being rational right now, but I can't help it. I remember all the years Annabel spent in and out of the hospital and the toll it took on my moms. I can't go through that again.

They cannot go through that again.

"Today was supposed to be a good day," I say, as if we'd been mid-discussion instead of me making my big grand escape. But I need him to understand something that I don't understand myself. "My husband left me, in a note, and today is the anniversary of my divorce. Can you believe that? A note!" I snort and continue talking. One of my mothers is Cuban, so I tend to use my hands a lot in conversation, especially when I'm worked up about something. It's genetic. If he takes half a step closer to me, it is possible I may slap him unintentionally. "Anyway, it's been hard, and it completely blindsided me. I thought I would die." I laugh without humor and wipe my palms down my pants. "Silly, right? As if you could die from a divorce. It's not like a tumor or anything. But I thought I would, because at the moment, I felt an insurmountable amount of pain and sorrow and defeat. But today, it's been a year, and I put an offer on a condo, which I'm super nervous about because the mortgage, it's a little more than I feel comfortable paying, but I did get a big promotion and well, anyway, I survived the year. I did it, and tonight I am going out with my two best friends, and for the first time in a long time, I'm happy and I'm looking forward to tomorrow. No offense to you, but you just took a big, huge poop on my parade. Everyone deserves a little bit of selfishness in their life. One day. Today is supposed to be that one day for me. So please don't be offended, but I'm choosing not to have menangia-whateverthehell today. I can have one tomorrow, but today, I'm choosing denial." I say it all in one long breath, and when I'm done, I notice for the first time a crack on the serious man's face.

"That seems like a lot."

"It is," I say, uncertain if he's talking about the oversharing of information or all the crap that I've been through this year.

"Promise me you'll call Dr. Chen next week. He's the best neurosurgeon in Florida. I'll make sure your records are sent over to him. Or you can set up another appointment with me and we can talk further. Okay?"

"Promise." I place two fingers over my heart like a scout.

"I don't want you to put it off, but I also see you need to process this on your own time."

"I do." It's jarring, the complete shift of emotions. From bliss to despair in less than an hour. I'm trying to catch up.

"Okay, then. Have fun at your divorce party," he says and gestures to the door behind me. I reach down to the knob and open it and then slide out.

Wouldn't life be grand if you could so easily compartmentalize things like I told Dr. Devi I would? Go to my party, celebrate, and forget the terrible news I just received and don't quite understand yet? Alas, I tried to forget about the tumor. I really did. Every time the word popped into my head, I tried to bury it back down.

Spoiler alert . . . I suck at compartmentalizing.

CHAPTER TWO

Can you guess what's the most important letter in the word *clock*?

Yep, that's right. It's the *L*! *The* L*!*

Without the *L*, you turn a very important corporate meeting into a frat house with snickering boys.

"That was hilarious!" Bernie, the heir to AutoRey and my friend and not yet (because his father is still very much alive) boss says as we walk back to our respective offices after my failed presentation.

"Hilarious for whom?" I grunt.

"For me. Definitely for me."

"Everyone's entitled to a typo every once in a while," I say. I am always super prepared for everything, but after the doctor's visit, I half-assed my PowerPoint presentation and almost died of humiliation in the process.

"You okay?" Bernie asks. "You seem . . . distracted."

Am I okay? Hmmmm. I think I have cancer even though the doctor said it wasn't cancer, but everything with an "oma" at the end feels cancer-ish, right? And tumor—aren't most tumors cancerous? And how am I going to tell my mothers?

God, I wish Annabel were here to talk to me about this. She always had the optimistic gene that I sometimes lack.

"Alex?" He waves his hand in front of me, and I realize I've been staring into space and clutching my chest. Thinking of my sister literally gives me an ache in my heart.

"Uh . . . yeah, just excited for tonight, I guess."

"Margot hasn't stopped talking about it." Margot is Bernie's wife and one of my best friends. "She hasn't been out with the girls in ages." He air quotes it and says it in a loud, pitchy voice. I suppose he's imitating either women or a dying cat.

"It's going to be great. I can't wait." Maybe if I say it enough, I'll believe it. Before Dr. Devi, I was excited. Now, however, I am numb.

"When do you think you'll have a new pitch ready? I'm sure you have a plan B in your arsenal."

"I always do." It's a lie; I never bomb, and therefore I've never needed a plan B. I sometimes miss the mark and plan A turns into plan A 2.0, but there's never been a need for me to have to start from scratch. "Three weeks," I say confidently, even if I have to pull that confidence out of my ass, because there's no way I'm not going to try again and nail it. The Rey family has entrusted me to help them land this account; they've promoted me and given me the tools to succeed, and I can't let them down.

"Two weeks," he says. "And see if Victor has any suggestions."

Victor, ugh. I don't have any personal issues with Victor Serrano *per se.* He's a nice guy; he's bright, a hard worker. Hell, I hired him. He's my second-in-command. When I'm not here, he's in charge of the department. Except I've never not been here. But hypothetically, that's how it would work.

But he's, well . . . a man. The Reys are not sexist, but the men in this company do play golf and hang out at the country club and are in a baseball league, all things I'm simply not invited to do. They did invite me once to a charity racquetball tournament, but they said I was too intense and too competitive. I like to win, and I'm in good shape, tumor notwithstanding. I don't have a beer belly or high blood pressure like the rest of them. The bar isn't set that high, if I'm being honest. But I think they expected me to play like a "girl," and instead I played like they wished they could play.

I was never invited to any more sporting events.

But Victor's always there. He's basically that perpetual pebble in my shoe.

So no. I don't want to ask him for help. In fact, I ask my staff to execute my ideas and visions, but I don't necessarily ask my staff for *help*.

Should I, though? But then, if he does come up with something brilliant, will I lose my job, be demoted?

"I mean it, Martinez. Two weeks," Bernie says, and this time with his serious work tone. After fifteen years of working together, I know when my friend has left the conversation and my future boss has walked in. "You've been a little off your game lately, and Dad is anxious to finalize something to present to PriceMart. We're counting on you to make it happen."

Off my game? Because of one flopped presentation? My posture changes at the comment.

"Whoa. I screwed up today, I admit. But off my game? That's harsh."

"Well, it's true, Alex. You've been distracted and, I don't know . . . you don't seem excited about PriceMart. You haven't seemed excited about much lately. I thought that this new project would rile you up."

"I am excited." My tone is sharp. "I haven't been distracted, Bernie; I've been focused on this pitch. I've slept, eaten, and breathed PriceMart." I don't like to be questioned on my work. How excited does he want me to be about auto parts? How much riling up does he expect? "What the hell did you want, Bernie? Maracas?"

He holds up his hands in surrender. "Okay, okay. Maybe I'm wrong. Just do better and do it fast."

I press my fist against my mouth. He shouldn't question my work and then make light of it.

I have been hyperfocused on this campaign. Granted, it's not exciting and it doesn't get my creative juices flowing, but I still tried what I thought was my best. How dare he question my passion?

PriceMart is opening an automotive department inside their stores, and we are bidding for the exclusive right to have our products sold inside. As the chief marketing officer at AutoRey, it's my job to convince PriceMart that AutoRey is the company they should choose. But there're only so many ways you can make auto parts exciting.

"I'm on it. Don't worry," I say.

This would be a major deal for our company. For obvious reasons, I need to nail this pitch. And with this news from the doctor, will I even be able to focus enough to come up with a brand-new pitch? This tumor wasn't in the plan.

Ugh . . . tumor. *No, no, no. No thinking about it today.* I had a little headache, went to the doctor, and came out with a tumor. *How is that even possible?* A few weeks ago, I googled and WebMD'ed my symptoms. There were, of course, the doomsday diagnoses. The ones that are rare and you tend to ignore because *you* are never the person who gets the cancer or the strange (and disgusting) parasites that live and breed in your brain. It's always your friend's coworker's cousin twice removed who has the misfortune of being that odd man out. You never expect it to happen to you.

Migraines and stress, which are the common diagnoses listed under my symptoms—I was prepared to hear *that* bad news. Maybe I'd need migraine medication. Nowhere was a tumor even in the realm of possibilities.

But today is not the day for tumors. Today is a day of celebration.

I should leave early and take a hot bath or maybe make an appointment to do my nails before the party. If there were a definition next to *mental health day*, the results of my doctor's appointment would be next to it.

Instead, I do the next worst thing.

I fish out the folded paper from my purse, and in the search bar of my computer, I type in *Cerebral Meningioma* and brace for the results.

Cerebral meningioma: a brain tumor, although it is not a tumor of brain tissue. It is actually a tumor of the meninges, the thin layers of tissue that cover the brain and spinal cord.

What the hell does that even mean?

Dr. Devi made it very clear that it was unlikely to be cancerous, but until the surgeon goes in, removes it, and does a biopsy, it would be impossible to say for certain. He also made it clear that not removing it wasn't an option. *But why not, exactly?* According to Google, many people never even know they have a meningioma, and when they do, they merely monitor it. Why can't I just monitor it? Monitoring sounds better. I can monitor the hell out of this tumor. Thinking of the years that Annabel was in treatment and how she basically lived in hospitals, being poked and prodded all the time . . . I don't want that for me or for my mothers.

Just yesterday, I went on my usual jog, and last weekend, I went on a fifteen-mile bike ride at Shark Valley. Obviously, I feel fine. I mean, I get occasional headaches, and once in a while I do have an ache in my legs that radiates to my back. But it's not tumor pain. Doctors get things wrong all the time. Plus, Dr. Devi's not a tumor doctor—is that a thing? Oncologists are for cancer, and this isn't cancer—allegedly. Being a woman of action, I decide to ask Google to direct me to the correct kind of doctor for this kind of problem, and it turns out that a neurologist is the correct kind of doctor. But I can't leave the fate of my health in the hands of one person I don't even know. Someone who called me by the wrong name—twice.

By the time I walk out of the office to go to my divorceaversary party, I've made an appointment with another neurologist for a second opinion and have requested my medical records from Dr. Devi.

Now that I've had my moment to process, I can start compartmentalizing again and have fun at my party. Because you already know how good I am at that.

———

Nestled in Coral Gables, an upscale area of Miami, is Purple Haze. It's an obnoxiously loud and overpriced restaurant and bar. Sylvie, my best friend since third grade, chose it because on Friday nights, the happy hour is full of good-looking businessmen hanging out by the bar area, where Sylvie and Margot are already sitting at a high-top. Also, the loaded nachos are divine.

"Woo-hoo!" Sylvie yells when she sees me walk in, her sharp, dark brown bob swinging side to side. "It's the lady of the hour!" A Miss America–style pink sash is suddenly placed around my torso by Sylvie, as she hugs me, followed by a plastic silver crown from Margot. I look down. It's definitely not fitting for a Miss Anything. It says Ding Dong the Dick Is Gone.

God, I love these women. I sit down, and a margarita is slid my way like magic. I don't know if it's fresh or if it's one of theirs, but I immediately take a big soothing gulp. I feel better already. I eye the big plate of nachos that's already sitting in the middle of the table, and my empty stomach rumbles.

"We are so proud of you, Alex," Sylvie says, holding up her own margarita.

"I'm kinda proud of myself too," I say and lick some of the salt on the rim.

I know people divorce all the time and there are thousands of things that are worse (like a tumor, but we're not going to think about that now). But I wasn't *just* married for ten years; I was with Michael my entire life. Our lives—financially, emotionally, and socially—were so entangled, I didn't know where my life started and his ended. And one day, completely out of the blue, he left me, and I was not equipped for the fallout.

I knew how to balance a checkbook; I knew our accounts and passwords and all those important adult things people need to know.

But just because I knew them didn't mean I *knew* them. I didn't pay the bills. That was Michael's department. Mostly because I was busy and didn't want the hassle, and I trusted him. He was my husband and my best friend. And then he left, and I didn't know when bills were due and what needed to be paid. Not a huge deal. Except that when we did divorce, he wanted, and was entitled to, half our assets. That included the house, which I couldn't afford by myself—nor did I want to, once I realized it was upside down. So we sold it and ended up having to pay off the underwater part of the mortgage. So, now broke, I found myself without a home, with a new cell phone plan, and with other little life hassles.

And that's only the financial pain-in-the-ass part.

The emotional part was so much worse.

I hadn't slept alone for years, and I missed him. Hell, I loved him. Just because he stopped loving me didn't mean I magically stopped loving him. For a few months, it felt like I'd lost a limb. If I'm being honest, I still wake up and think I'm going to see him walk out of the bathroom with tousled hair as he gets ready for work. And then, to top it off, I feel some sort of way for even missing him. I should be stronger. *He* left *me*. I should not want him anymore.

I never cried, though. Not a single tear. I was shocked and devastated, and everyone waited for the moment I would fall apart. In my own way, I *did* fall apart, but it was mostly in private and with dry eyes. I'd pace my room with an anxious energy that some days made my legs ache from the number of laps I would do around and around my room. I was hitting my Fitbit goal by midday.

My mind wondering: *Was there another woman? Did I do something wrong? Would I ever love again? Did I want to love again?*

It was awful, and I knew, as a rational woman, that I'd ultimately be okay. Countless people divorced. There are so many problems in the world, I felt selfish, privileged, and petty for being devastated.

But he was the person who'd listen to my office woes and my silly jokes that no one else got. He was the person who knew how to jiggle the key in just the perfect way that opened the latch to the side door of our ex-home. He was the only person in the world who knew I was cranky in the mornings and liked my café con leche with almond milk because regular milk made me bloated and that I was a grouch until that first sip of coffee. It wasn't the end of the world, but for me, it was. The bottom line was: he was my person, and now I was person-less.

But I was getting over it, and I was starting to see my future, and it looked promising. I was happy(ish). Notwithstanding the ridiculous freakin' doctor appointment this morning.

Michael would have been the first person I told the news. He would have comforted me; we would have researched and made decisions together. But none of that's possible. I am alone with this information, and I will have to deal with it alone. And I will get through it alone. Of that, I am sure. But it doesn't mean I don't want to share my woes with someone.

A lump forms in my throat, but I push it down.

"Hey, how'd that doctor appointment go today?" Margot yells over all the noise.

I shake my hand and reach for my drink. "Uh-uh. Not the time for doctor talk. It's time for margaritas," I say and clink my glass against their own. The topic is quickly overlooked as we toast to a great night.

When Annabel, my younger sister, died, that was truly a tragedy. I was fifteen. She'd just turned fourteen, and it sort of felt as if we'd been waiting for the day for years. But nothing prepares you for death. I remember sobbing as if someone were physically tearing my heart out of my body. I remember watching my mothers fall apart. Losing a child, losing my sister, that was the kind of pain that deserved tears. Michael leaving me was something different. A betrayal. There's different kinds of pain, I've learned. Michael leaving me was anger-fueled pain. Annabel's death was grief and a general sense of loss. I'd have to live the rest of my life without my sister. My mothers would never see Annabel grow up, find love, get married, have children. It was finite, and then shortly thereafter, I lost Mima too. Not physically—she's still alive, but our relationship was never the same after that. Hell, *Mima* was never the same after that. The Latin flair, that spicy personality that made her, her . . . it was gone.

Thankfully, Purple Haze is loud enough that you can't focus on your own thoughts too long, plus dark enough that my friends won't notice my eyes start to mist.

"You're my hero!" Margot says, holding up her margarita to me. "I'd be lost without Bernie."

"Oh, shut it," Sylvie says with a roll of her hazel-colored eyes. It's in good humor, of course, and she has a smile as she says it. I quickly sniffle and shift my thoughts to the present. "You'd be fine. We don't need men." Sylvie is what one would call a *man-hater*. She's had too many bad relationships, and therefore, all men are evil.

"I didn't know how I'd survive this year, to be honest. But I figured it out. And if I could do it, you could too, Margot. Not that you'd ever have to. Bernie worships the ground you walk on." I thought I had that with Michael once, but I don't say that out loud. Instead, I finish my margarita and order another one.

"Excuse me," a voice says from behind me, followed by a tap on my shoulder. I turn around. A man wearing a navy-blue suit and thick black glasses, hair parted too perfectly to the side, is standing uncomfortably close. He has a beer in hand and an arrogant smile on his smug face. "You're Alex Martinez from Saint Teresa Catholic High School, right? I'm great with faces."

I look at him carefully, and he does look vaguely familiar, but *I'm* not great with faces. "Yes." It comes out more like a question than an answer.

"Robert." He points his thumbs at himself. "Come on, you remember me. Tight end for the varsity team. Prom king." He sounds like a tool. We're much too old to bring in frivolous titles from our high school days. I'm not trying to play coy; I really don't remember him. *And who introduces themselves with just a first name?* Unless you're Sting or Madonna, I need a first and last name. "You tutored me in—"

"Chemistry," Sylvie cuts in while snapping her fingers. "I remember you. Alex, you tutored him in chemistry after school."

He looks over my shoulder. "Sylvia Roberts, right?"

"Robbins," she corrects him.

"Oh yeah, that's right."

"You look different," I say.

"It's the glasses," he says to me. And it clicks.

It's not the glasses. His hair is blacker than it used to be. *Someone's been dyeing their grays with a bit too much black dye.* He was a jerk back then. I remember he was forced to get tutored in order to play in the weekly football games, and he always made the hour-long sessions a total pain in my behind. And now I know why he didn't tell us his last name!

"Wait, you're Bob!"

"I go by Robert now. Robert Blobel." He was known as Bob the Blob. He wasn't a blob. He was actually the opposite of a blob, but he was a douche and deserved the nickname. He would correct everyone: *"It's Blobel, with a short e, like* blow *and* bell. *Not* blob *and* el.*"* Unfortunately, kids are mean, and when you say *blow* and *bell* one too many times, you will forthwith be forever known as Bob the Blob. I catch myself giggling, and I see Sylvie is holding it back too.

"And you are?" He's trying to recall Margot.

"I'm Margot. I didn't go to Saint Teresa," she says.

He then pulls out the fourth chair and sits. I do not want company right now. I want familiar. I want drinks. I want my girls. I certainly do not want Bob, prom douche and captain of the football jerks.

"You ladies here with anyone?" Ugh, the sleazy smile.

"We're actually just having a nice quiet girls' night," I say, hoping he gets the hint. And also, it doesn't go unnoticed that there is nothing quiet about Purple Haze.

"Oh. Nice. Well, maybe I can buy you a drink?" he says, looking at me with smoldering eyes. It's fake and too forward and I want to throw up.

"Nah, we're good, thanks."

"Oh, come on, one drink? For old times' sake?" And he winks. I gag.

Again, I say no. Then he has the audacity to turn to Sylvie. "How about you, honey? You were always fun," he says, and I notice he's swaying a bit. Drunk fool.

Sylvie, being Sylvie, leans forward, almost as if she's going to kiss him, and you can immediately see Bob's excitement at the prospect. "Unless you want me to pour this entire margarita over your big fat ego-inflated head, I'd suggest you turn right around and walk away, Bob," she says, twirling her fingers dismissively at him.

His smile drops, and he pushes his chair back. "Bitches," he says under his breath as he walks away. I look back at Sylvie, then at Margot, and we burst out laughing.

"That's one way of getting back into the dating scene," I say, and then we laugh some more.

"He was an ass," Margot says.

"Same as in high school. I can't believe you didn't remember him right away. Michael used to get so jealous," Sylvie replies.

"Of Bob the Blob?" I say, and we quickly explain the nickname's origin to Margot, who laughs loudly. "Anyway, I don't remember that. Hell, I can't remember one single time Michael was jealous."

"You were oblivious. He was always in a terrible mood when it was your tutoring day."

"I guess I was busy being annoyed that I had to hang out with Bob for an hour."

"I dated a Bob before Bernie," Margot adds as she takes a sip of her drink. "He was kind of annoying, too, now that I think about it. It must be the name."

We all chuckle.

"Anyway, what were we talking about before we were so rudely interrupted? Oh yeah . . . back to Alex! It's your special day. I almost want to send Michael a text telling him to suck it. I wish he could see how far you've come this year!" Sometimes I think she's more upset at my divorce than I am. It's not true, of course. I was not upset. I was devastated. Heartbroken. Scared. Pissed. The entire spectrum of the emotional sphere, I lived it.

Michael, Sylvie, and I were childhood friends, which I think is why Sylvie is so upset. She didn't see it coming. No one did. Michael, a glasses-wearing, self-proclaimed "computer geek" with a small gut and a receding hairline, dumped me with a freaking note. I may not be a supermodel, but I still look damn good, if I do say so myself. He couldn't do better. At least that's what the vengeful part of me told myself, repeatedly.

A year's worth of therapy and self-help books made me see how imperfect my marriage actually was. He never even proposed. It took months after our marriage ended for me to even see that. It was just the evolution of our relationship to then marry. And we did. And it was good. No. It was great, but my meter is obviously off, since I have nothing to compare it to. First kiss. First date. First love. First (and only) sexual experience.

We were a team. He supported me through my master's. I supported him through his PhD in philosophy. We argued like most couples and then made up. There were no signs. And then one day, I came home, and he was gone.

At first, I thought it was a mistake. Until I found the stupid note:

21

Alex,

You know I don't do confrontation and I hate seeing you hurt. I thought a letter was best. I accepted a professor position in Cincinnati. I start next week. It's better to make a clean break. I think we can both agree, it's been over for a long time now. Fall in love, Alex. Find the perfect man for you. You deserve it.

All my love, Michael

"It's been over for a while now?" I say out loud, full of righteous indignation, as I take out the note (too short to be a letter. He couldn't even give me a damn letter) from my pocket. "Bullshit! He made things over when he left." *I thought things were fine.*

I can recite the entire note, I've read it so many times. But those seven little words tore deep into my soul. Sylvie and Margot know about the note. "Do you think there was another woman?" I ask, then hold my hand up. I've asked this a dozen times over the year, and they've both said no. He just didn't seem like the type. But is there a type of adulterous man? Thin, fat, tall, short, rich, poor—anyone could cheat. "Nope. Nope. Don't answer that. I don't want to know." This is a party. This is closure.

"Burn it. Burn it. Burn it," my two friends chant while beating the top of the table. Thank God it's loud and no one can hear us. I take the little crystal candleholder from the middle of the table and look down. "Shit. It's fake. Battery votive."

Sylvie, of course, is prepared. She pours the half-eaten nachos into the bread basket and then takes a lighter from her purse and points to the now-empty plate. I place the stupid breakup note on the plate, and she flickers on the lighter, setting the corner of the paper on fire.

"Yeah!" Margot cheers. "Michael did you a favor, Alex. You're killing it at work, you went for the overdue promotion, and you got it. And now you're going to be a homeowner in a few months. You seem happier and less stressed out than I've seen you in the last five years. It's a blessing in disguise if you think about it."

I've thought those very words in my own head a few times. I vacillate between thanking Michael for giving me the motivation I needed to ask for the promotion I deserved and wanting to fly to Cincinnati, find him, and sucker punch him right in his balls.

What can I say: I have good days and bad days.

But the truth is, I'm more independent because of it. I never realized how much I depended on Michael. *I mean, there were better ways I could have learned the lesson, of course.*

It was a hard road, and I know it's not over, not at all, but I'm getting there. I feel like I've reached the peak of the climb and now it's going to be a smooth descent into happy.

"Uh-oh," Sylvie yells as we observe fire eat up the paper and smoke billow into the air. Before we have time to go into a full-blown panic, the plate is doused with ice water, most of it dripping down the sides of the table and onto my lap. I yelp and stand up, ice rolling onto the floor.

"You can't do that in here!" a server shouts as she puts out our little tabletop bonfire. "What's wrong with you?"

Then a very angry and very tall man with a thick hipster beard and a purposefully messy full head of hair rushes over as he yells, "What the hell?" By the way he commands authority, I assume he's the manager or maybe even security.

"It's my divorceaversary, and I was getting closure," I say with indignation, wiping my legs with a napkin.

"I don't give a shit what it is. You are not going to set my restaurant on fire. Settle the tab and get out of here before I call the police," he says.

"That's a little melodramatic, don't ya think?" Sylvie says, her hand on her hip.

"No, I think I'm being the right amount of dramatic considering you almost set the place on fire," Mr. Hipster shouts back.

Margot hands her credit card to the server. "It's fine. We're fine. We'll leave."

"I don't want to leave," I say, knowing I'm sounding petulant. It's the first time I've had fun in a year. Hell, in years. I was really looking forward to tonight. I'm trying to get goddamn closure, and I'm trying to forget all about the doctor's appointment from this morning. I'm not going to leave.

"Excuse me?" he says. "You absolutely are going to leave."

Shit. I didn't realize I'd said that out loud. Oh well, I may as well say it again. "I'm not leaving."

"Maybe I can help." Oh hell. It's Bob again. He leans against the table and inserts himself into the conversation. "I'm sure that these ladies are very sorry for their antics—" He takes out his wallet, but I've had enough.

"Bob, get the hell out of here," I say, pushing him aside. The last thing I need is for him to try and mansplain his way out of this for me. "I don't need your help."

"Are you sure about that, honey? And it's Robert now."

"Eff off, Bob," Sylvie says.

"And stop with the *honey*," I add, annoyed. I turn and repeat to the manager trying to ignore Bob's exit, "I'm not leaving."

"Oh, but you are," he says and takes his phone out of his pocket, presumably to call the cops. "We can do this the easy way or the hard way." The smell of burned paper lingers in the air. The bar is loud, so we're yelling. And also, I'm mad, so I'd be yelling even if the bar weren't loud.

"Alex, it's fine. Let's just leave. We can go somewhere else," Sylvie says. Which is surprising—the feisty one in the group is trying to calm me down. I'm not a pushover. Not at all. Hell, in a man's world, I work in a man's profession. Trust me when I say, I can hold my own. But I'm not ordinarily rude. Except right now. *I am not leaving!*

"Sit down!" I sit with clenched teeth and point to my friends, who look at each other questioningly. I haven't even drunk enough to be drunk, and they know this. "Listen, you, you manager guy, it was a piece of freaking paper. You're acting like I came in here with a flamethrower! Nothing was going to happen. It would have fizzled out. Relax." I wipe some of the water off my trousers with a cloth napkin, not that it's doing much, since my nice work pants are drenched. "No harm, no foul. I apologize for how we went about it, but nothing happened. Now, we'd like some more drinks." Then for good measure, I say, "Please."

"Are you crazy?" he asks and then turns to my friends. "She's crazy, right?"

My friends don't respond. For a split second, I think they're going to agree with this guy.

He's beginning to really tick me off.

"Why am I crazy? Bet you wouldn't say that to a man."

"Actually, if he set a table on fire—yeah, I'd call him batshit crazy."

Hmph! I didn't expect that answer. I'm biting my bottom lip, a little disconcerted. "Well, it wasn't the table. It was a piece of paper." The server brings back Margot's card, and she quickly signs it and hands the slip back to the server.

"No wonder the guy left you," he says, looking at the silly sash I have around my chest and the crown, then mutters under his breath, "Bitch." He doesn't even have the nerve to say the word to my face. This is the second half-whispered, spineless "bitch" I get in less than twenty minutes.

I lose my shit. Big. Time.

"I'm the bitch? *I'm the bitch?*" I push back my chair and get right in his face. "I was a great wife. The freakin' best wife. And I got a stupid breakup note after ten years of marriage. No, not a letter. A note. But for three hundred and sixty-five days, I survived. And this one damn day that I want to celebrate, the first sliver of happiness in the shitty year, I'm told I have a brain tumor. A tumor! In my brain! Not to mention that I spelled *clock* wrong at work. It's been a bad day, mister. You listening to me? I'm not a bitch. I'm just a woman who's had a bad, bad, bad day. I'm sorry I set the note on fire. There's just so much shit one person can take before their cup runneth over, and my effing cup has runneth the eff over, you hear me?"

I'm pretty sure the entire bar hears me, because I'm screaming. Not yelling. Screaming. I'm even jabbing him in the chest.

Mr. Hipster's eyes soften. I'm not sure if it was the tumor, the note, the misspelled word, or all of the above, but something in my speech struck a nerve.

"You have a brain tumor?" Sylvie whispers. Her hand is on mine. I turn my head, and both of my friends are in utter disbelief.

I didn't mean to say that all out loud. Not today, at least. *Cat's out of the bag now.*

Thankfully, Mr. Hipster gives us some grace as his shoulders sag, and then he says something to the server before turning back to us. "No more fire! Understand?" he warns, pointing directly at me. "I'm keeping my eyes on you." I nod, and then he walks away.

A busser comes our way and clears the mess of ice and water from the table, and we all sit back down. My friends are looking at me, and I know they want answers, but I just fuss with the fresh plates and napkins on the table, trying to delay the moment as much as possible.

"Oh my God, would you stop that?" Sylvie says, sliding the plate away from me. "Start talking."

"I really, really don't want to have this conversation today."

"Yeah, well, it's too late for that. You can't drop a bomb like that on us and then tell us you don't want to talk about it," Margot says.

I sigh defeatedly. "The migraines I was having, well, they're not migraines. It's a tumor. It's the icing on the crappy year, right?" I laugh, but it comes out a fake, nervous laugh that is too loud and high-pitched. "It's just something annoying I have to deal with . . . you know, like Bob over there."

"Stop making light of this. Do you . . . are you . . . do you have cancer?" Sylvie asks somberly.

"Supposedly no. But I have to get it removed or else things could get worse."

"Worse how?" Margot asks.

"I could have seizures, and I could even lose control of my legs and lose my memory."

"Oh my God." Margot gasps. "How long have you known? Why didn't you say something to us? I just asked you how the appointment went, for God's sake."

I fold a paper napkin over and over again. "I just found out this morning, and my goal was to try and forget about it. To enjoy the evening and deal with it later."

Sylvie's eyes open to the size of saucers. "You can't hide your head in the sand with this one, Alex. We need to deal with this. It sounds dangerous."

I stop fidgeting with the napkin and look up. "I don't hide my head in the sand. I just want to make sure that I'm working with correct information. Before everyone starts overreacting, I wanted to get a second opinion first. That's completely reasonable."

She exhales and then reaches across the table and places her hand over mine. "It is. I agree. I just want to make sure you're asking all the right questions and listening to your doctors."

"Part of the reason I don't want to tell my moms until I absolutely need to tell them is because you know how Josefina Maria de la Cruz Martinez gets." That's Mima's full name and what we call her when she's in full-blown mama-bear mode. "She becomes super overbearing. I don't need her checking my temperature every five minutes or worried about every headache or broken nail." Even though I'm talking about Mima, I'm trying for them to understand that I don't want them to hover either. "You know it makes me uncomfortable when people dote on me." After Annabel's death, Mima became a worrywart, understandably so. We sometimes lovingly poke fun at her and call her Dr. Mom because she will hover, google, print articles, pray rosaries over us, all because of a toothache.

"I know. Trust me. We all know about your allergy to emotional conversations."

I give her the finger playfully.

"Just make sure you ask about the consequences of the surgery. Does your doctor recommend a specific surgeon? Does your insurance cover all of this? I can help pay for anything that you need."

"AutoRey has great benefits. I can help you figure that out with the insurance if you need, sweetie."

I pull my hand away and tsk. "I'll make sure to add all those questions to the list of questions I have. But let's not start with *sweetie* or any kind of baby talk and no holding hands." New drinks are placed on our table, and I grab my margarita and down half of it in one pull. "Go on. Drink."

"Alex—" Sylvie says.

I take a huge gulp, which I instantly regret because, well . . . tequila burns. In a firmer tone, I say, "I'm not doing this. This is not a pity party. This is a triumph party! And no stupid fire or tumor is going to ruin my evening."

They eye me frustratedly.

"I'm not going to cry or sit here and watch you both fall apart. I feel great. I swear."

"If you felt *great*, you wouldn't have gone to the doctor," Sylvie says, exuding all that Cuban attitude, her head and hands moving in sync. Unlike me, Sylvie is 100 percent Cuban; she was born in Havana and came to the US when she was seven years old. Sometimes when she gets very excited or angry, she reverts to a very fast Spanglish.

"I didn't feel great when I made the appointment at the doctor, obviously. But I haven't had a single migraine since. Whatever this tumor thing is, it's still going to be there tomorrow. In fact, it may have been there for years and years. One more day isn't going to change anything. Can we please table this TED Talk for later? Please?" I reach for each of their hands and squeeze. "If we start talking about it now and you two crybabies start sobbing, they will definitely kick us out. A small tabletop fire is one thing, but the much-dreaded group of crying women is another. Mr. Hipster's head will explode. Do you want to get us kicked out? Do you?"

"Well, if you actually cry, it would be worth it," Sylvie says.

I give her the finger playfully, again. "Maybe you two just cry too much."

They roll their eyes. They don't cry too much. They cry a normal amount, which is to say, not very often and only when it's warranted. Me, on the other hand, yeah, well, I just don't have tears.

"I think your tear ducts are broken. They should check that when they check your brain," Sylvie says, and that makes me actually laugh out loud.

"Too soon, Sylvie!" Margot yelps and elbows Sylvie, which makes me laugh harder. I needed this laugh.

"So we can just stop talking about this for now? Pleeeease?"

They look at each other and, as if they reach a secret agreement for a moratorium on the conversation, they both take their drinks and sip. I can tell they don't even want to drink them; they're just trying to appease me. Unfortunately, even after telling them all about the misspelling mistake and Sylvie telling us all about her online dating mishaps, the mood is not the same. Like tumors tend to do, they spoil the evening.

Our conversation is stilted and awkward, and I think I see sorrow on their faces, which is why I'm tucked in bed and fast asleep by ten. After the reaction I received from my friends (and even from the manager), there is no way I'm sharing the news with anyone else. God forbid my mothers find out. I wouldn't be able to handle their tears.

Worst divorceaversary party ever.

CHAPTER THREE

"I'm coming. I'm coming!" I yawn-yell as I grab my old and frayed terry-cloth robe from behind my bathroom door. *Who could it be at this time?* I wipe the sleep from my eyes with the back of my hands. "It's tomorrow, Alex! Open up. Time to talk." *Argh.* I know that loud voice all too well. It's Sylvie. And, if I was a betting woman, I'd bet that Margot is standing right behind her in some sort of cardigan set and sensible yet cute linen capris and matching flats, asking Sylvie to lower her voice. Unlike Sylvie's blunt bob, which makes her look intimidating, Margot has blonde highlights, and her hair is either perfectly straight or in a neat bun, not a hair out of place, and she screams sweet suburban housewife.

"Shhh . . . ," I say as I open the door. The bright morning light momentarily blinds me. "Stop yelling. You'll wake them up." They know who *"them"* is. I've been living in my parents' guest room for the last year. It's more like an extra room with a door that leads to the outside. Unfortunately, there's also a door that leads to the inside, which means I am frequently visited by my mothers. Whom I adore. But am also driven bananas by with all their fussing and snooping. "I don't want my moms to know."

Mima's depression, following Annabel's death, lasted almost three years. It was the kind of depression that keeps you in bed for weeks on end. Mom was so preoccupied with her own grief and the state of Mima that I was often forgotten. I vividly remember being left at school or having to go without lunch because they'd forgotten to give me lunch money. Of course, when they'd realized they'd forgotten me, Mima's guilt would send her spiraling into a worse state of sorrow, or she'd get upset at Mom for forgetting and that led to another bout of depression. Needless to say, there were countless times I'd find a ride home or scramble around for food so as to not put any more burden on them.

My moms still have bad days every now and again, Mima more than Mom. Sometimes I see her gazing out the window, as if she expects Annabel to walk in at any moment. Honestly, once in a while I think it's all a nightmare, and I'll wake up to find Annabel singing to *The Wizard of Oz* on the television. We never talk about her, and we're always treading lightly, especially for Mima's sake. This is why I cannot tell my mothers about the monster living in my brain. They would not be able to handle it, and I would not be able to live with myself if I caused them any more pain. They've been through enough.

"You promised yesterday that if we dropped the subject, today you'd tell us all about the t-t—" Margot says. Poor thing, she can't even get the word out.

I put her out of her misery and cut her off. "Fine. Let me get dressed, and we'll go out for breakfast. Not a word about anything until we're out of this house, you hear me?" I close the door behind them.

Sylvie mimes zipping her lips, but not before she adds, "Can we at least talk about that godawful robe? You know, if you ever start dating again, a trip to Victoria's Secret wouldn't hurt."

I roll my eyes. The last thing I'm thinking about is dating or lingerie.

By the way, I was right about Margot's outfit, except she's not in flats. She's wearing platform espadrilles, the picture of a suburban housewife, straight out of a J.Crew catalog.

Sylvie, on the other hand, is wearing jeans that have big tears in strategic places—the kind of tears that are made by an expensive retail establishment. She has on yellow Converse sneakers and a simple black T-shirt that probably cost more than my monthly car payment. "How are you guys so perky at this time?" I ask. They drank too. Shouldn't they have a little bit of a headache?

"Let's not do pleasantries. If you don't want to chat here, then hurry up and get dressed." Sylvie snaps her fingers.

"Fine. Fine," I say, but there's a quick knock on the inside door to my room, and Mom peeks her head inside.

"Helloooo. I thought I heard voices. You're up?" she says, letting herself right in. "Oh, and it's the girls. Hi, ladies."

"Good morning, Claire," my friends say to my mom as she hugs them both.

"Morning, Mom," I say. "We're going to go get breakfast."

"Okay, honey," Mom says. "Did you ladies have a fun evening?" she asks as she goes straight to the bed and starts making it. That's the problem (and blessing) with being at home; I'm babied and spoiled, but also maybe I didn't want my bed made right this particular second. Regardless, I don't want to be ungrateful; I am living with them rent-free, after all.

"Let's just say it was interesting," Sylvie says, and I open my eyes wide, admonishing her from across the room.

"Yeah? How so?" Mom asks as she tucks the sheets tightly underneath the mattress.

"Just a little ritual burning and incantations. You know . . . the usual," Sylvie says.

I let out a breath. I trust Sylvie, but you never know . . .

"Did you meet any nice men?" she asks.

"Just Bob," Sylvie says and eyes me to hurry up.

"Bob?"

She waves her hand dismissively. "Long story. Just an annoying guy who seemed really stuck on Alex."

I think she's talking about the tumor, not Bob. Maybe both.

"How cute," Mom says. "You guys are going to go gossip about this Bob fella?"

"Yes!" Margot says. "We want to hear all about how Alex met Bob and how she's going to get rid of him. He seems very taken with her, ya know."

I give them both an evil stare.

My mother is so excited about the prospect of a man.

"Settle down, Mom. It's nothing."

"Well, your mother and I are very proud of you, honey. I know it's been tough. If I ever saw Michael again, I don't even know what I'd say. It wouldn't be nice, that I can assure you. But meeting someone new is a great way to start moving on." Mom's sweet that way. I know she'd give him an earful even though it would be without curse words or a raised voice. But it would cut deep. Mom tends to go the guilt route, whereas Mima doesn't refrain from using colorful words and saying them loud enough for the neighbors to hear. She would do a lot more than give Michael an earful. She'd probably cut off his ears! Mom's way is actually more effective, if my childhood is anything to gauge by. Every time Mom would sit me down for a lecture, I'd leave heartbroken, in tears, and feeling as if I'd totally let her down. Whereas with Mima, I may have left with a switch to my behind, but within a day, it was as if nothing had happened.

The point is—if I had to sic one of them on Michael, I'd pick Mom. Although I'd love to see Mima try and beat Michael with a switch from the big tree out back. That would be something to behold. I almost giggle out loud at the mental image. "Just for fun, you know?" She winks twice. She's so cute, trying to be the cool mom. "It's too soon for something serious, but some action never hurt anyone."

"Mom!" I yelp, surprised she'd say that.

"Oh yeah, Claire. That's what I'm talkin' about." Sylvie grins and gives Mom a high five. I shake my head in disbelief even as I smile at the ridiculous conversation.

I leave Mom and my friends to chat while I'm pulling out clothes from the closet. I run to the bathroom with the clothes I've blindly picked out and quickly get dressed. The longer they're with Mom, the more the chances are that they'll let my little diagnosis slip.

Eventually, we walk out of the house. All of us automatically head straight to Sylvie's Tesla. I have a Toyota Corolla. It's white and only four years old. Michael thought it was a sensible and reasonably priced car. Not to mention the safety features, which are top-notch. But it's no Tesla. Did I mention that my best friend is an environmental engineer? She's not only bighearted and overprotective, she's also pretty damn cool.

"You sit up front. Get comfy and spill the tea," Margot says, sliding into the back seat of the four-door SUV, which magically opens as Sylvie approaches.

"I haven't even had coffee. Can't we chat during breakfast?"

"No," they both say simultaneously.

"Ugh. Fine. You guys are worse than this brain tumor," I say.

"What is wrong with you? Too soon, Alex. Too soon," Margot says, shaking her head.

I sit back and look forward, the palm trees passing us by as we propel forward onto the busy street. I live in a suburban community in Miami, and on Saturday mornings, instead of the relentless traffic, there are mostly families riding bikes around the neighborhood or people walking their dogs. It's early spring, but from the weather, it may as well be the middle of summer. I really love Miami at this time of the year. Most of the country is still fighting winter, and we are already beach ready.

I exhale loudly and start explaining. "I've been having some migraines, as you already know. Well, I thought they were migraines. A few weeks ago, I was walking out of a long board meeting, and my legs just sort of gave out from under me, and I fell."

"Oh, I remember Bernie mentioning that," Margot says. "He said you collapsed. I called you that night, and you said you were fine."

"Your favorite word," Sylvie says under her breath.

I look over my shoulder. "I did not collapse," I reply indignantly and then look over to Sylvie. "*Fine* is a perfectly . . . fine word. I'm not perfect, nor am I terrible. I'm fine. And anyway, Bernie grossly exaggerates. I fell, that's all."

"Collapse, fall. Tomato tomahto. Keep going with your story," Sylvie says, focusing on the road.

"There is a massive difference between collapsing and falling. Collapsing implies something more serious. Dramatic. I merely fell. But it's not worth arguing about."

"I'm pretty sure you just did," Sylvie adds.

I almost stick out my tongue at her, but a thirty-something wouldn't do that. Right? Instead, I roll my eyes, maturely, and continue recounting the story while cursing her in my brain, like a civilized adult. "I took a couple of ibuprofen when I got home and slept it off. I thought it was stress, to be honest. You know we're working on that huge bid for PriceMart, and this is the first big project since my promotion." I look back to Margot because I'm sure her husband has filled her in on it. "I've been putting in a lot of hours on it and . . ." And I feel as if my job depends on it, but I will not say that out loud. It's a niggling feeling that's really been weighing on me. I've struck out once already. After working at AutoRey for almost fifteen years, starting as a cashier and working my way up the ladder, this has never happened. Even before my promotion, I had been making pitches to the board for years. My official capacity was vague. I did some marketing, but I also helped in finance and even did some HR. About six years ago, I had seriously considered quitting. I studied marketing because I liked to think outside the box and use my creative muscle. I was stagnant at AutoRey and bored to death. Michael and I had discussed it, and he had asked me what exactly I wanted to do instead. I didn't have an answer. I only knew that working at AutoRey for the rest of my life wasn't it. But we'd needed the income, and he hadn't been making enough to support us.

I wouldn't say that Michael made me stay at AutoRey—hell, he didn't even try to convince me. He didn't, however, encourage me to leave or empathize with the monotony of AutoRey, and since I wasn't even that sure what I wanted to do, I stayed. As the company grew and they needed to formalize positions, I was given the official title of chief marketing officer and a substantial raise, but my role has not really changed in more than six years. And this last year has been different. There are more closed-door meetings, and Bernard seems perpetually grumpy, and Bernie's definitely tougher to please these days. There's an added level of pressure oozing through the office that wasn't there before. I often wonder if the company is having financial trouble, but then I see expansion upon expansion and realize the company's doing better than ever, which makes me think maybe I'm the problem.

"And?" Sylvie asks, glancing over to me.

I shake off the negative thoughts and insecurities coursing through my veins. "Uh . . . and what?"

"And the divorce. Work and the divorce and all you've done this year, it's probably all starting to catch up to you." Margot finishes my sentence.

"Um, yeah. The divorce," I say, because I had not been thinking about Michael or the divorce when I'd fallen, but the events of the last year are the best explanation for my stress, right? "So Nora, my secretary, scheduled an appointment for me to see my primary doctor the next day, which I did. But then my PCP referred me to a neurologist, thinking we were dealing with migraines. She said I'd been having too many headaches, and there were migraine medicines I could be prescribed, but I needed a proper diagnosis."

Nora is like a third mother to me. As if I didn't have enough. She's in her late sixties and types everything using only her index finger. It takes approximately forty-nine years for her to type an email and send it. But what she lacks in technology, she makes up in her knowledge of the business. She can give me a contact phone number in thirty seconds, using her ginormous Rolodex that sits proudly on her credenza. We tease her about it often, but it's efficient and, aside from the slow typing, so is she. She's also caring and sweet and brings us peanut butter cookies on Mondays.

"Dr. Devi, the neurologist, ran a bunch of tests. I also had an MRI done last week, and yesterday I went in for the results. They wouldn't give them to me over the phone, can you believe it?" When they called to schedule an appointment, I kept asking for them to just give me the results over the phone, but they wouldn't. They made me drive all the way to them to hear the bad news in person. I will never understand why people think that bad news should be given in person. It makes no sense. Bad news should be given in private so you can process your emotions without having to worry about who's watching.

"Of course I can believe it! You don't give that kind of news over the phone," Margot says indignantly.

I shrug. "Anyway, he told me I have a cerebral meningioma, which is a tumor in the cerebral part of the brain. Evidently, that's the part that controls walking and coordination."

There's dead air after that. I suppose it's not often someone gives you intimate details about their brain tumor.

Sylvie parks the car as we arrive at the café, then turns to me. "What happened next? Finish the story."

I hold my hands out questioningly. What else is there to say?

"That cannot end there. What is the rest of it?" Margot demands.

"What do you think this is, a novel? I went to the doctor; he told me the results. That's it. There's no more to tell. It's a tumor that I have to have removed. Most likely it's benign, but it's creating havoc nonetheless. It's what caused my legs to feel like spaghetti that day I fell and what's causing my headaches, which, by the way, do not happen often." I need to make that very clear.

"I don't like how any of this sounds," Margot says. I'm glad I can't see her face. Margot wears her heart on her sleeve, and if I turn around and her face looks anything like her voice sounds, trembly, I'll break out in hives. I'm scared and stressed out as it is; I can't handle it coming from someone else. I'm done with this conversation. I can't stand being pitied.

"How long have you had it?" Sylvie asks.

"Who knows? I may have had it since I was a kid." Google taught me that.

"So when's the surgery? What are the side effects? Recovery?" Margot asks.

"I don't know yet. The doctor gave me the surgeon's information, and I'm supposed to call and make an appointment, but honestly, okay, so . . . don't get mad."

"That's how you've always started shitty ideas, Alex," Sylvie says.

I ignore her and continue. "I've been thinking about this, and I think it's bullshit. I feel fine."

"There's that damn word again," Sylvie says.

"Bernie had to carry you to a chair," Margot adds.

"Okay, okay. That day I didn't feel fine. But in general, I'm fi—great. Amazing. I jog, I hike. I ride my bike. I'm on my feet all day. I would know if I had a tumor, for God's sake."

They're staring at me wide eyed.

"You are so smart, Alex, yet you're being incredibly naive right now," Margot says, and Margot never says things that aren't positive.

"Look." I exhale. "It's a lot to take in, okay? I'm still processing it. Honestly, I think it's a mistake. But just in case, I made an appointment with a neurologist for a second opinion."

"Good. Okay, that's good. Finally, something that makes sense," Sylvie says. "What else did the doctor tell you?"

"He wanted to talk more. I guess he wanted to explain things, and he was hoping for more questions, but I was caught so off guard and I had the presentation at the office and the divorceaversary to get to, so I didn't know what else to ask. I've told you everything I know so far. There's nothing else."

"I don't like that you're acting so blasé about this!" Sylvie says.

"I'm not acting blasé!" I unhook my seat belt and open the door. The girls follow.

"Wait. She didn't mean—" Margot begins, but Sylvie doesn't let her finish.

"I did mean it. This will not go away by ignoring it."

"I'm not ignoring it. Jesus, I just found out yesterday. It hasn't even been twenty-four hours. What the hell do you want me to do? Fall to the floor in tears? Yell? Scream?"

"Yes. No. I don't know!" Sylvie throws her hands up in the air. "You always have the strangest reactions to things."

I've heard this before, especially after the divorce. I didn't tell my friends for almost a month after Michael left. At first I thought it was a mistake, an awful practical joke. Then I thought he'd had a midlife crisis and would waltz back home in a few days. By the time I'd told them, I was already somewhat numb to the idea, and therefore there wasn't a lot of outward emotion on my part. Or rather, the emotions I did show didn't match the situation, according to Margot. *I'd be devastated. I don't think I could sit there and eat a meal knowing Bernie left me. How are you ordering dessert?"* Margot asked.

"Why is it strange? Because I'm calm? It's only on the outside, trust me. Inside I'm freaked out. I just don't see the point in coming apart without knowing exactly what is happening."

"How about we get coffee and sit?" Margot asks, and I almost roll my eyes. I've never met anyone who hates confrontation as much as Margot. She opens the door to La Vana, a nearby restaurant that serves breakfast. She knows we're not going to yell in front of people.

After we're seated and we've given the server our order, I've had a second to think and drink some coffee. If Sylvie or Margot gave me the news that one of them had an illness, I would be acting the same way. They love me; of course they're worried. "Listen, I appreciate your concern. I really do. And I'm not going to ignore this. I already made an appointment for a second opinion, and I'll see the neurosurgeon and then make a decision. I am not trying to be difficult. I really think that this is all a big mistake."

"Alex . . . ," Margot says sadly.

"I know you're thinking I'm in denial. But wouldn't I know, deep in my heart, if I had something as devastating as a brain tumor? I'd know if something was truly wrong, and I feel it in my gut that I'm fine. Sorry, I mean good. I'm good. This is a mistake. A misdiagnosis. I just know it. I don't know how, but I do, and I need you to trust me. It's why I didn't want to tell anyone anything."

"Alex—"

I know what she's going to say, but I don't want to hear it. "Last year it was the divorce, and now there's a tumor; what's it going to be next year? We're talking about brain surgery. I can't just book an appointment for surgery as if it's a manicure. I need to know that this is truly the only option. For all I know, I've had this my entire life, so what's another week or two while I figure things out?"

"Paralysis, apparently," Sylvie says.

"I don't think it works like that," I snap back.

"Well, to be honest, you don't really know how it works because you haven't asked. You really need to find out exactly what is going on, Alex," Margot says.

Sylvie is getting frustrated, and it seems that Margot is too.

"I may not have asked enough questions, but I did ask how quickly this thing would grow, and he didn't say it was something that needed to be removed tomorrow. Even if I take his estimation conservatively, I have a few months to figure things out."

"Does Bernie know?" Margot asks.

"No!" Crap. I really don't want him to know, especially since we have this big presentation going on soon. "Oh, Margot, promise me you won't say anything to Bernie. Shit, you already did, didn't you?"

"No. He was asleep when I got home and left to go to the office early this morning."

"He's at the office today? On a Saturday?" My worry meter is going crazy.

"Board meeting or something. I think they're interviewing someone. Who knows? But then they're going to play racquetball. He'll be in a terrible mood when he gets home and has to ice his knee and his lower back." She shrugs and waves it off. "Anyway, I'll make you a deal. If you go to the surgeon and report back exactly what he tells you, and then you make a reasonable and informed decision, I won't tell Bernie."

Interviewing someone? I didn't know they'd be hiring anyone. Why wouldn't they tell me this? Since when do the Reys interview staff themselves? Unless it's someone high level.

When I don't say anything, Margot adds, "Or your moms. If not, I'm telling them as soon as we drop you off."

"You play dirty."

"You have to do what the doctor says, Alex. Just because you say it's fine doesn't make it so," Sylvie points out.

"You have a t-t—" Margot begins.

"Let's call it something else. You can't say the word, and I'm tired of hearing it," I say.

"Bob the Blob," Sylvie says without missing a beat, and I laugh out loud. I love my friend. She can be a pain in the ass, but she's the best.

"Seriously! What is wrong with you two?" Margot practically yells. "You guys have a dark, sick sense of humor."

We do. I feel terrible asking them to keep this secret, but it's only until I know for sure that Bob is real.

Sylvie smiles at me and winks. I know she'll have my back no matter what happens, and I know she's concerned, but she knows she needs to give me a little space to figure this out before she completely loses her patience.

CHAPTER FOUR

"Good morning, Nora," I say as I walk past her desk and into my office on Monday morning, two weeks later.

I've tried my best to forget Bob. It's been surprisingly easy, since I've been so focused and excited over my presentation. I can't remember the last time I worked this hard, but it was worth it. I love the concept, and I had fun coming up with it. Also, with the second-opinion appointment with the doctor coming up, there's not much I can do, and stressing never solved anything. But today is the day. I have an appointment at eleven. Meanwhile, I've put Bob into a small box in my brain and then pushed that box way back.

"Good morning, dear. Glenda left those mock-ups for you," she says. "They're on your desk."

"Thanks, Nora," I holler over my shoulder as I put my purse down and pick up the boards with the new website idea. This is a Hail Mary move. I want to propose a complete branding overhaul. I've wanted to do it for a long time. I've sketched ideas for years and have contemplated going to the Reys with it, but I've held off because Bernard is not a man who likes change or innovation.

But I think we need to be bold. Our competitors are going to try and present a model where their parts, logos, and philosophy are an extension of PriceMart. But PriceMart doesn't do auto parts, and consumers know this. PriceMart is all about economy, not quality. AutoRey is about quality. People trust us. We are the leading manufacturer of auto parts in the country, and they don't want to buy PriceMart's generic brand—they want to buy AutoRey's trusted products from PriceMart's shelves at a reduced price. That's the pitch.

But we need to get the word out that we've branched out and are selling within the PriceMart company. How do we do that? We go bold. We rebrand but in a way that it's the same philosophy and idea but in a more modern setting.

"Is that the new pitch?" Bernie asks, walking in and making himself comfortable on the chair across from my desk.

"Yep," I say, scanning the board and finally taking a seat myself. He takes the other one and looks at it.

"There are misspellings," he notes, but I had already seen them. "Let me guess: Glenda?"

I don't bother responding because I know what he's going to say next.

"She's awful. When are you going to fire her?"

"We need another female in the department. She's the only one who applied, and I really thought she'd work out."

"You really thought or you really wanted?"

I groan. He's right. It was probably wishful thinking. She wowed me at the interview with her power suit and her stilettos, as well as her innovative ideas. I'm not ready to let her go just yet. She's not the sharpest tool in the shed, but those original ideas, if given the right opportunity, could work. Unfortunately, AutoRey doesn't usually have those opportunities available, since it's the same ol' ideas, day in and day out.

"She reminds me of me a little."

He scrunches his face. "Of you? How? You've always been on your game—you're a go-getter and a perfectionist. I haven't seen any of that with Glenda."

I shrug. He's not wrong, but I've always been a bit of a dreamer, and in my mind, I always want to push the envelope a bit when we're coming up with a new campaign, except I know that's not what the Reys want, so I always stick to what's tried and true. Glenda isn't seasoned enough yet to know that her ideas are too big for the company, and it's fun to hear her thought process, which isn't too far off from my own. Also, I'm a bit jealous of her wardrobe and assured sense of style. Even though we work out of the corporate office, AutoRey is not very corporate-y. I'm usually in sensible trousers and a polo or a no-frills buttoned shirt.

Bernard went from a mom-and-pop shop to a major multimillion-dollar corporation in a very short time, and the company culture hasn't progressed with the growth. Bernard had been a mechanic himself and was still a "roll up your sleeves and work" kind of man. He may wear a suit and tie these days, but on his days off, he still tinkers with the engine of his 1968 Corvette Stingray.

"Well, thank God we have time to revise these," he says. "There's nothing here about PriceMart."

"I know. We're going to be inside their stores. We are not selling their product. They're selling ours. So I thought we'd work on our own branding first—"

"I dunno . . ."

"It's time, Bernie. This is outdated and bland." I show him the slides with our current logos.

"Dad doesn't like change. He's never going to be okay with this."

"He hired me to do exactly this. Trust me."

He looks at one slide, then another and finally places them down. "Well, get your shit together, fix the misspellings, and do a good job, otherwise Dad's going to have a heart attack. I've never seen him this on edge." He squeezes my shoulder as he walks away.

He's right.

Bernard Rey will not find the misspelling funny, especially if the typo turns *clock* into a very vulgar word in front of a pitch to the biggest retail chain in the world. I'm sure their directors would not be amused either. I cringe at the thought as Glenda walks by the open door of my office. All perfect hair, perky personality, and professional ensemble. It makes me smile.

I went from climbing trees and chasing lizards as a kid, to making sure that Mima got out of bed and showered every morning, to making sure that there was enough milk in the fridge for our morning café con leche. Mom usually went to work before anyone woke up, and I was left to my own devices while Mima recovered.

And at work, I'm a serious take-no-bullshit top executive—I'm in charge of their marketing department and have seventeen employees under me. I'm the only female in the C-suite. Which is why I really wanted it to work out with Glenda—you know, to counteract some of the Eau de Testosterone in the air.

My mothers taught me that anything a man could do, I could do. From hitting home runs at Little League to kicking a soccer ball in middle school to becoming president of the debate team in high school and a national math scholar in college. Or, now, selling car parts. Even though the concept of gender was not something that should have held me back, I've always known better. I'm not naive. I know what some of the men say behind my back and what men think when I leave the room. But gossip doesn't bother me. Numbers speak for themselves, and I've brought the company millions with my creative, outside-the-box approach to marketing.

But have I lost my *mojo*?

I sigh and look up at my screen, the blankness of it pretty synonymous with what's happening inside my head right now. I've run out of new ideas.

I glance at the affirmation sign right next to my keyboard. Do SOMETHING YOU LOVE AND YOU'LL NEVER WORK A DAY IN YOUR LIFE.

Ha! Ain't that a lie? I flick it down onto the desk with a loud thump so that I don't have to see it. Then I groan out loud.

"Everything okay in there?" Nora hollers from her desk, which is right outside my office.

"Just peachy," I yell back and hear her chuckle even through my closed office door. She knows I'm not peachy. Not even close. She's seen (and heard) about the failed presentation.

I wonder if she knows what the board was meeting about on Saturday. I can't ask Bernie, but I can't really ask Nora either. She's their family, after all.

"Keep on smilin'. It's the best medicine," she yells back, and I know she's looking at the affirmation on her own desk. It was a gift from Mima, who is obsessed with T.J.Maxx. I swear, T.J.Maxx got her out of her depression.

I know, I know. It's not possible. Well, it isn't really exactly that T.J.Maxx was the cure for her depression, but Mima was always the one who cared about fashion and makeup and all those things. Even though I never gave her a thing to worry about, I was trying to do my own makeup on the day of my prom, and she walked into my room. She was wearing the same nightgown she always wore, and she looked as frail and defeated as ever.

"What are you doing, mi amor?"

"Remember? Tonight's prom. I think I should . . . I don't know, wear some makeup."

"Claro que sí." *Of course*, she'd said and then proceeded to help me. It was the first time I'd seen her smile in years, and it was like I had my Mima back. She showed me what shade looked best on my skin and what was too much or not enough. She also did my hair in fat curls using a curling iron I didn't even know she had, and then finally she helped me with my dress. I had forgotten how Mima and Annabel did these kinds of things all the time, precancer. They played with makeup, did their nails, and they went shopping. They weren't just mother and daughter; they were friends.

Not that I wasn't my mother's friend as well, but our relationship was different. It wasn't less loving; it was just different. I didn't enjoy shopping or makeovers, but I enjoyed listening to them talk about it. Just like they enjoyed listening to me tell them all about the latest book I'd read. And, on days when Annabel wasn't out with Mima, we'd lie around the house talking about "when we're grown up" adventures. We were going to have so many. I suppose she wasn't just my sister; she was my best friend, so I can see why Mima missed her so, so much.

"No, no. That purse doesn't match," she had said. I shrugged. It was all I had. She looked at her watch. "Stay here. I'll be back." In record time, she had been dressed and out the door.

"Where'd your Mima go?" Mom had poked her head into my bedroom, fiddling with a camcorder.

"I don't know. She said something about my purse and left."

We'd both shrugged. "You look beautiful, Alex."

"Thanks, Mom."

Twenty minutes later, Mima had walked back into the house with a shopping bag. She turned it over, and at least seven different purses in different sizes and colors came tumbling down onto my bed. This is a scene I recall too often between Annabel and Mima. They loved to shop together and even more, they loved to show Mom and me all their finds, even if we weren't interested. It was always amusing to see them excited when they found a bargain—tags from T.J.Maxx everywhere. After that day, I noticed every few weeks she'd make a run to the store. It was the only place she really went, and then she'd show us all the things she'd purchased. It was the time she was most chatty and animated.

If she ever goes missing, that's the first place we'd look. Because of this obsession, I have about two dozen wooden affirmation signs in varying colors and sizes, and I've had to spread them out to others around my office. Even with the $7.99 price tag, my kooky mother believes that the boxes were handmade, storm-weathered, and written by an enlightened savant who's wandered the earth imparting knowledge via T.J.Maxx. Normally, they don't bother me, and I even like some of the wisdom on them. Some are corny, some funny, and some are genuinely deep.

Except this one.

This one sitting right beside my computer screen, staring at me, is a big fat lie.

I thought I loved my job, but it is work, and right now, I do not love anything about it!

I send an email to my staff, who're as deflated as I am, mostly because I've made them rework these boards a dozen times in as many days. I want to meet with them after lunch to finalize this presentation. I want it to be perfect before I pitch it to Bernard.

Call me the moment you get out of the doctor today. Margot texts me just as I'm about to call Glenda in to correct the misspellings.

I will, I reply, and she sends back the prayer emoji.

I tap my nails on my desk over and over. You know when you can't sleep and the later it becomes, the more anxious you get, and that leads you to be even more sleepless? Well, that's what's been happening to me. I'm stressed out about my ideas and whether they're too bold, which leaves me depressed, and that kills my creativity even more. It's a never-ending cycle.

Eventually, it's time for me to head out to my appointment. Maybe I'm more nervous than I thought I was. There's a knot in the pit of my stomach.

There's a wooden sign hanging on my closed door that says:

IF OPPORTUNITY DOESN'T KNOCK, BUILD A DOOR.

I give it the finger before I head out the door.

You can say that my stress level is at DEFCON One while I drive to the doctor. Everything is hanging on this appointment. When I went to Dr. Devi, I hadn't been nervous. Frankly, I'd been annoyed. With all the work I had piled up on my desk, the last thing I wanted to do was drive across town to have a doctor read me a diagnosis that he could've easily told me over the phone. But I'd also thought it was something less serious.

Now, on my way to see Dr. Gibbons, I'm actually nauseated, and this eyebrow twitch I've developed is driving me insane. Within thirty minutes of leaving my office, I'm already in an exam room of a very modern-looking office building. Dr. Gibbons, a middle-aged woman with a blonde bob and wire-rimmed glasses, comes in. She introduces herself but barely looks up from my chart.

"I see you sent everything over from Dr. Devi. Good. Good." She keeps reading. She flips the page. Reads some more. Flips back to the first. My leg bops up and down, and I want to yell for her to hurry up.

She grabs her stethoscope and signals for me to hop on the examination table, which I do. She tells me to breathe in and out while she listens. Of course, this all makes me even more anxious since I just want her to get to the tumor, which is why I'm here.

"Everything okay?" I ask.

"Yes. Everything sounds good." She sits back down. "I've had a chance to review it all before you arrived today, and I made a call to Devi. We took our boards together. Good guy." *If she's already reviewed it and spoken to the other doctor, why is she still looking at the chart in that way that makes me think she's searching for an answer? Is she not sure? Why is she taking forever to tell me what's wrong? Why the hell is she talking about her board exam?*

She takes one last glance, then closes it and finally makes eye contact with me.

"Ms. Martinez, how do you feel?"

"Emotionally? I'm falling apart." I point to my eye. I wonder if she can even see the way it's fluttering. "I've developed a nervous tic, so that's super fun." She doesn't seem to care, but humor has always been my default setting during stressful situations. "Physically, I'm perfectly fine. That's why I'm here. Dr. Devi says I have a cerebral meningioma, which I've been researching, and I think he's wrong."

"Why do you think he is wrong?" Her tone is clinical. She's not surprised or annoyed by my statement.

"Because I don't have memory loss, seizures, severe pain of any kind. That's what it says online I'd be feeling. I'd barely be able to get up and move from the weakness in my legs. Notwithstanding the nervous twitch, which is probably eyestrain from my stupid work presentation, I'm in great health."

"Something must've prompted you to go see him in the first place. A healthy thirty-five-year-old female doesn't simply go to a neurologist on a whim," she says.

"Well, I do get headaches every now and again."

"How often is now and again?"

"A few times a month. They're not excruciating or anything. I take Advil and get back to whatever I was doing. Ironically, though, I haven't had a single one in a month or so. I had thought they were migraines, which is what brought me to Dr. Devi."

She clicks on the top of her pen and then writes something in the file, then clicks the pen closed. The click echoes through the room.

"Not painful, just a dull ache," I add. "I don't even miss work for them." I hope she writes all that down. No need to make a mountain out of a molehill or anything.

She looks up, pen still in hand. "Anything else? Nausea? Weakness? Lethargy? Mood shift?"

"Nope," I begin and then add, "well, there was this small incident. But it's really nothing. A few weeks ago, I was in a board meeting that lasted an eternity—you know how men can ramble on and on." I snort nervously, and then a small blush creeps up my neck. There's no reciprocity or even embarrassment from her on my behalf, so I soldier on. "Anyway, when I stood up and took a step, I fell. But I'm sure it was from sitting so long." I wave my hand dismissively.

She clicks the pen and starts writing again. Argh. *Stop making notes!* "Before you fell, did you feel numbness in your extremities? Dizziness?"

"My leg had that normal pins-and-needles feeling."

She starts to write again. What the hell? Is she penning a novel or something? I want to rip it from her hand and make her listen to me. *I'm fine.* There's silence in the room while she continues her dissertation, and then I finally feel the need to break the silence. "Um . . . so . . . what do you think? You saw the scans, right?"

She looks up at me and places her pen down. Finally! "Ms. Martinez, you have a large mass on the area of your skull near the cerebellum. Consistent with the radiologist, I would confirm a meningioma."

Damn it.

She continues to speak in a very clinical and removed manner. "It is quite large, and I'm surprised you are not having more manifestations caused by the way it's pressed against the nerves. I recommend immediate resection."

"But . . . but . . . you don't understand, Doctor. I eat well; I exercise often. I have a yearly physical, no high cholesterol or any of that. I don't smoke. I don't do drugs. I'm healthy."

"Ms. Martinez—" she begins, but I interrupt.

"Alex. Please call me Alex."

"Alex, cerebral meningiomas are very slow-forming tumors, and you did nothing to cause this. What you eat or don't eat would not have made a difference."

When I don't say anything for far too long, she says with a trace of humanity that wasn't there before, "Alex, you have a brain tumor. I'm sorry to have to be so blunt, but the sooner you come to terms with this, the sooner you'll go see the neurosurgeon and have it removed.

You will have a much-improved quality of life." Her empathy actually makes it worse. I do not want anyone to feel sorry for me. I prefer the cold robotic diagnostician.

"I read that radiation is preferred over surgery."

"Yes, of course. It is less invasive. Unfortunately, you'd need to discuss that with the surgeon. He'll develop a plan with you, but, in my opinion, this tumor is far too large for radiation. In fact, you may need both surgery and radiation if he cannot resect it all."

Now I'm really going to throw up.

"I'll let Dr. Chen decide that. He's the best neurosurgeon in Florida."

"I know. Dr. Devi suggested him too."

"I'll warn you now, his bedside manner leaves much to be desired."

Damn, her bedside manner hasn't been stellar, so if his is worse, I'm scared of what he's going to say.

"What happens if I don't have the surgery?"

"That's not advisable. You're young and otherwise healthy; there's no reason to—"

"But what if?" I cut her off, my voice shaky, and I cannot help but find the similarities between my diagnosis and Annabel's cancer. I understand we don't have the same thing, but the doctors were optimistic about her prognosis. My mothers did everything they were supposed to do. They followed every single recommendation and advice from the extensive team of doctors, and Annabel still died. Hell, I think that what was worse than the actual death was the awful year leading up to it.

"First, your headaches will not improve. They may worsen in the next few months, in fact. As the tumor presses on the nerves, you may eventually lose your ability to walk or balance. It all depends, but your speech can be compromised, and it can even impact your mood. It's difficult to say for sure, but these are all within the realm of possibility."

"Immediate possibility?"

"No. Not necessarily immediate. Like I said, this is a slow-growing tumor, but it's already significant in size. It's hard to say how fast things would progress."

"Meaning it could be slow or not at all. That is a possibility, correct?"

"An unlikely one."

"But one nonetheless."

She exhales. "Alex, I wish I could tell you that this is the worst you'll feel, but I cannot tell you that. No one can. It can happen next week or next year or years from now. But the fact is, you have a tumor, and that is not something I advise you leave to chance."

"I appreciate your honesty, Doctor." But this is a lie. I need a little less honesty and a lot more positivity. Why can't she just say that I'll be all right and that everything's going to work out? As a rational person, I understand she can't lie to me, but as a person who received the worst news, I need some optimism.

"Good luck, Alex," she says and stretches out her arm. We shake hands, and she steps out of the room, leaving me shell-shocked.

———

I am exhausted by the time I get home. After the appointment, I went to the office to meet with my team, but my head wasn't in it. I assigned everyone a task, putting Victor in charge of execution, and left early. It was a first for me, and everyone was shocked, but no one asked any questions.

Before I walk inside, I call my friends on a double line. I don't want to risk my mothers hearing the call, and I don't want to explain this twice.

"Hi," they both say at once. "What did the doctor say?" Sylvie asks.

"She agrees with the first doctor and suggested I see the surgeon." I try not to sound as dejected as I feel.

"Oh, Alex . . . I'm so sorry," Margot says. We were all holding on to hope, I guess.

"Yeah, so I'll see what the neurosurgeon says, and I'll take it from there."

"You okay?" Sylvie asks.

"Aside from Bob, yep, I'm great."

"Har-har," Sylvie says.

"Oh, and I'd like to report I've developed a super-flattering nervous tic."

They laugh, but there's not much humor behind it.

"It's okay to be upset, you know. We understand. This is a big deal."

"I am upset and worried and all those things," I tell them. "But until it's time for surgery, all I can do is keep on moving forward, right?"

"That's a good attitude, Alex," Margot says. "You're strong and you're scrappy. You'll be fine."

"Yeah, I know." But I don't know. I have a brain tumor; I can't even wrap my head around this news.

"And he's still hopeful it can be removed and it's not cancer?" Sylvie asks.

"It was a she and yes, she agreed with the other doctor."

"You know we're here if you need us?" Sylvie says. "I don't know what to do, but I want to help somehow."

"I know. But I'm okay. There's nothing to do at the moment." When my mothers told me about Annabel's diagnosis, I was young and naive. The doctors were optimistic, and therefore I was optimistic, even when I saw my mothers falter. There was no googling or second-guessing the doctors, and I knew only what was shared with me. I never asked anything more. Mostly, I realize, my young brain didn't understand the severity of the diagnosis. I accepted that she had cancer and I accepted that with the correct treatment, she'd be okay.

I remember knowing it was bad because cancer was bad. Leukemia was bad. The pale, drained faces of my mothers when they said the

C-word were bad. But I processed it in that indestructible, immortal way that kids process things. Death is a foreign occurrence that just doesn't even register as a possibility. One of my grandmothers had died years earlier, and it was sad; I had cried, and then I'd moved on in that way kids move on. Annabel was positive too. Even as her tiny body became frail and weak, she smiled and cuddled her dolls and mostly complained about the inconvenience of cancer. *"Why can't I go outside and play?"* or *"The hospital bed is uncomfortable."* But I can't recall her complaining about pain. Now, as an adult, I realize she must've hurt. Did she not say anything, or did I just not pay attention to it? The thought nags at me. And even though my diagnosis is so different from Annabel's, all the things I had not thought about when she'd been diagnosed and sick are now all I can think about.

They sigh into the phone, and we say our goodbyes.

I'm seriously tired of getting bad news. I may not be able to control the tumor, but I can control the way my presentation turns out at work.

CHAPTER FIVE

You know what's great about dealing with a major amount of stress at work? You can't think of the brain tumor that has set up residence in your skull. *Look at me being glass half-full.*

"Do you think the ol' man's going to go for it? You don't think it's too much?" Victor asks as we finish revising our last slide. Victor was the first person I hired when I was given the authority to start a marketing team six years ago. He'd take my job in a second if he could, of that I'm sure. I used to think it could never happen. To be in my role, you have to have a particular set of cojones that Victor just doesn't possess; he's indecisive and scared of risks. But he has a penis and I don't, and lately (mostly because of my failed pitch and the meetings I'm not invited to), I worry that I could be replaced. Plus, I am going to need a week or two of time off for this Bob situation. Will this be the moment where he swoops in and takes my job?

Victor goes to the country club with the other executives and some of the department heads, and they golf. They have drinks and complain about their wives, after hours. He's part of the baseball league. They do "bro-dude" things that I'm not invited to do. I don't want to be that whiny kid who cries about being excluded, but right now, I want to be let in to the cool boys' table. And I hate myself for feeling this way.

"Bernard is old-school." I take a step back to look at the finished boards. "But if he just listened with an open mind, he'd love it."

"Old-school is an understatement," Victor says.

"Our online presence just isn't reflective of the times," I say.

"And while I do agree we need to step that up"—He leans in closer, studying the presentation carefully—"is this too much, maybe? I dunno, Alex. We've had the same brand forever, and it's worked. Why fix something that isn't broke, ya know?"

I throw my hands up in the air. "Exactly! Forever. Things evolve and change. This logo and our website aren't reflective of the times! You know it, I know it, hell Bernie knows it, even though he'd never admit it. We should've done this years ago. We need to ramp up our e-commerce. PriceMart needs to see us as a real player in the game. If we sell, they sell."

"You tried to change the home page of the website years ago, and he said it was too bold. *This* is so much bolder," Victor says.

"Well, now he wants something that he's not going to get unless he does something grand. Fresh. New."

"And you think this is it?" Victor says with uncertainty in his voice.

"No. No. No. None of that. You've got to believe in the product in order to pitch it. You can't sound doubtful."

"I love the new logo, the layout of the new online platform. I love it all, Alex. But will Bernard?"

I wish he would have voiced all these questions while we were coming up with the concept. I knew he wasn't thrilled, but I didn't realize he thought it was a bad idea. Well, either way, I can't change it now. This is the most sure I've been on anything I've ever done at work. "I guess we'll find out soon enough."

Victor exhales and then gathers everything and heads to the conference room to prepare for this afternoon. We have a run-through of the pitch that I'm giving tomorrow. If Bernard and the rest of the directors approve it, then we'll get things ready for the meeting with PriceMart in the next few months.

"I'll see you later. Have an errand to run before our meeting," I say, and I run to the neurosurgeon for my appointment.

———

"Good morning, Ms. Martinez, I'm Dr. Chen. Pleasure to meet you." I'm less scared than I was when I went to Dr. Gibbons last week. Maybe the stress of it all has made me numb. Maybe Bob's affecting my ability to feel. Whatever it is, I just want to get it over with. Schedule the surgery, spend a few weeks in recovery, and get back to living my life. I calculated that if I have the surgery next week, I'll be fully recovered by the time we have to meet the PriceMart people in Seattle. There's so much logistics, planning, and number crunching that needs to take place before the big presentation.

My part in the scheme of things is only one piece of the puzzle, but a very large piece. Once our plan is approved, the execution will take months, but I can do a lot of it from home while I recover. I've thought it all through, and I feel a little less anxious about it. Things always look better when you've planned it out. I take after Mom in that respect. Mima and Annabel were always the spontaneous adventurer types. This presentation feels like something Annabel would love—it's creative, fun, and unexpected. I'm so proud of it.

"Please, call me Alex." If he's the person who's going to possibly cut into my brain, we should be on a first-name basis, right?

I'm sitting on the chair that is adjacent to the examining table, and he's sitting across from me, a file on his lap, much like the other two doctors I've seen this last month.

He takes off his glasses and puts them aside. "I see you have a grade-one brain tumor." I'm not sure whether he's trying to make me at ease by being playful or if he has zero concern for my feelings right now. Either way, it's not funny.

My heart is beating a bit faster now. "And you're the man to remove it, right?"

"That is correct. It's grade one, so that's good."

Oh, he's being serious? I thought he was joking a second ago; grade one is an actual thing, apparently. Like when men say, *She's a grade-A piece of ass.* Jesus, I've been hanging around men too much. "What does grade one mean? How many grades are there?"

"Grade one means that it's likely not cancerous and it possibly hasn't invaded the brain. Grade two and three are more likely to be cancerous and invasive. Your tumor is mostly superficial, but unfortunately, because of where it is and its size, we need to go in through the cranium."

My tumor. As if I purchased it or asked for it. Wouldn't it be great if I could return it? "And that's bad?"

"Not bad. Not good. Some of these can be done with minimally invasive approaches. For instance, we sometimes go in through someone's sinuses. But that's not an option for you. I'll go in through here." He reaches toward me and bends my ear forward. He pokes and prods my skull. "We'll do what's called a keyhole retrosigmoid craniotomy, where we open a small hole right here in the cranium to get to the tumor."

Make a hole. In my skull.

The smoothie I had for breakfast is climbing back up. Obviously, somewhere in my subconscious, I knew that brain surgery involved my skull, but for some reason, I never considered exactly what that meant. And now all I can think about is a drill literally making a hole in my skull.

"I read that radiation—"

He shakes his head. "You need surgery, Ms. Martinez. There's no getting around it. The sooner the better. If the mass continues to compress this nerve area, your headaches will intensify, and there could be other secondary manifestations." He points to the tumor on the MRI with the back of his pen. I can see the mass clearly. It looks out of place, as if there was a smudge on the lens of the camera.

I look away from the image. "How soon? And what am I looking at in terms of recovery? Is it a risky surgery?"

"It will only get worse if left there, but for your age, the surgery is not as risky. You're still young, and you want to be able to feel better, don't you?" He takes out a pen from his shirt pocket and opens up the folder. I guess it was a rhetorical question because he doesn't wait for my answer.

"I'm not in pain. I feel fine."

"That's surprising. It's a pretty substantial mass."

"You've done these surgeries before? Is it common? What's the recovery time?"

"I don't want you to worry. I've done this countless times. You're in the best hands. You'll have to stay in the hospital a week or so for observation post-surgery. We'll run scans daily to make sure there's no bleeding. Then, because of the location, you'd probably need about four to six weeks of recovery before you can return to work. Depending on how you do with recovery, you can go on light duties for about five weeks after that. Sometimes, there's swelling, and you may need some PT, OT, or ST."

"PT, OT, ST?" I ask, feeling extremely overwhelmed all of a sudden. That was a lot of weeks of recovery; I kind of lost count.

"Physical therapy, occupational therapy, speech therapy."

I'm about to hyperventilate, and I don't think he's paying enough attention to the severity of what he's telling me. "So you're saying that it's going to take twelve weeks?"

"Twelve to sixteen weeks. Give or take," he says, unfazed by my squeal or the magnitude of the timeline he's just given me.

"And even though you're saying it's just a small hole and you've done this many times and it's no big deal, I may need OT, ST, and PT?"

"I never said it's no big deal, Ms. Martinez. I said I have done this many times. But I don't want you to make light of this. You have a tumor that is only going to wreak more havoc as time goes on. This is major surgery, but there's no reason to believe that everything will not go well."

Did he just say he doesn't want me to take it lightly? I'm about to have a full-blown meltdown while he's just sitting there all cool, calm, and collected, and he thinks I'm not taking it seriously enough?

"As for the therapy," he begins. "It's brain surgery, Ms. Martinez. We are good, and we've had great success using this technique, but, as in all surgeries, there's the risk of clots, infections, bleeding, but that's a less than ten percent chance. There's always the anesthesia itself, which can be risky. Like I mentioned, with swelling, the recovery can take a little longer, and the swelling can cause speech issues, memory loss, or even paralysis. Because of the size, you do have an increased chance of some temporary issues, which is why PT, OT, ST are possibilities. It's a fifty-fifty chance, Ms. Martinez, but I can't know for sure until I go in and see how entwined the tumor is with the nerves. You will feel pressure and headaches for some time afterward."

"Usually?" My voice cracks. "Usually doesn't sound hopeful. Could it be permanent?"

"Well, your tumor—"

"Please, don't call it my tumor anymore. It's not my tumor. It's a parasite that I want gone." I'm sure I'm as white as a ghost. I feel my hands shake. "I went to see a neurologist for a headache, and now I'm facing brain surgery that may give me more headaches? How did we get to this point? I wish I had never gone to Dr. Devi in the first place."

Dr. Chen opens the door and barks to a nearby nurse, "Bring Ms. Martinez some juice.

"Breathe, Ms. Martinez," he says. "Ignoring the problem isn't going to solve anything. Like I said, you're young and healthy, and you'll get through this. It's my duty to tell you the risks, and yes, some of those could be permanent, but that is rare. A less than two percent chance. There's no reason to believe any of that will occur. This is not an elective surgery, Ms. Martinez; that mass has to go." The nurse comes in, punches a tiny straw through an apple juice box, and the doctor practically shoves it in my mouth. After I gulp a few times, he tells me to breathe in through my nose and out through my mouth.

"We'll need to schedule you for pre-op labs and some additional tests. My office will call you to schedule everything, including the date of the surgery and the pre-op instructions. I'm sure you'll need to make arrangements with your employer. We will provide medical documentation to show them as well."

"But, but . . . I feel fine." How many times have I repeated these words? Not just to Dr. Chen but to everyone. And still, they want to cut me open. Memories of Annabel blur my vision.

"That's great. Let's keep it that way," he says and scribbles a few other things in my chart. "Are you married?"

"No. Why?"

"Do you have someone who will assist you post-surgery? You'll need some help, a support system."

My mothers. My poor mothers. They'll have to be my support system like they were with Annabel. My mothers and I were at her side all day every day. More than once, Annabel was too weak to make it to the bathroom on time, and I learned how to change the sheets and wash her up without having to move her off the bed. I knew when she needed crackers to help with the nausea or when she wanted to talk about regular teenage girl things happening at school because she was having a good day.

This makes me even angrier at Michael. This is the "in sickness and in health" part I needed him for. I hate having to put my mothers through this again. "Y-yes, I have a support system."

"Good. Good." He says a few other things that are surely import-ant, but I don't register any of it. He squeezes my shoulder on the way out. As if he's sorry for the news but also, it's another day at the office for him. Then he's gone, and I'm given a pile of papers with a packet of instructions, the title CRANIOTOMY PREP. Such a life-altering procedure, and I am just given preprinted instructions before I drive off to work in a state of confusion and slight panic.

The ringing in my ears is making me dizzy. Is it Bob or the emo-tional breakdown that was bound to occur?

I walked into the appointment feeling a bit more optimistic, and I'm leaving feeling like I've just been issued a life sentence. Hell, I *have* been issued a life sentence. What would I do if I couldn't walk? And memory loss?

My phone's ringing with an incoming call from Bernie, and I know I have to take it because I have deadlines and people depending on me, but I'm not in the mood to talk. I answer it anyway. "Hello?"

"Hey. There's an issue at the Omaha store, and Dad's flying out tonight. He wants to go over your pitch before he leaves. Are you on your way back?"

"Uh, yeah. I'm driving."

"Good. He wants to do it now."

"Now?" I echo.

"Are you listening? Dad is leaving—" And the rest is a blur. I'm underwater, and there's noise around me, but it's muffled. That's how I feel. I think I "ahem" and "ahaa" a few times, but I don't know what I'm responding to.

"Uh . . . yeah, uh . . . I'll be there in twenty minutes." And I hang up. The last thing I need to do is go to work and start presenting any-thing to anyone. I have not taken a sick day in . . . in . . . I have no idea when I last took a full sick day. I park my car at the office and hope I stopped at all the red lights, because I cannot recall driving here.

I take the stairs up the three flights. There's commotion in the boardroom, which is where I'm supposed to be, but instead, I take a left and head straight to my office like a zombie, where I plop down on my chair. *Dr. Chen wants to drill a hole in my head. I'm going to have headaches for weeks, not to mention the possible complications from surgery. What if I'm that statistic who becomes paralyzed?*

"Good, you're back. Are you ready, dear?" Nora peeks in my door, and I jump. "Oh, sorry," she says.

"No. It's fine. You just startled me."

She eyes me suspiciously. "You okay? They're waiting for you in the conference room. You want some water? A PowerBar? You look a little pale, sweetie."

"No thanks," I say, not even sure what I'm saying. I robotically stand up and walk to the conference room.

I am not ready.

I close my eyes, count to ten, and try to forget about everything except for the presentation I have right now. My job depends on it (I think). I need to focus. But this is not just any marketing meeting. There's a sense of dread that's been ebbing and flowing throughout the office. The tension is palpable, and it's making me even more anxious. The fact that Bernard moved this pitch up instead of just waiting to do it on Monday when he returns just adds to that sense of urgency and unease.

This is a new feeling for me. I began at AutoRey right after high school at their flagship store. I needed a job that was close to home so I could check in on Mima during the day when Mom was at work. I applied for a bunch of minimum-wage jobs, and AutoRey hired me. It was convenient and just hectic enough that I didn't have time to think of the black cloud that waited for me at home. It was the perfect escape.

Eventually, I was promoted to manager, and the Rey family was super accommodating while I went to college; they even paid for my master's degree in marketing. I've always felt indebted to them, not to mention indispensable. Hell, Bernard's told me I'm indispensable. I felt like a Rey. Until recently.

When we began buying out small auto-parts stores, I was very vocal on how to rebrand those stores. Phasing them into our folds slowly is the key. People like their small neighborhood shops and hate the big, bad chain stores. And because we weren't a big, bad chain store yet, it wasn't too difficult to fit right in to the small-town feel. We always keep the employees (my idea) and get the owners out of debt. You may think we're terrible for buying out the small shops, but if it wasn't us, it would be someone else. At least we do it with a heart. That's my motto, and I've been lucky that Bernard has always agreed. But now we're going into new territory. Now we're going inside a store, an already established big, bad box store, and we're putting our merchandise inside. This would take AutoRey to the next level. Yet it all falls on my shoulders. I have to admit, creating this new pitch, coming up with the concept, seeing it on the presentation boards gave me a new sense of excitement. It's not often I can flex my creative muscle when it comes to automotive parts. But now I'm scared that I went too far with this proposal. *Damn it, Victor. Why did he have to put doubt in my head?*

When I walk in, Bernard is at the head of the long wooden table. Bernard, like Bernie, is about six feet tall, with broad shoulders and a thick mustache. Unlike Bernie, Bernard's mustache is white from age, much like the hair on his head. He's wearing a black polo with the logo of his company over his pectorals. If he were standing, he'd tower over most of the staff. He exudes command, but since I've known him for so long, I know he's actually a big teddy bear. Today, however, he's less teddy bear and more lion. The warm smile I've grown to love is gone. He's all business today.

For the first time since I met him, it surprises me how I've never seen this side of him. My heart's beating like a drum, and I can feel it in my ears. He needs this deal as much as I do.

The rest of the executives, including Bernie, start walking into the room. "You're up, Alex," Bernard says when everyone takes their place. I have three of my team members with me, one of whom is Victor, who places the boards on the easel.

I've always been comfortable pitching ideas. This is where I shine. Today, however, my hands are shaking when I point to the first poster board, but I try and power through.

My new idea is a bit out there. But it still fits their concept of "Rey."

I place the mock-ups against the easels and step back.

I start off awkward. Stilted. I'm just reading the boards without any feeling. When I see Bernie yawn, something inside snaps. I need to focus.

"Sorry. Sorry," I say and place the first board back and glance at Victor, who looks nervous on my behalf. "Let me start over," I say, and I see confused faces. It's not like me to be unprepared. I take a sip of water, and this time I start more assuredly. I move from one board to the other, feeling more confident as time passes. Victor then turns on the slides, which are projected on the wall behind me, and every other worry melts away as work takes over.

I'm laser focused on pitching this new idea to this table of men, grasping their attention, making them lean in to see the details of everything. Asking questions, which I have answers to, making them smile and nod. I can read a room, and this room is liking this idea.

"In the commercials, there will be a king in cartoon form, and it'll be King Auto talking." I show them the new proposed logo, and the mock-up animated figure is projected behind me in tandem. "Simple font, no frills. White lettering, black background. But we'll incorporate the cartoon king into the website and on the ads." *If you can't beat them, join them* was my thought process when coming up with this. I wanted something cleaner and simpler. I didn't want anything gimmicky, and here I am proposing the biggest gimmick of them all. "The goal is to have this king be as known as the GEICO lizard or the duck from Aflac."

I talk for about forty-five minutes, the jitteriness of earlier long gone.

And then I'm finished.

And no one speaks.

Normally, I can read Bernard, but now, there's just silence. I look around the room, and Bernie is smiling, and so are the other executives, but Bernard is just quiet, except for the drumming of his fingers against the mahogany table.

The silence is deafening, and all the smiles in the room begin to dissipate as we all come to the realization that Bernard may, in fact, hate my pitch.

Someone clears their throat, and Bernard eyes me. "I'd like a moment alone with Alex, please."

Quickly, everyone scatters, even Bernie, who looks worried on my behalf. He squeezes my shoulder as he walks past me. I've decided, right here and now, I hate that gesture. Was I a shoulder squeezer too? Did Bernie do this often? I'd never noticed before, but after the earlier placating squeeze from Dr. Bad News, this one from Bernie leaves me feeling dreadful.

"Have a seat, Alex," he says, and I think I'm going to throw up. I pull the seat across from him.

"How do you think that went?" His voice is neutral.

"I think it went very well. I took what this company is all about, family and tradition, and made it more relatable to this day and age. The website will be very user-friendly and—"

"You've always been unpredictable but reliable."

I open my mouth and then close it again. I'm actually speechless. I am unsure whether this is an insult or a compliment. Am I predictable and unreliable now?

After an awkward beat, he says, "I see that you're excited about this, and I hate to crush that enthusiasm, but I don't like it, Alex. It's not what I expected from you. It's not in line with the AutoRey vision."

I feel like I've been hit in the face. My cheeks flame, and I have to hold back tears. Yes, actual tears. They don't actually come out, but I feel that telltale sign as my throat closes up and my nose clogs up. "It's my opinion that the best way to get PriceMart's attention is to rebrand."

"Rebranding is not what we need. I'm not changing what makes us, us."

"AutoRey sells car parts. With all due respect, Bernard, what does this crown have to do with that? This is old-fashioned," I say, grabbing a sample of our current logo and sliding it over to him. "PriceMart is about efficiency, and if you study their website, it's user-friendly, geared toward tech-savvy consumers who are just as comfortable walking into a store or shopping online. We need to give the same perception of being accessible and reliable."

"It's been our logo for fifty-one years. It's a staple. Imagine if tomorrow Coke made their logo purple or Nike changed from a swoosh to a star?"

"Pepsi has rebranded a dozen times. Google, IHOP . . . I can give you a hundred major corporations that have rebranded, changed with the times, and it's been great for business. It's been the thing that has needed to happen. Bernard, you know how many dots the consumer has to connect to understand what a crown has to do with AutoRey?"

Rey is their last name, and it's the Spanish word for king, and thus the crown. It's a play on their name, and I hate it, mostly because it's not even a cool-looking crown. It's literally a big, overly adorned, medieval gold crown with red felt lining. Right under the crown, the word *AutoRey* is written in an ornate font. Edwardian Script, to be exact. Before I began working here, fifteen years ago, I didn't even know that was a font. The kicker is, all emails and correspondence within the company must be written in Edwardian Script, per company policy.

The staff can't understand half the emails they receive because it's all swirly lines jumbled together. It's the default font on our company computers. "Are we selling automotive parts or are we blacksmiths from the Middle Ages?"

"Rebranding is what a company does when they're not successful. It's the equivalent of a washed-up movie star doing a reality television show."

"I respectfully disagree. Rebranding is a way a company changes and adapts to the times. We're competing with big-name auto-parts stores and major retailers. We need to catch up to this decade. Hell, to this century. We need to make buying parts online easier and more accessible. Most people want to buy their windshield wiper fluid online—they don't want to get dressed, fight traffic, go to a store, and wait in line."

"This just isn't working for me."

I think he means me: I'm not working for him.

His mind is made up, and there's nothing I'm going to say to change it. I know him enough to know this.

"I've been thinking, maybe we need fresh eyes to take a look at this?"

"Fresh eyes?" It's happening. I'm getting fired.

"I'm thinking that we need to go outside. Get a professional marketing company—"

"Are you firing me?"

"No!" He says it without batting an eye. "I just think we are in over our heads on this. We need this bid, and I don't think we're going in the right direction. I'm sorry, Alex. It's not personal."

Bullshit. Of course it's personal. Maybe it isn't personal for him, but it is for me. It's my whole life. If Victor had proposed it, would Bernard have liked it? Is it because I'm a woman, and changing aesthetics seems like an insignificant thing that a female would fixate on?

"Bernie and Victor liked it," I blurt out, to see if that makes any difference. It angers me that I even have to say this, but I say it anyway with my teeth clenched, as if the words had to be pried out of my mouth.

"Okay," he says, seemingly confused. "It's still not the direction I want to take." It gives me a tiny bit of relief that he says that, because on a personal level, I love Bernard, and I would hate to think of him as sexist. "I want to start vetting marketing firms, and I'm counting on you to assist with this." He smiles. I think it's his way of placating me, but I don't feel placated. I feel like I flopped, and I'm mad and hurt, and there're a lot of feelings brewing that I just cannot pinpoint. "You'll take the lead? Be the liaison between them and us?" He frames it as a question, but it's really a demand. Suddenly I have a different role. I've gone from chief marketing officer to liaison for the marketing company we're bringing on.

"Sure," I say, barely getting the word out.

With this, his mustache tips up, and I see all his perfectly white teeth. He smiles at me sweetly, as if he doesn't realize he just gave me devastating news. The second of the day.

"I already have Luisa looking up some names. She'll send you a list, and we can go from there." Luisa is his executive assistant, and the fact that she's already looking them up means he assumed today would be a failure. I was out before I even walked in.

I press my lips together and push my chair back. There's nothing else to discuss.

He leans over the table with his arm. "This is going to be great; you'll see."

I nod, not at all "seeing" how this will be great for me, but nevertheless, I lean over the wide table to shake his hand, and a tinge of pain radiates from my neck to the back of my eye. I try to hold in the whimper that escapes my lips, but he must've heard it. "Did you ever go to the doctor, Alex? After you passed out that day? You don't look so well."

I didn't pass out, I want to say, but words are failing me right now. "Yes," I say. He's waiting for me to tell him, and I should. I should tell him, but I don't feel like being vulnerable right now. The last thing I need is for him to feel sorry for me. "I'm fine. It was nothing."

"It's been hectic around here lately. Take some time off, Alex. You deserve it. I don't remember the last time you took a personal day. I even told you to take some time off after that bastard left you, and you never did. I appreciate your work ethic, but everyone needs time off every now and again. It's good for the soul."

I take the papers and my notepad, not wanting to meet his eyes. I'm mad. Sad. Hurt. Betrayed. Scared. All the negative emotions.

"Seriously, Alex. I insist. Take some time. Come back refreshed and feeling better. I insist," he says again.

I look up at him and swallow. "Yeah. Okay."

"Great! A break—it'll be perfect," he says.

"A break?" I parrot back. It's as if all the words he's saying just aren't computing in my head.

"Yeah, a vacation. Don't worry about a thing, Victor can work on vetting those agencies." This new role is so insignificant that Victor can just do it. I'm not needed at all. "Yeah?"

Leave work during a major transition and put Victor in charge of things? I feign a smile. "Uh . . . yeah. Okay."

"Wonderful," he says, slapping the table emphatically. Then he walks out of the room, completely unperturbed that he's thrown my entire life into a loop.

I walk right into my office, grab my purse, and walk out. Nora looks at me questioningly, but I just wave to her and say, "Good night." Which must be weird because it's not even two yet. But I have to process what just happened.

Not just what happened in the office but everything that's happened today.

Today, the day my world fell apart.

PART TWO

I WAS MUCH HAPPIER BEING IN DENIAL

CHAPTER SIX

"You're home early," Mima says, looking over her shoulder from a crouched position by the garden, a handful of weeds in one hand and a dirt-laden glove on the other. She has on a huge floppy hat and a bright sun-kissed smile and dark jean overalls. I close the door to my car and then walk to her and help her to an upright position.

"You cut yourself again," I say, noticing the small scratches that look like she got into a fight with a disgruntled cat, but I know it's that she's been trimming the bougainvillea that has taken over the front of the house. I've suggested they have it removed and the house repainted before it rots the foundation. But my mothers love it. Annabel used to love it, too, even if it wasn't nearly as wild as it is now. Maybe that's why they keep it. I wonder if they remember that about Annabel. She loved flowers. Pink flowers, specifically.

"No big deal," she says, waving off my concern. "Honey? Are you okay?"

"Yes. No. I don't know." They cannot know the full story. I don't even know how to process the full story. "I think I'm going on a vacation."

My mother looks at me, completely surprised by my off-the-wall comment. I've never suggested going on vacation, though I've always wanted to travel. Always. It was something Annabel and I talked about all the time, long before she got sick. We had a big map in our shared bedroom, and we dreamed of all the places we'd go.

"We'll take a gap year and backpack through Europe," she'd say and put thumbtacks on all the places we were going to go.

"A gap year? Cubans don't take gap years," I giggled.

"Sure they do. Mima will probably want to come with us. We'll have to figure out how to get them to stay so we can go on our own."

"You're a year behind me, Annabel. I'll have to start college and then take off my sophomore year."

"As long as we go, Alex. We have to go! There's so much to see and do. One day we'll be married with our own kids and husbands, and we'll never have the chance of going on an adventure together. Just the two of us. The stories we'll tell our kids!"

And then she died, and traveling didn't seem as exciting anymore.

Michael wasn't a big traveler—he was a homebody. During our marriage, I fell into a routine, and that dream kind of faded. That's not to say that I was miserable; I was good. We were living our lives, having lovely meals, going to museums, the beach; we boated and fished. It was a good life, and I hadn't thought of traveling in years.

Mima tosses the weeds into the trash she set by her, takes off her gloves, and wipes her hand down her jeans. "Vamos," she says, ushering me into the main house. "I just made some café. You can sit and explain, because no entiendo, mija." I've thoroughly confused her. Hell, I've confused myself.

I don't want company, but there's no way of getting around that now. I live here; I can't hide from them. I want to hide from everyone right now. Maybe I *should* get away. I haven't completely come to terms with my divorce, and now the tumor and termination or vacation or whateverthehell it is . . . I need to get a handle on all this. I wish I could lock myself in my room for a month to think, but that's impossible with my mothers and my friends hovering with questions that I just don't have answers for.

And as I think of this, a plan starts to form. Maybe I can leave. I have vacation time. I've never taken a vacation. I have money saved—maybe not enough, though. Stupid deposit on my condo. But maybe this is exactly what I need—a vacation, before I have to have this stupid operation.

"Hey, you're home early," Mom says as she sees Mima and me walk into the kitchen.

"Alex says she's going on a vacation. No luce bien. Estara enferma? Loca?" Mima says as if my Spanish-speaking ass is not right in front of her.

"I'm fine, and I'm not crazy."

"Vacation?" Mom echoes.

I sit at the kitchen table, and Mima pours me a small cup of Cuban coffee. The whole house smells like café with the brown "espumita" at the top made with a lot of sugar. "My presentation today did not go well. Bernard suggested, or rather insisted, I take a vacation."

"He insisted?" Mima asks.

"Josefina Maria de la Cruz Martinez," Mom warns. "Let her finish before you jump to conclusions."

"Okay, okay," Mima says with her hands up.

"I think I'm getting fired. Or maybe I got fired. I'm not a hundred percent sure what happened. One minute I was giving a presentation, and the next he said he was hiring an outside marketing firm and I should take some time off."

"What? You need to tell us exactly what happened," Mom says.

"Bernard did not like the presentation. Or rather, he did not like my idea. He said he had decided to go with a marketing firm. With a marketing firm taking over, why would they need me? He suggested I take some time off and I think, in my confusion and shock, I agreed."

"Hmm," Mima says.

I turn to my mother, annoyed and frustrated. "What does that mean? Hmm?" That's not helpful at all.

"I think," Mom steps in, "we are just trying to figure out how you went from time off to termination."

"I don't know. It was all sudden; I don't think I've processed it."

"When life gives you lemons . . . mi amor," Mima says, pointing to an affirmation box on the wall by the microwave.

"Tone it down, Mima. I'm not in the mood for positivity right now."

"I'm just suggesting that maybe a little time to relax and regroup may be exactly what you need. It's not a terrible idea, you know? I'm sure once you go back refreshed, everything will make sense."

"I agree, sweetie," Mom says. "Take a few days, a week, sleep in, relax, and then go back rejuvenated and with a clear head."

I gulp down the café in one swallow and then stand up. "Maybe," I say noncommittally. "I'll see you guys later. I need to think." I kiss them both on the cheek and then go to my room.

"Why don't you stay? I was about to start on dinner."

"Thanks, but I'm not hungry," I say sadly. "Love you both."

———

It's early in the day, and I'm not used to being home at this time. I'm not a person who can just sit around and do nothing. I try, don't get me wrong. I lie down and attempt to take a nap, but ten minutes later, I'm standing up again. It's too hot at this time for a jog, so that's out of the question. I turn on the TV and go through the one hundred zillion channels, and there is nothing on.

I blow out a big breath and lie back down and look up at the ceiling. This house, this room, it brings me so many great memories of my childhood. This is where Annabel and I would come play pretend when we were little girls. I would always want to be a teacher or a doctor, and she wanted to dress up like Indiana Jones with khakis and a rope, binoculars, and a compass. We would argue for a bit and then compromise: I'd be Indiana Jones's teacher.

While Mom graded papers in the main part of the house, Mima would play loud salsa music and show us her favorite dance moves down here. This is where we opened Christmas gifts and where we built play forts. The spot where my mothers measured our heights is in a corner, wonky lines in pencil creeping up the wall with dates and initials.

Shortly after Annabel died, Mom converted it into a big guest room. I don't know if she did that because it brought her and Mima painful memories of Annabel, too, or because we didn't need a play-room anymore by that time. Regardless, this room was the heart of the house from the time I was born until I was fifteen.

Maybe I'm different from my mothers, but it doesn't bring me pain to be in this room; it brings me comfort.

My phone rings, and I see it's Margot. "Hello," I say, clearing my throat from the lump that has formed. I don't want to be paralyzed or lose my memory or anything that, in my opinion, is just as debilitating as death. I don't want to have terrible years where I'm withering away, regretting all the things I never got around to doing.

"I heard things didn't go great at your meeting today," she says. Damn Bernie and his big mouth.

"That's an understatement," I say. "Did Bernie tell you that his father insists I take some time off?"

"No. Bernie said his father did not like the concept and that he'd felt terrible for having to tell you."

"And then he told me to go on a vacation."

"Well, it's not the worst idea." She sounds like my mother, except she adds, "After you have your surgery, maybe we can do a girls' trip. Maybe a cruise or something involving a beach and a piña colada."

After my surgery. What if there is no "after my surgery"? Fifty-fifty are not good odds. Annabel didn't get an *after her surgery*. After battling leukemia with medicines that made her sick and thin, bald and frail, the cancer won. There wasn't much left to be done. And then we got hope. An experimental surgery that had been successful with all the candidates. We were able to get her into the program, and she never made it out of the operating room alive. So excuse me if I'm not as optimistic of an *"after my surgery."*

"Alex? You still there?"

"Yeah, yeah. I'm just . . . It's been a rough day."

"I know, sweetie, but listen, don't take Bernard's decision to heart. You know they all love you over there. You're family. You need to tell them about your surgery and then take the time to recover. It's all going to be fine."

Easy to say when it's not your head that's being drilled. I don't want to be snarky with Margot. It's not her fault that my world's falling apart.

Margot may be married to Bernie, but she is far removed from the company dealings. She knows the tidbits Bernie shares and anything important that she should know, but for the most part, Margot just isn't interested. She's happy as a clam as a part-time librarian in our community library and the rest of her time making sure their home is pristine and food is on the table every day. I know that if I asked Margot to get more information for me, she would. I, however, would never put her in that position.

"Yeah," I say noncommittally, and she surely hears the deflated sigh. Let me just figure things out and wrap my head around everything and then I'll tell them.

"Okay. Well, you know you're not alone, right? We're here for you. Just a phone call away, Alex. I could talk to Bernie—"

"No. It's okay, Margot. Really, it's fine."

"Well, if you need anything . . ."

"I know. Thanks, Margot." We hang up, and I drop my phone on the bed.

I never stopped and assessed the last twenty years and, being in this room and in this headspace, all I can seem to think about are the last twenty years that just flew by. When you're in the crisis, you're just trying to survive. I think that's what I've been doing, living my life in survival mode and trying to make as few waves as possible because Annabel's death was a tsunami that almost drowned us all.

I turn my head, and the wall of boxes that were neatly stacked up and ignored for the last year stare back at me. When the closing of my new home happens, I don't want to lug unnecessary clutter into the new place. Maybe I shouldn't even move. If I need this so-called support system while I recover, staying right here with my mothers would be for the best. Not to mention, if I'm unemployed, moving forward on the condo closing wouldn't be the prudent thing to do, right?

I grab the contract and review it; I'm still within the period of time to back out. Actually, I have three days left on the contingency period. I need to make a rational decision. Just one today.

Meanwhile, I decide to make myself useful and look through some of these boxes. Why not? I've got nothing else to do.

I sit down on the floor, drag over a box, and start pulling out things. This is a bunch of stuff my mothers gave me a few years after I left home, after they'd cleaned out the attic. It's mostly memorabilia from my youth, things I haven't seen in years. No, decades. There's a first-place medal from when I won the spelling bee in third grade, a bunch of report cards, pictures held together with a rubber band, a trophy from my cross-country days. I push the box aside and sit back and go through the photos. So many memories, and Michael is in most of them; even through grade school, he's there with Sylvie and me. There's some of Annabel, always so pretty. Her hair was lighter than mine, and she always kept it long and combed out her waves.

What would she be doing if she were alive? What would she say about my diagnosis? I know we would have been the kind of sisters who would have stayed close. She would have been there for me through my divorce, and I would have helped her during childbirth. As I imagine the life she would have had, the lump in my throat returns. *Oh, Annabel, how I wish you were here. So many what-ifs and could-have-beens.*

There's a bunch of photos of a trip we took to Disney when I was thirteen. Mima and Annabel were sitting next to each other, their arms up in the air and faces full of excitement as they're hurled down a roller coaster. Mom and I, on the other hand, have our eyes closed and are gripping the safety bar.

It's been so long since I've seen this carefree side of Mima, the one who dove headfirst into things and let me sneak an extra cookie after dinner. Mima smiles and joins in conversations, but there is always sadness behind her eyes. I'm constantly waiting for her to start crying or to hide in her room and not come out.

I lost my mom and Annabel twenty years ago, and I hadn't even really processed that until right this moment.

Emotionally, I can't go any further with this box. It's been too hard of a day. I stand and get another box and open it. I can see just from the papers that fall out, it's all the miscellaneous crap I didn't know what to do with when the house was sold. Anything on the kitchen counter or on my nightstand or thrown in a corner of my closet was tossed into this box. It's crap that I probably should've gotten rid of a long time ago. There's a sewing kit that I've never used nor would know how to use. I've had it since I can remember, and I can't seem to throw it away. I just know I'll need it one day. But I need to purge the clutter. I should have done this a while ago. Purging is a great way to really start moving on with this new single life. I start to form a little pile of things I'm going to toss. There's an empty Advil bottle, a bunch of pens, dead batteries, old bills, and magazines. The throwaway pile keeps getting bigger and bigger. There's a grocery list handwritten by Michael from years past, a keepsake from a baby shower of a coworker, some old receipts, and business cards. Toss. Toss. Toss. Then I take out a book. A thick travel book called *100 Most Beautiful Places to Visit.*

I sit back on my haunches. "Oh, I forgot about this," I say out loud to no one. This was Annabel's. It was a book Mima gave her on the Christmas that she was diagnosed. She'd read that a way to tamp down anxiety and depression when you're going through a rough time is to focus on things that you are looking forward to. Traveling was one of the examples, since she knew how much Annabel wanted to travel. So she'd bought this big, glossy coffee table book for Annabel as a present.

We sat around and dog-eared every place we'd visit when she got better—most of it, unfortunately, done lying down next to her in a hospital bed. But it gave us all hope. "When I grow up, I'm going to work on a cruise ship so that I can travel the world," she said.

"You get seasick just standing at the dock," I replied.

"That's true. Then I'll be a flight attendant." It was something to look forward to.

She never went to any of these places, and neither did I. It was her dream, and I just wanted to follow along. I'd follow along anywhere she wanted to go if she were around. She was my favorite person in the world.

I remember showing this to Michael once. *"Maybe we can go to one of these places one day."*

"One day, honey. One day," he had said and kissed me on my forehead tenderly. But the book was put away and forgotten, and then life got in the way. He was always too busy, or it was too expensive, or, "Maybe next year."

I open the first page and see the inscription.

To Our Sweet Annabel,

Pick a place. The sky's the limit. This time next year, when you're better, we'll all go. Stay strong and always remember how loved you are.

Love, M & M.

She had spent months nonstop chattering about the Grand Canyon, and then she'd changed her mind and decided on Puerto Rico so she could see the bioluminescence; then she decided on whale watching in Nantucket. She'd dog-eared, wrote on, and researched each place, carefully changing her mind on her dream location at least a dozen times, which meant that the book had a lot of marks in it. We'd talked so much about traveling as kids that this book just seemed like the first step in making it actually happen. It wouldn't be a distant dream but a reality. She'd get better, and we'd go on our adventures. "We can't wait until college, Alex. As soon as I'm better, we'll go, even if the moms come with us. What if I get better, and then it comes back, Alex?" she had said with desperation. I'd never heard her sound as mature as she had at that very moment.

"That won't happen, Annabel. Don't say that. I don't want to hear it."

"Well, you have to hear it, Alex. We don't know what'll happen, and I'm not going to wait until later. As soon as I'm better, we're all going somewhere fun. Plus, I'm tired of sitting in this mint-green room. I want to hike the Grand Canyon or, if it's winter, go skiing in Telluride. And if I make it to college, we'll go somewhere else. It's a big planet. And if I don't make it, you'll go without me."

"Stop saying that!"

She took my face in her hands, squishing my cheeks together, something she always did when she wanted to get my undivided attention. Except the skin on her hands was bruised from where IVs had been placed, and they were bony and clammy, almost foreign-feeling.

"No, you're not listening, Alex. Not really. I want you to promise me." Again, that desperation was so clear, how had I missed it? It was such an intense conversation. Maybe she did know how sick she really was. Was I the only one who wasn't aware of the severity of the diagnosis? This had been a plea, and I hadn't taken it seriously enough.

"I swear, Annabel. As soon as you're better, we'll go wherever you want."

And then she held out her pinkie, and we entwined them in a promise that I never fulfilled.

How the heck had I forgotten this? I remembered she wanted an adventure. I remember the book. But until right this moment, that promise had been forgotten. Those years were a blur, and now little memories are coming to light as my own mortality looms near.

Maybe this is a sign. Maybe I do need to go on the trip that Annabel wasn't able to take. The one I'd pinkie promised to do. If I lose my memory or ability to walk or to see, this may be my last chance.

What are the odds that today, of all days, I pick up this book?

There are no coincidences. Isn't that one of my mother's sayings?

I skim through the book, specifically the pages that look the most tattered, and then by the time the sun comes out the next morning, I've booked a ticket to Arizona; I've contacted my Realtor and asked to have the offer on my condo rescinded. She emails me back asking me to reconsider, but my mind is made up. I send her the wire instructions for where to send my escrow and sign all the pertinent paperwork. I tell her to keep $1,000 for the hard work she put into finding me this place. And then she confirms that the wire returning my deposit is in transit.

It's the most impulsive thing I've ever done in my life. It's also the most Annabel thing I've ever done in my life.

Adventure, here I come.

CHAPTER SEVEN

"Are you sure you've thought this through?" Mom asks as we park at the airport. *Annabel, sister, this is a bad idea!* And I can almost hear her giggle.

"No. But I've been 'thinking things through' for thirty-five years, and it's time I do something wild and fun. Annabel never had the chance, and I'm not going to squander it. I should have done this a long time ago."

We don't speak about Annabel much, so it quiets the moms for a moment. There's a soft smile in their eyes and a sense of understanding.

"Ay, mija. I just don't like that you're doing it all alone. Can't you do something wild and fun at home? Or maybe give us a few days to plan and we'll go with you."

"I need to do this." I told them about my trip. "If I don't do it now, I'll chicken out and something will come up and then I won't go. I need to go. Don't you remember how many times Annabel and I talked about traveling before she got sick, then even more while she *was* sick? I promised her, and I never went." She would have been the absolute worst travel partner. She loved adventures, in theory. She wanted to go everywhere, but she was also scared of just about everything. She'd surely overpack, want to stay in hotels that were way over our budget, and she'd probably meet a bunch of strangers and they'd follow us around for the entire trip just to be able to hang out longer with her. She was just that infectious. God, I miss her so much.

"But, honey—"

"Mom, how many times have you told me the story of the time you took four buses from Miami to DC, all alone, when you were only seventeen, to join a women's liberation march? Do you regret that?" I know she doesn't. She was always fighting for women's rights and volunteered for NOW for years.

"That was different," Mom says.

"And you, Mima; you were fearless. You came to this country alone, without any money, without any family, and you paved your own way and had fun while doing it."

"Like she said, that was muy diferente," Mima adds.

"Yes. It was different," I say and point to them one by one. "You were too young, and it was a radical march. And you crossed an ocean on a raft, which was extraordinarily dangerous. I'm going on vacation, and I'm almost middle-aged. Life doesn't come with a remote. You have to get up and change it yourself."

"Don't use my inspirational quote against us, Alex," Mima says, but there's a silly grin on her face.

They both exhale loudly and give me a big hug. "Call every day."

I haven't told them about the condo or the tumor yet. I will. Just not yet. Once I get a handle on my emotions and set the date of the surgery, I'll tell them. I need to do this first. Alone.

"I will," I say. "Love you."

"Te quiero, mi amor," Mima says at the same time that Mom says, "Love you, honey."

I lift the handle of the case and roll it into the airport doors and head to gate twelve to start my trip.

While I wait for my flight to board, I do the cowardly thing; I text Sylvie and Margot instead of calling them. I know they're going to object or worry, which will cause me to second-guess my decision.

Good morning. I know you're both going to be mad. I know I should pick up the phone and call you. But I really need to do this, and if I call you, you'll be rational and talk me out of it. I don't want rational right now. Even if it doesn't make any sense to you, I need to do this. So here goes . . . I'm going on a trip. If I have to undergo surgery, I need to do one last exciting thing. Annabel never got her chance, and I need to do it for me and for her. I'm going to Arizona, and then after that I may go to Costa Rica and who knows what next. I'll be gone only a few weeks. The Grand Canyon was one of the places Annabel, my moms, and I were going to go when she got into remission. I had forgotten about it, but last night I found the book that she and I used to plan our adventure.

It's a sign, right?

And I know you're thinking that I don't believe in signs, but you do, Sylvie, so I'm going to take that sign and run with it. I can't do this when the tumor gets bigger, and I don't know what's going to happen after surgery. Right now, I feel great; I have the money and the time, so I'm going. I hate to ask you to keep this a secret, but I'm asking. I don't want anyone to know yet—it's just going to make everyone worry unnecessarily. I promise that the moment I get back, I'll schedule the surgery and tell everyone. I love you, and I hope you'll still love me when I return.

I hit "Send" and switch my phone to airplane mode.

Next stop: Arizona.

———

A few months ago, if I were to envision a trip to the Grand Canyon, I'd think of having coffee on my balcony overlooking the natural wonder.

I'd do some short hiking trips, maybe a helicopter tour to the bottom, and just absorb the grandeur of the canyon. That was pretumor Alex.

Post-tumor Alex has an itch to be adventurous like Annabel. Maybe I need to prove to myself that Bob is not in charge. I'm going to show my tumor who's boss. And I'm also going to remember every single second of this trip so that there's no possible way I can forget it if something were to happen during surgery.

Have I mentioned that I'm a runner? I run every single morning. I'm in great shape (aside from the obvious). Which is why I feel completely confident that booking a four-day adventure hike into the Grand Canyon, labeled "expert," will be totally fine.

Plus, you can't think about your problems when you're exhausted and in survival mode, right?

"Ready?" David, our tour guide, asks the group. David could be eighteen or thirty-eight. Between the gaiter covering his neck and mouth, his Oakley sunglasses, and his hat, I can't see his face. We spent half the day yesterday, the day after I arrived in Arizona, going through the rules, the packing, and all the things that we need to be aware of.

Aside from David and me, there's a group of four guys, midtwenties, all jacked up on Red Bulls and wearing worn-out hiking boots and backpacks. They look like they woke up five minutes ago and just decided to go on a hike. Do they know this is "expert" level? There's also a young couple holding hands who I overheard say were on their honeymoon. They look like fitness models with their new athleisure outfits and hiking gear. *Who goes on an extreme hike on their honeymoon? Definitely not sexy.* But who am I to judge? Maybe that's the kind of fun thing I should have done to hold Michael's interest. Except he wouldn't have come. Maybe if I'd pushed Michael to be more adventurous instead of just accepting his constant *"no"* or *"later"* to all my plans, I wouldn't be hiking this canyon all by my lonesome.

Last is an older man, maybe late fifties, whose professional camera and clothes fit the "expert" category—lightweight cargo pants, well-worn hiking boots, and a khaki shirt with more pockets than I've ever seen outside a backpack.

"Everyone read all the forms with Jane, right?" David asks. Jane is the nice lady from the office who went over everything with us yesterday. There's a collective "yes" from the group. "And everyone understands that this is not a novice trip? We'll be roughing it in tents, walking long distances."

Again, everyone just nods. Jane was very clear about this too. I wonder how many people change their minds halfway through. It doesn't matter, because I will not be changing my mind. I'm hyped. I'm ready.

"We'll be going from rim to rim, and even though it may seem easy now as we walk down, once we start back up in two days, it's going to be tough, and there's no turning back once we start. First up, we'll be trekking seven miles to Cottonwood Campground. It'll take about half the day, so we should be there by lunch."

I guess there will be no sightseeing on this trip. I send a quick text to Sylvie and Margot and then a separate one to my moms. The last thing I need is my mothers and my friends on the same text group and someone accidentally saying more than necessary.

I know you all think I've lost my mind, but this is the clearest I've ever been. I'm going on a four-day hike, and they've made it clear that I will not have any reception. I've emailed you all the info on the tour company. Please try not to worry. I'll call you in four days. Love you. I press "Send," turn off my phone, slide it into my pocket, and forget the photos I was planning on taking.

At the office where I rented most of the gear and paid for the tour, they explained the hydration situation carefully and gave us a list of essentials to pack, which I purchased yesterday. I'm ready. So damn ready.

"Ready?" David asks, as if reading my thoughts.

The energy from the canyon, from the others, from this new experience is radiating out of me. "Yes!" I say and pound my fist up, and everyone turns their head to me. I bite my lip and slide my arm down; the group of guys all laugh.

"I like that attitude, champ," David says and then slides on his pack. "Remember how we taught you. Let me know if you need help."

The tour company taught us how to put the thirty-pound packs on and take them off. I was able to do it yesterday, but it feels so much heavier today.

"Let me give you a hand," David says, but I wave him off.

"I got it." I bend and use my thigh muscles to stand up with the pack securely on my shoulders.

"All right, good job," he says and then looks around to see if everyone's ready. "Let's hit the road. Remember, these trails can be narrow, so stay vigilant and walk one behind the other instead of side by side. Look around. Take it all in. For some of you this may be a once-in-a-lifetime experience. Be present."

For some reason, his words hit me hard. This may very well be a once-in-a-lifetime experience for me. I may never be able to physically do any of this again. I regret all the trips and opportunities I've missed. I take a deep breath. *Be present.* Those words resonate through me. Annabel was always present, even before she got sick. She felt things intensely and loved fiercely. She told everyone how she felt, when she felt it, unapologetically. If she loved you, you knew. If she disliked you, you also knew. When we went to the beach, she didn't bring a book or headphones. She was all in for that specific activity. Sand buckets and shovels, snorkels and fins, and fun. Everything seemed like the most fun she'd ever had. I, on the other hand, am not as vocal or expressive. I'm not someone who enjoys being the center of attention. But that doesn't mean I'm not happy or that I'm not having fun, but I don't wear my heart on my sleeve, and I wonder if Annabel knew that even if I didn't giggle or skip all the way to the beach, that I was having a wonderful time just like she was. If I dwell on all the what-ifs and could've-beens, all I'm doing is missing out again. I can't change the past, so I may as well focus on the present.

I want to be the last one in line. Miami is as flat as it gets; I'm used to running on a flat surface with humidity in the air. Arizona is hot and dry; it feels like I'm standing behind the exhaust of a public bus every time I inhale. If I'm too slow, I won't hold anyone up. But of course, when David says we need to use the "buddy system" so that everyone can keep an eye out for their buddy, I'm the odd man out. The honeymooners are obviously together, and the photographer evens out the five guys, so that leaves me, which means I am moved up to the front of the line to buddy with David. "Looks like you're stuck with me," he says, and I give him a small, unsure smile.

If I slow down, everyone will have to slow down. I don't love this plan, but I've never been a complainer, so I just trek behind David quietly.

It's an eight-thousand-foot downhill hike and, an hour in, it's mostly our steps that I hear, the occasional bird from afar, the crunch of boots against pebbles, and the clicking of a camera. No one is talking except for David, who occasionally stops to check in on us, which makes me the leader of the group for a brief moment as he makes his way to the back of the line and then back to the front.

It's late April, and the weather is perfect. The sweltering heat of summer hasn't arrived yet, nor is it cold. When David asks how we feel, I do a self-assessment. Headache? No. Nausea? No. Weak legs? No. In fact, I feel strong and able as we make our way down the canyon.

"Beautiful, isn't it?" the photographer says as he points the camera above us at a flock of birds. I know nothing about birds, but I agree, they are beautiful. Obviously, I've seen birds before, but between the silence around us and the contrast of colors from the reddish rocks and the cloudless blue sky, they seem to be dancing for us—gliding and weaving through the wind and changing from a V pattern to a horizontal row and back like a well-orchestrated symphony.

"How are they in such perfect sync? It's amazing," I say. "The cliffs, the foliage, all of it. Wow."

Click-click. "I'm a photographer for *Landscapes Digest.*" *Click-click.* He's looking through the lens as he speaks, like it's an extension of himself. It doesn't feel like when someone speaks to you while texting or swiping through their phone in that rude way we all do at times. "Third time here and I always see something new. Always awed by the magnificence of it."

"That's cool—traveling all over taking photos," I say, pushing aside a branch with my arm. "I'm Alex, by the way."

"Greg," he says, releasing his camera and letting it hang by the straps around his neck. Deep lines around his mouth and across his forehead mar his skin. I think it's as much from being in the sun as it is from age, but his smile and the crinkles around his eyes are kind. "Very nice to meet you, Alex."

"I'm Conner," one of the guys from the back of the line hollers, which makes me chuckle. I wave sheepishly, and Conner adds, "Let me know if you need help. This is my fifth time. I'm practically a pro." He winks. He's flirting with me, which is completely unexpected but also very endearing. He has to be ten years younger than I am. He, too, has been under the sun for too long, and I almost toss him sunblock for his face. In thirty years, he'll be the spitting image of Greg. But it's not my business. I'm not the mother hen of this group. I have my own problems to deal with.

Instead, I smile. "I'll keep that in mind," I say and keep on moving forward.

"How about you?" I ask David, who is a few steps ahead of me. "You must've done this a thousand times."

"Not quite a thousand," he says. "I only do it when my sister is in a bind. She and her husband own the company and were short a guide this week," he says. "But yeah, it's always amazing."

"So Jane's your sister?"

"Yep," he says.

"And the Grand Canyon is your backyard. Lucky you," I say.

"I grew up in the area. Have gone down more times than I can remember." He steps to the side and motions to the floor. "Watch out for that log," he says to me and then yells it back to the rest of the group. During the mostly quiet walk, he stops a few times to point out plants, special views, to give us some history on the area.

"What's that?" I point to something hanging from . . . well, from a rocky mountain wall way up high. So high, in fact, I have to place my palm over my brows and squint because of the sun in my eyes. The bright orange cloth seems out of place on the untouched reddish surface.

David and Greg look up. "Oh, that's just a portaledge," David says and continues walking.

"What?"

"It's what people sleep in when they're canyoneering," Greg says.

"So many words I don't understand," I say, and they both laugh.

"Canyoneering is kind of like rock climbing, but there's usually more rappelling from walls, since the canyon is so smooth and it's hard to find purchase to climb. When it's time for bed, you can just build the canvas ledge, tie it, tie yourself to it, and go to sleep."

My mind boggles. "You're telling me that those people are just taking a nap all the way up there? They're literally dangling from the side of a mountain."

"They're strapped to the ledge, and the ledge is strapped securely to the mountain," he says, as if I am the insane one.

"Doesn't seem safe."

"But it is fun," he teases. He really is a mountain man.

"You do this, don't you? You sleep on something not wider than a gurney against mountains. For fun. And you rappel from cliffs."

"When I have time," he says with a shrug. "I actually have only done it a couple of times, and it is scary, but the sound, or lack of sound, up there is the closest thing you'll ever get to being a bird."

"I don't want to be a bird," I mumble under my breath. I look back up, the portaledge thing swinging slightly with the wind, and I wince. I then continue moving forward, making sure I don't fall off a cliff myself, while looking up at the true daredevils on the mountain. And here I thought I was living on the edge, going on this little adventure.

At one point, I have an impressive but intimidating red wall of limestone on my right and on my left, a very significant drop to the bottom of the canyon. I try to adjust my nerves and focus on putting one foot in front of the other, avoiding looking toward the left. There is no fence and no railing—one wrong step and . . . splat! My thighs are trembling, and my breath is labored. "Take it slow," David says in a low, soothing voice. "Conner and the rest of the Boy Scouts are way behind; there's no need to rush. Don't look down. You're doing awesome, Alex." My heart is racing, and my hands shake as I try to hold on to the wall—which is futile, since it's flat and hot to the touch from the beaming sun.

"This doesn't seem very safe. How have people not died here? Jeez, this can't be more than the width of my body."

"As long as you don't fall, it's safe."

Oh my God, is he making a joke? This is not the time for jokes. I can't even glare at him because I'm too scared to make any movements. He holds out his hand to help me with my balance, but I hesitate because I'm actually scared of falling off the cliff, so I grab his hand and he helps me up and over until I'm in a clearing.

"You did great, champ."

I exhale and bend down, my palms against my thighs.

While I regroup, David helps Greg and then the bigger group of guys. The honeymooners are way behind. "Stick with the group!" David yells and has us wait in the clearing for the lovebirds.

Now that I'm calm, I realize it wasn't as narrow as I felt it to be. The fall to the left is certainly impressive, but it was my fear making it look worse than it actually is. In fact, it's wide enough for the honeymooners to walk side by side if they wanted to.

Luckily, there are no injuries and, just like David said, we make it to the river by lunch.

"Who's hungry?" he asks, and everyone raises their hand, which makes him laugh. He pushes down the bandanna he has covering his face. "I've never gotten a different answer," he whispers to me with a cheeky wink.

Oh . . . he has a beautiful smile with perfectly straight white teeth. I kind of don't want him to cover up again now that I've seen his face. If I were to guess, I'd peg him for late thirties, maybe early forties, and very handsome in a rugged, mountain-man sort of way.

"All right, find a spot. This is where we'll be camping out tonight. There are pit toilets over there, and there's potable water as well. Remember: leave things as you found them. Everything needs to be taken with you. I recommend setting up camp before eating." We all get to work.

I pick a spot that is mostly flat and also a little away from the group of guys and the couple but still close enough to the firepit. I read it gets a little cold here in the evenings. I pull out my one-person tent and easily figure out how to set it up; then I put in the sleeping bag. *I hope I remember how to repack all this gear later.*

Meanwhile, I see the honeymooners wandering around instead of following David's instructions. The guys are goofing off, but for the most part, they're slowly following directions, and Greg set up camp so fast, I didn't even notice.

"How's everyone feeling?" David asks. My calves and shoulders are on fire, but I'm otherwise great. Tip-top, actually. There's a bunch of "good," "great," and "awesome" from the group.

I sit down at a picnic table off to the side made of thick logs and start to unpack my lunch. There are four days' worth of meals neatly and efficiently packed in my bag. I wonder what happens if you don't carefully ration and eat it all in one or two days. I side-eye the group of guys and take a guess that Conner will be starving by tomorrow night.

"Was going to check if you needed any help," David says as he takes a seat across from me with his food.

"Nah, I got it, but thanks."

"Word of advice? Move your tent to the other side." He points to where his own tent and Greg's are set up.

I furrow my brow. "Why? If it rains, that tree will give me shade."

"It's not gonna rain, and all that tree is gonna do is give you too much shade. Temps drop quickly when the sun goes down, and you want to be out in the open to let that tent catch every bit of sun it can."

Hunh. Makes sense. "Thanks," I say and take a bite out of my sandwich.

"I'll help you move it when we're done."

"I can do it—don't worry," I say, watching in fascination how he eats his sandwich in two big bites and is done. "Did you even taste that?"

"I was starving," he says, looking satisfied now that he's eaten, if you can even call that eating. "Are you going on the hike?" There is a short hike to Roaring Springs. We can stay here and wander around on our own or go with the guide, according to the itinerary. This is what they call "downtime" if we want it. My mind immediately goes to work. I know you'd think it would go to Bob, actually, but it goes to Victor. Is Victor weaseling his way into my job? How about the new marketing firm? I don't want to be a liaison between the firm and the Reys. I want to use my brain and my creativity, not my ability to delegate. I want a job where I can make meaningful contributions. If I am pushed aside, I'd feel useless, and that's the last thing I need right now. Like I did all those years ago when I started working at AutoRey, I need to stay busy. Unfortunately, I can't afford to quit, not when I'm going to need medical insurance more than ever.

"Yes," I yell frantically. The last thing I want is "downtime." Downtime makes my brain wander, and I don't want to think or focus. I want to feel my thighs ache and hear my heart pumping as I expend energy.

I still haven't finished the first half of my food and the man's done, so I speed it up. The sun's still out, and I want to see more. I want to take everything in, since this trip may be a once-in-a-lifetime experience. *Ack. Damn tumor thoughts.*

Speaking of taking everything in. David is hot, and I'm not the kind of woman who says *"hot."* He's not handsome in the classical sense of the word, now that I'm looking at him head-on. His eyes are a deep blue, much like Jane's, but they look more intense against his suntanned skin. He has a five-o'clock shadow at midday, and his hair is dark blond and longish, as if he's about two months overdue for a haircut. He's also tall and lean, probably from the hiking. I have a feeling he doesn't just hike when his sister needs his help. Also, he has an interesting scar that goes from the middle of his right cheek almost in a straight line up to his hairline, causing a tiny little bald spot on his right eyebrow.

"Cool. It's not far. About a mile and the view's great."

"Should I take anything?" I ask.

"Just water. It's a short walk," he says and hops off and whistles to get the attention of the rest of the group. "Listen up. If you're coming with me on the hike, meet here in twenty minutes. If not, remember to stay close by. When night falls, it gets very dark. Carry a flashlight and be careful with cliffs. Remember, the most common injury down here is a broken ankle. Make sure you watch where you're walking. Getting back up with a broken or sprained ankle is no fun."

After I've scarfed down my lunch, I easily move my tent to the other side. It isn't difficult at all.

As I'm tidying up the inside of the small enclosure, I feel a shadow darken the inside of my tent. I stick my head out and come face-to-face with Conner. "Hey, Alex, you going on the hike?"

"Oh, uh . . ." I move back for a bit of space. "Yes. You?"

"Nah. Was wondering if you wanted to hang out. Jepson brought a ukulele, and we have some booze." He shows me the flask.

"Um . . . that's cool." I think of a ukulele fitting in my already full-to-the-brim backpack. Of all the necessities that I wanted to fit in there, a musical instrument was not on my list. To each their own, I guess. "But I really want to see the spring, so . . . rain check?"

"Sure," he says and gives me a cheeky wink, and I think I blush. How hard up am I in the male-attention category that I'm actually affected by this guy? He's sweet and cute and young. Too young. I wait a moment for him to move out of my way so that I can make my escape to the meeting point for the hike.

David is sitting on a boulder whittling a stick. I've never actually seen anyone whittle. I'm not sure if he's making something specific or if he's just killing time with his pocketknife and a random stick he found on the floor. "Think it's just you and me, champ."

I look around, and the honeymooners are in their tent, the guys are laughing heartily at something, and Greg is setting up his camera. David closes his pocketknife, stuffs it into his pocket, and places the stick on the ground. "I guess so. You don't have to go just for me. It's fine—" I read that the guides have to be allowed to rest and that we need to respect their downtime. It was in the instructions. If David is tired, I don't want to make him go on another hike, one he's probably done a hundred times.

"No, it's cool. Let's hit it," he says, waving his palm forward, and I follow behind him. At first, we're mostly silent, and I notice either I've picked up the pace or he's slowed his because we're next to each other rather than in a line.

I watch him for a moment, so calmly finishing whatever he was carving into wood before putting it away in his backpack. *What an interesting job David has.* Obviously, he loves nature and hiking because this isn't a job you'd do for any other reason. I can't imagine the pay is that great.

Do I love my job that much? Hell, do I love anything that much? I want to do well at work and I want to help land the PriceMart account, but it's not sitting-on-a-boulder-whittling kind of love. The Reys are family, and I don't want to let them down; those are things I do know for certain. Whether I love my job . . . I couldn't say.

"Is Alex short for Alexa? Alexandra?" he asks.

"Nope. It's just Alex. I was supposed to be a boy, and my mothers had everything already embroidered with Alex and were used to thinking of me as Alex. So the name stuck. Plain ol' Alex Martinez," I say. My mothers were absolutely certain I'd be a boy. Some of that assurance came from the ultrasound, but mostly it came from the Cuban side of my family tree.

I'm not sure exactly how the world of Catholic saints works, since I stopped attending mass the year I graduated from Saint Teresa Catholic High School, but the way it was told to me was that Mima's parents, my grandparents, prayed to San Lazaro every day for a month, and San Lazaro, through dreams or prophecies, I'm unsure, told them that Alejandro would be born on a hot summer day in June, specifically June 19. Alas, San Lazaro, and consequently my grandparents, was wrong, since I am not a "he," and I was born on January 29.

"So . . . plain ol' Alex, how hard-pressed are you about Roaring Springs? Ribbon Falls is a little longer, but it's my favorite waterfall. What do you say? You want some real adventure?"

"Absolutely! That's why I'm here." The more off the beaten path, the better. If I'm trying to survive a grueling hike, all the other things swirling in my mind will be forgotten—at least temporarily.

"You're fast, and I'm sure we can make it back before nightfall. With a big group, it's hard to deviate, but if it's just us, we'll be fine."

He thinks I'm fast. That makes me happy. Would someone who was fast and able to go on an adventure with an experienced hiker have a brain tumor? Obviously not. Just the thought of that sends my adrenaline pumping, and I can feel my legs move quicker.

Pebbles crunch underneath my hiking boots as we climb and walk and move over fallen logs and hop over creeks. "We don't get a lot of singles," he says matter-of-factly. "Unless they're here for work, like Greg. We get a lot of photographers."

"Is that a question?" I ask, a little breathless as I keep moving. "Or an observation?"

"Trying not to be intrusive, but I guess I'm failing at it. It's definitely a question."

I chuckle. "It was a last-minute decision. I had a real shitty few days, sort of got forced on a vacation, maybe. So here I am."

"That's a lot of sort-ofs and maybes."

"Yep," I say, not necessarily wanting to relive the last week. The way it came out of my mouth in a question form is how it's still tied together in my brain. Everything seems uncertain right now.

"You needed to escape. A lot of people come here to escape their problems."

I almost trip on some rocks when he says that. I hadn't thought of it as an escape. Escape seems like a cop-out, and that's not what I'm doing. I'm trying to figure things out, not escape them. *Right?*

"Oh shit. Sorry. Didn't mean to offend," he quickly adds.

"No. It's fine. You just happened to put things into a different perspective is all." I stop for a moment and take out my canteen and drink some water. He follows my lead and does the same. I wipe off my mouth with the back of my hand. I didn't come here to escape. I know I have a tumor, and I know I have to have it removed. I came here to get some clarity and some memories before my surgery, right? *Crap, am*

I running away from my problems? "I think I came here to figure some stuff out but also, now that I'm here, I don't think I even want to think about what's going on back home. But I wouldn't call that escaping my problems, right?" I don't let him respond. "I want to focus on the next four days and making it back to the top safely. Right now, this is all I want to focus on." I shrug.

"Seems like pretty big stuff you're not trying to escape from going on at home."

I laugh. "Like I said, it's been a difficult few days," is all I say, and we don't talk again for a bit. But then, as if midconversation, I blurt out, "Why is it that taking a mental health break to unwind is considered escaping or"—I air quote it—"running away?"

"I think if you had taken a break on a tropical island and were in a bikini sipping daiquiris, it would be a vacation. But being that you are literally in the middle of nowhere, without any communication, doing dangerous shit . . . some may perceive it as trying to escape something. But I'm not here to judge. This is my happy place."

"Hunh. I don't think I have a happy place."

"You may want to look into finding one."

I smile. I agree; I need a place that brings me peace. "So you're saying that my choice of location is what is giving out the escape vibe?"

"I don't know you enough but . . . yeah, sort of."

"If your sister went on a hike, would you say she's running away?"

"My sister is a tour guide, an adrenaline junkie, and a naturist. She loves hiking; she cliff dives and rock climbs. If she went to a tropical island to sip daiquiris, I'd question her motivation."

I laugh. "Well, maybe I'm like your sister. Maybe I'm the kind of person who goes on hikes for vacations."

He eyes me suspiciously. "If you say so, champ."

We're almost yelling now, and I realize it's the loud sound of the waterfall muffling our voices. It's deafening. We're obviously getting closer. "In the summer, this fall is the best place to jump in for a swim, but it's still too cold in the year."

We pass a group of trees, and then I feel the mist of the water on my face before I even see the fall.

"Oh wow," I whisper. It's breathtaking. I cup my brow to cover some of the sunlight as I look up and up and up.

He points to the top, where the river flows down. "We walked most of that," he says. "Come on, let me show you the best part."

"I can't believe it gets better."

"Oh, trust me, it does."

I follow him carefully. The rocks are slippery and jagged underneath my hiking boots. Between the bright sunlight beaming down like ribbons, I see the red rocks and the mossy green fall hit a clear lake. Oh . . . Ribbon Falls. I wonder if that's where it gets its name.

David takes off his pack and sets it on a big rock. "You can leave your stuff here."

I do as he says; then he climbs a boulder. He's agile and skilled, and I'm not sure whether I'm going to be able to follow. I don't possess the same upper-body strength that he does. Once he's up, he bends down and extends his hand. "Put one foot there," he says, pointing to a jagged rock that can fit a foot. "And the other one there." He points to another rock. *Is this the "experienced" part of the hike?*

"David . . ."

"You can do it. I got you. Take my hand."

I hesitate for a moment. "Screw it," I say and accept his help. How am I going to undergo major surgery, with major post-op recovery, without allowing anyone to help? I have an aversion to causing other people worry or stress, but I'm not going to have a choice after surgery.

I exhale loudly and do as he says; his palm wraps around my forearm and my palm wraps around his and before I know it, I'm on the same boulder, teetering to get my footing. He has the balance of a tightrope walker. We are super close, almost nose to nose, and between hoping I don't fall down the boulder and break an appendage, I also feel something new. My heart rate has increased, and it has nothing to do with the hike. I think I perceive a slight intake of breath from him, too, but I must have imagined it when he turns carefully around and hoists himself up the next boulder.

"Good job, champ. One more and I promise you'll thank me."

My thighs are on fire, but I push myself up, much like I did a minute ago, using our interlocked arms for support. "Look," he says once I'm up.

"Is that the Colorado River?" It's gorgeous, and also scary, as it moves viciously down the canyon, hammering all its pressure against rocks and boulders and winding around and over small cliffs.

"Yep. Follow me. We're not done."

"Wait," I say, still enjoying the view and getting wet from the waterfall, but I follow him, and he sneaks into some opening that makes me apprehensive, but I can tell where this is going and I'm so excited, I practically run after him.

Then we're here.

We're behind the waterfall!

"Oh my God!" I yell, both from excitement and because it's the only way he'll hear me. What I can only assume to be thousands of pounds of water pressure pounds down in front of me. It's both intensely scary and also wonderfully thrilling and beautiful. "This is amazing, David."

"Look." He points, and there's a rainbow caused by the fall and the light.

"Damn, I wish I'd brought my phone. This needs a photo."

"No photos. Just enjoy it. Your memories are the only photos you'll need."

"Memories, yeah," I say, mostly to myself, and that lump forms in my throat again. It's becoming too familiar. What if I do need the surgery, and then I lose my memory? I don't want to forget this moment, this view, the physical effort it took to get here. I want to remember it all.

"Thank you so much for bringing me here. I'm truly in awe."

"It's one of my favorite places in the world. If I didn't have a group waiting for me, I'd sit here the rest of the day."

"I don't blame you. I think I'd do the same. Hanging out with us at a campground must be a drag."

"Not at all. I like it."

"You do? It doesn't get monotonous?"

"Sometimes, but people's faces, people who get it—it makes it worth the while. Your face at every turn is what makes it worth it. You don't always get that genuine reaction. It's like I have this secret that I'm showing off. Like this is my playground. It makes it worth it."

"You're territorial about it."

"A little. It's my special spot. Unfortunately, however, we have to go. I don't want to get caught in the dark this far from camp."

I take one last look over my shoulder as we start the hike back to camp.

I take a mental picture and hope that I'll be able to remember this moment forever.

CHAPTER EIGHT

As I suspected, the next morning it is nearly impossible to get everything into the backpack. It takes me three tries, and the last time, when no one is looking, I smoosh my clothes into it and then pray to all my mother's favorite saints that I'll be able to zip it up. Plus, my thighs are burning from all the climbing I did yesterday.

From the tic in his jaw, I think David is annoyed—two of the guys didn't have the same luck, so we're running about an hour behind. *Mental note: David likes punctuality.*

It's another long day, made longer by the sore muscles from yesterday's hike. Things I didn't know could ache, ache. Since everyone is complaining about the same muscle groups, I know it's not related to my tumor in any way. A month ago, I'd relish the pain. As a fairly fit person, I like to sweat and work out. Now it worries me. And I hate this feeling. This extra brain activity I have to put into something so normal, like being sore from strenuous exercise, worries me. Anyway, I'm fine. Or rather, as fine as everyone else.

The seven-mile hike down to Bright Angel Campground feels like an eternity. This hike is flatter, less inclined downward than yesterday, which makes it more taxing. The little chitchat from yesterday's hike is gone. It's mostly silence except for David checking in from time to time, and most responses are grunts or thumbs-ups.

"How's everyone holding up?" David asks at one of the rest areas. We hang our packs from metal poles. I stretch my arms and massage my shoulders before grabbing my canteen and a PowerBar.

"The mosquitoes are the size of birds," Conner says, and I have to agree. I've spent a lot of the day smacking bugs off my skin. We all brought repellent and sunscreen, and I take the opportunity to reapply both. Luckily, I don't have much exposed skin, since I wore pants and a long-sleeve rash guard under a T-shirt, mostly to avoid the sun, but now I'm happy it also helps with the bugs.

"Here," David says. "Put some of this behind your ears. It helps. It's a mix of tea tree oil and lotion." He passes around a small bottle, and we all do as he says.

"All right, let's hit the road," David continues, and one by one, we place our bags back on. "I call this the ankle twister. Look down and watch where you step."

It's a path that's mostly pebbles. Large, small, and medium, but an easy way to twist an ankle the wrong way. I'm really careful where I step, and I'm super concentrated when David stops to grab something from his pack, and I slam right into him.

Umph!

"Are you all right?" he says as I shake off the impact.

"Yes. Oh man, sorry about that. Are you okay?" He could've tumbled over.

"All good," he says with a smile. I can tell he's smiling only from the crinkle around his eyes because his face is mostly covered again today.

Then there's a loud yelp and the sound of something, or rather someone, falling, dust plumes everywhere. "Shit," David mumbles and makes his way to the back. We all drop our packs and go to help. Conner tripped, and three of the guys fell after him.

"We're okay!" they yell as David evaluates the situation. I think this pit stop is going to take a while, because as soon as Conner begins to walk, there's a noticeable limp, and David makes him take off his shoe to examine his ankle. The guides are all first aid certified, I learned from the pamphlet I was given when I signed up.

By the look on Conner's face, he's hurting, but he's not going to admit it. Men. Yeesh. Even in the middle of this crater, I'm surrounded by men who can't admit when they've been bested.

Eventually, we start walking again, but between the morning delay and this stop, we're running very late. David goes back a few times to check in on Conner, and it's obvious that Conner is in pain, since he's limping, so we slow down our pace.

"You okay, Conner?" I ask when we stop for a rest before crossing a long bridge.

"Great. It's nothing. But if you want to hang back with me, I would feel so much better."

I roll my eyes and smile. "Come on, you can help me over the bridge. I hate heights," I lie.

"You got it," he says, his chest puffing out.

I don't have a fear of heights, but the bridge feels as if it's swinging with the wind, and Conner doesn't seem very steady on his feet.

Even with the white noise from the wind and the river below, it's quieter than yesterday at the falls, because this part of the Colorado River doesn't have any rapids. It's serene and peaceful, and by the time we arrive at our campsite, I don't have the energy to set up a camp. I look around and, I'm happy to report, neither do my cohikers.

"How's your foot? Let me help you with your tent," I say. Conner has plopped himself down by a tree. I scoot down next to him.

"Nah, I'm good," he says with a flirty bro-dude wink, and I roll my eyes.

"No, you're not good. I saw you limping. I twisted my ankle once, and it hurt like hell. I can imagine walking on it for this long isn't any fun."

"No, seriously, I'm good. Done this a few times."

He's not going to admit he's hurt. Typical man. "Okay. If you say so." But at that same moment, his friends snatch Conner's pack, ignoring his protest, and take out his tent. They're a good bunch of guys. They don't tease Conner about the ankle, which is clearly hurting him. They just help.

I start to move and then halt. It's like I've been smacked right in the face with a realization.

Whoa! Am I Conner? Sylvie accused me of saying fine *all the time, and I admit I don't ask for help . . . Oh crap! I am Conner! I've turned into "one of the guys." For me, it's not about seeming masculine; it's about not imposing on or inconveniencing anyone. But maybe Conner has some deep-seated issue as well. Maybe I shouldn't chalk it all up to "boys being boys" anymore.*

Well, look at that . . . Conner, of all people, has taught me something invaluable.

"Are you okay? You zoned out for a moment," Conner says.

I blink a few times. "Yeah, yes. I'm good."

"How about some company until we have the energy to move?" he asks.

"Sure," I say. "So you do this trip with your friends every year?"

"Nah. Not every year. Not anymore, at least." He seems sad by that. "They're my fraternity brothers, the ones I've kept in touch with. Travis is married, and Jay and Ned also have small kids, so it's hard for them to get away. We used to plan a big adventure trip every year until they decided to get married."

"So selfish of them."

"Right!" He laughs.

"And you? You still single?"

"Too many adventures left to have to settle down," he says.

"Ah. But if you find the right person, you can have those adventures together."

"That doesn't exist. That's a unicorn. Once you're married, then you're tied down to a mortgage and kids and PTA meetings and shit that I am not interested in at all."

I laugh. Is it a unicorn? Finding the right person, the person who wants to do the same things as you? Who's willing to go on a hare-brained trip to the Grand Canyon from rim to rim? I don't think Michael would have objected to coming along, but it wouldn't have been his first choice. He wasn't much of a traveler and absolutely not a hiker or someone who'd sleep in a tent in the middle of nowhere. To be fair, Michael never knew this side of me. Honestly, though, I didn't share it with him either. I took the lead in a lot of parts of our relationship with my need to make everyone feel comfortable and at ease. I didn't want to burden him with the tragedy of losing my sister and, well, my mother during that loss too. But wouldn't someone who loves you, who's supposed to know you better than anyone else, know this part of you? Or shouldn't I have wanted to share this with him?

"Ah, I don't know. Maybe you're right. I'm not much of a romantic anyway. Plus, is it so bad to do things on your own?"

"That's what I tell the guys!" he says animatedly. "They're whining about their wives and kids, but I'm free and can travel on a whim. I answer to no one." But that doesn't sound great. Michael hated spontaneity. He hated anything that *he* didn't love. I never realized that until just now. If it wasn't something Michael wanted to do, he'd complain and moan and ultimately sour my experience. Which is why I never traveled. This trip he would have found to be crazy and dangerous. And on the off chance I convinced him to come, I would have spent the entire trip trying to prove that it was worth it. It would have been more stress than it was worth.

Don't get me wrong, Michael was a great guy and, had I spoken up about my feelings, he'd probably have been okay to do whatever I wanted to do. I think the thing I loved most about Michael was the stability he gave me. He saw me, he loved me, and in my screwed-up way of trying to please everyone, I just became what he needed in a wife and forgot what I needed out of life. But stability does not passion make. And that realization makes me sad. Sad for me, but also sad for Michael. He deserved better than someone who basically just needed an interested human.

"So what's your story? You're here solo; I guess you're having trouble finding your unicorn?"

Ten years ago, I'd thought I was married to him. The perfect man. Sensitive, compassionate, intelligent, funny. Hell, a year ago, I'd have bet he was a unicorn. Not until the rug was pulled out from underneath me did I realize I was living in some sort of self-preservation bubble. Actually, it's taken me a divorce and a trip to Arizona to realize that.

"Nope, I guess I haven't."

Luckily Conner is either preoccupied with his pain or too self-centered to care, but he doesn't follow up the question and, with relief, I don't divulge more information. So we sit in companionable silence until my stomach starts rumbling.

"I guess I better get moving on my tent so that I can get some food in me. I'm starving."

"I think I'll just sit here for a little while longer."

"When you want to admit that your ankle actually hurts, let me know."

He smirks. I feel sort of sad for Conner. Luckily, he's still young enough that he will eventually find love and see the error of his ways.

David's set up his tent, and he walks to Conner and drops to his knee with a first aid kit. "Okay, let me take a look." While they work on that, I decide that's my cue to get moving on my own tasks.

———

Dinner tonight is a bowl of lentils each, which we heat up by the campfire. Everyone is exhausted, so we all stay close by, chatting and laughing and getting to know one another. David must've picked up the stick he put down yesterday before our hike to the falls, because he's whittling again.

The guys talk about their wives and their children while Conner rolls his eyes, still refusing to say he's hurt, although David has wrapped his ankle and put one of those self-cooling ice packs on it. David doesn't think it's broken but offers to call in for help. Of course, Conner refuses. The honeymooners stay with us just long enough to eat, and then they disappear giggling into the woods, and Greg scoots next to me and shows me some other photos he's taken along the way. I heard a lot of clicks along the walk, but I didn't realize he had taken so many beautiful shots. I promise to give him my email before we leave so that he can send me some. As night falls, everyone starts heading toward their own tents.

As I lie down and look up at the nylon tent, I get lost in my thoughts, because I'm too tired to move but not tired enough to fall asleep.

What if I do have a tumor and I do have surgery and my tumor is removed together with my memories? If I can't remember something, it's as if it didn't happen, right? I can't will myself to remember no matter how hard I try. Maybe it wouldn't be as bad as losing the ability to walk. The doctor didn't say I'd be paralyzed, but I could have weakness, which means that what I just did, I could not ever do again. The thought makes me anxious. Like, I should be doing something. I have to remember every single view, feeling, sensation. All of it. I have to experience it and hope that the memory stays in my memory bank.

I self-evaluate. I did a lot this afternoon, and I still feel physically great. No headache. My legs and shoulders feel tight, but it's from the hike and the weight of the pack, I'm sure. Overall, except for the worry that I can't shake, even all these miles away from civilization, I feel good.

I take my phone from my pack. I wonder if the Reys miss me. I miss them. I am still so hurt by the way that played out. I never thought that two bad pitches could cost me my job. Because even if I'm not fired, I'm clearly not needed if I could be so easily sent on a leave of absence. I wonder what they think of my abrupt departure. Is Victor sitting in my office right now? Are they laughing at my failed presentations over golf? Well, it is what it is. I wasn't exactly given a choice, and I can't do anything right now from the bottom of the canyon. Or can I? I'd like to know if they've at least tried reaching out. Feeling needed is all I want. It'll cure this anxiety that is unnerving me.

I know that there's no reception down here, but I can't help but check. I reach my hand up and around every corner of my tent to see if I can get even one bar of signal. Nothing.

Maybe if I go a little higher. I unzip my tent. Every sound seems amplified in the quiet. I step out of the tent. People are enjoying their time doing different things. The guys are sitting around the fire and are passing a flask back and forth, chatting loudly and laughing. Greg has set up a tripod on a little cliff a few feet away from our campsite. The honeymooners seem to be still on their sort of hike or make-out session. Who knows? They kiss and hold hands often. It's cute, even if it's a bit much.

I don't remember ever wanting Michael that much, to be honest. I suppose everyone strives for that, being so in love and so full of passion that you can't help but touch each other all the time.

Anyway, I refocus my attention on the reception situation.

I wonder how my mothers are doing. I need to know what is happening at the office. If I am in fact replaced, what would I do? I have bills to pay. I don't even have a résumé because I've worked at AutoRey for so long. And then the what-ifs in terms of the brain tumor hit me. I need insurance. Shit, I can't be without insurance right now! I really need to check my emails. I need to know what's going on. I cannot lose my job.

But before I go into a full-blown panic, I remember that I just hiked down the freakin' Grand Canyon and I feel great. Never better, actually. Would someone with a brain tumor be able to hike seven miles and handle altitude change? I take in the crisp, clean air until my panic subsides.

I stretch my arm up, twisting and turning, moving from one side to the other. If I could just have five minutes of reception, just long enough to check my emails. I need to know I still have a job. I need *that* worry to vanish too.

Oomph . . . A strong arm wraps around my waist and catches me just as I'm about to trip forward.

"Gotcha," David says as I right myself and look down at the branch I didn't see. "If I knew any better, I'd say you're doing it on purpose."

"Oh my God," I say, patting my shirt and taking a step away. He reaches down and picks up my phone. I didn't even realize it had fallen. "I am so sorry. Again. Definitely not on purpose."

"No cracks," he says, looking at the screen. "I bet that's a relief." He hands it back to me.

"I'm more relieved *I* didn't crack in half. Thank you."

He chuckles. "You're welcome. If there is one place you should pay attention to location, it's this place. There are holes and cliffs everywhere. You can really get hurt. Ask Conner."

"You're right," I say, embarrassed. I didn't book this adventure to worry about work, and I certainly don't want a broken ankle (or worse). I place my phone in my pocket and, for the first time, look up and around. Where have I even wandered to? The campsite is at least fifty yards away. I berate myself for being so careless.

"There's no reception around here—trust me. Don't waste the energy looking."

"I know. I guess I was hoping."

"Lasted two days," he says with a *tsk-tsk*, but he's also smiling.

"I hate myself a little right now. I'm *that* girl, huh?"

He scrunches his nose in confirmation. "If it makes you feel any better, usually *that* girl or *that* guy, the executive who needs reception or the millennial who needs to Snapchat, can't keep up with the hike as well as you did, so I'll give you a pass."

I not only kept up with him, I'm still going. I'm not even tired.

"Where were you headed?" I ask. They read us the regulations about letting the guides rest at night, but David doesn't look like he's going to rest.

"Follow me," he says, and I do.

I walk over pebbles, that turn into rocks, that turn into big boulders. "Best place to see the sunset." He pats the space next to him, and I sit down. No climbing required, thank God.

"You sure you don't want to be alone? I read the regulations and—"

He turns his face toward me; his smile is soft, and his blue eyes are friendly as he says reassuringly, "I'm good, Alex. Just sit back and take it all in." I like the way he says my name. Have I ever thought that before? I'm usually annoyed that people call me by the wrong name, but liking something about Alex—I think this is a first. Anyway, I'm not here to swoon over this mountain man. I'm here to watch the sunset.

I exhale and look forward.

It's not fast. Shadows dance slowly across the sky. It's as if we're in the world's biggest movie theater and we have front-row seats to a cinematic-caliber sunset.

"You okay?" he asks. He's sitting right beside me, looking out at the sky, but I've been quiet for quite some time now.

I place my hand over my heart. "I think I hear my heartbeat," I whisper so as to not disrupt the sacred surroundings. This is what I envisioned the Grand Canyon to be. This right here. This is like the photo I saw in that National Geographic book. The sun starting to set and filling the canyon with an indescribable prism of colors and shadows.

"It never gets old," he says, seemingly as awestruck and deep in his own thoughts as I am. The sky turns hues of pinks and oranges as the sun begins to set over the canyon.

It takes about twenty minutes, and there's still some sunlight left when he hops off. "Let's go before it gets too dark."

I follow him down. "What'll happen with Conner?"

"Well, if it's still swollen by the morning, I'll have to call for him to be airlifted out. I don't think it's broken. If he keeps it elevated and doesn't walk on it tonight, he may be fine."

"Let's hope. I think he'll fight you before admitting he needs to be airlifted out."

David laughs. "Yep. I think you're right. But sometimes pain can make us lose our inhibitions. Self-preservation kicks in, and all you want is the pain to stop. So let's see what happens in the morning."

He says this as someone who understands pain, and I can't help but wonder about the scar on his face, but it's not my place to ask.

"I'm going to wash up," I say when we get back to camp, suddenly realizing how grimy I feel. "Thank you so much for letting me tag along. It was amazing."

"My pleasure, Alex." I like the way his eyes meet mine when he calls me by my name. "Make sure you take a flashlight. It'll be pitch-black in eight minutes."

How exact.

There's not a lot of washing up around here. I refuse to take a cold shower in a communal bathroom. I brought cleansing wipes that, when wet, create a lather. Mima would bring these along every time we went to the beach, because Mom hated sand all over the car. Annabel and I would whine over having to wash up in the public shower and then change into clothes, which would stick to our skin because we never dried ourselves properly. I smile at the memory.

My plan was to use the Colorado River to clean up. I crouch down and dip the wipe in the water, and as soon as it touches my skin, I yelp. "H-h-holy sh-shit . . ." There's no one around me to hear. How is it that some people actually went in the river? Maybe it's the Miami blood coursing in my veins. I'm used to warmth and heat. My body rejects this sort of temperature. David called it refreshing while we were hiking. Maybe it's that the sun has started to set, but oh my God . . . I quickly do my best to wash my face and my arms and underarms, and then I wipe everything down with a nonsoap cloth. When I'm done, and even colder because now I'm damp, I run to the "restroom" to change out of my stinky clothes and brush my teeth. I wrap the wipes in a Ziploc bag and put it back into my hiking bag to toss out when I'm back up in two days.

The air inside the canyon is nothing like it was above. It's like we've walked onto a different planet. I've heard the canyon in the summer, when all the visitors are here, is packed. But today, a nice spring day, there's not too many people around. When we left yesterday morning, it was warm, and the day got warmer as the sun rose. Now it's dropping, which I expected (thank you, Google), so I throw on a Miami Heat hoodie over the plain T-shirt I have on and fall asleep the moment my head hits the sleeping bag.

———

I'm up earlier than ever. Normally, I'm not a morning person, and I need coffee before I can even have a conversation with another human. Luckily, Greg's up and already making coffee by the firepit. According to the itinerary, today's hike is less than five miles. Unfortunately, I think we continue our ascent, which means it'll be a strenuous five miles.

"If you grab your cup, I'll pour you some coffee," Greg says.

"That would be heaven, Greg, thank you." I go get my cup, which is stored in my backpack, which is hanging from a tall pole, and Greg pours some thick black coffee into it. Since no one else is up and Greg seems busy with his camera, I take my mug to the spot where David brought me to see the sunset last night.

It's glorious. Both the coffee and the view. I sit and just take in all the nature around us. The birds are chirping, the river is bubbling nearby, and the sun is shining bright.

David walks by with his toiletry bag in hand. He looks fresh and rested, which causes me to run my fingers through my hair. I must look like a mess. Oh well, I didn't come here to look good. "Good morning, champ. How did you sleep?"

"Like the dead."

I guess he's back to calling me champ. I prefer Alex, even if champ's sweet.

"A full day of hiking will do that to you. The best sleep I ever get is on these trips. Even though the tent's no Ritz-Carlton, I'm so tired, I sleep deep."

"Ditto," I reply.

"Better go check on Conner."

When I finish my coffee, I walk back to camp to grab my toiletry bag. Most people are now up and getting ready. I quickly go to the bathroom, brush my teeth, put my hair in a ponytail, and then go back to camp to pack up. This time, I pack up easily, not just because of David's lesson yesterday but because I took very good mental notes when I unpacked so that it would be easy to redo this morning.

"Today will be a smooth uphill walk along the river. Keep an eye out for snakes."

Okay, I don't want to be the girl who yells about snakes, but I'm the girl who yells about snakes! Snakes and cockroaches. I hate them both. Just the words make me feel like they're crawling around me. Please, dear God, let the snakes be on vacation.

"Yo," Conner says from behind me, and I jump in surprise.

"Oh, hey. How you feeling?" I ask and look down at his foot, which is already covered with a hiking boot.

"Great."

I eye him suspiciously, and he laughs. "I swear. I took two Advil last night and two this morning. I elevated it, and it's good, but if it makes you feel better, I'll take it slow today."

"Yes, it will make me feel better." Obviously, it'll make *him* feel better, but if he wants to use me as justification for being a reasonable human being today, I'll take it.

"If you like adventure, you should come back during the summer. River rafting the Colorado River is wild," Conner says. Come back? White-water rafting? Will I ever be able to do anything physical again? I can almost see myself in a hospital bed full of tubes and needles and beeping machines, my mothers crying next to me. I am not ordinarily a pessimist, but I can't help thinking of all the things that could go wrong.

"In a river full of snakes? No thanks," I say, trying to lighten my mood.

"So you're saying that snakes is where you draw the line?" David says, overhearing our conversation.

"Hell yes. Snakes and roaches. Those are my hard limits. I detest them. The thought alone is making my skin crawl."

They both chuckle, and then Conner is distracted by a joke from one of his friends. This walk is less structured since the path is wider and we're not walking in a straight line.

"I'll tell you a secret," David says. He leans down a little and whispers, "I feel the same way about spiders. Nothing should have that many legs, and nothing should be that fuzzy."

I shake my head. "If I promise to take care of any spider attacks, will you promise to wrangle the snakes?"

"That's a deal." We walk the rest of the morning, mostly chatting and getting to know each other. The honeymooners met while getting their scuba diving certifications. They are avid thrill seekers, and he proposed while they were skydiving. One frat guy, Jay, shows me his daughter's photos on his phone. Conner fake gags when another guy,

Travis, talks for twenty solid minutes about his wife's cake-decorating business, which went viral on TikTok.

For years, I've tolerated this bro culture at work, and it always just felt "normal," something that "men did," but right now, on this trip, after detoxing from the men at work, I don't want to hear it from Conner. I roll my eyes and look away, making it very clear I'm not in on the joke and I'm not one of the guys on this. Instead, I ask Travis questions about his wife's business and smile at the way he's so proud of her. I hope that one day, Conner will see that there's nothing unmanly about having a family and loving your wife. It also occurs to me that I don't look forward to going back to work and having to deal with men who push me outside for the sake of their own egos. I shouldn't have to hide that I'm competitive and better than them at softball.

We stop midday for a quick lunch, and David prepares us for the rest of the hike. It's not a long hike, but it's a little strenuous, he says, because it's going to take some actual climbing. We're going to have to go through tight, rocky spots.

He lifts his glasses over his head, and I laugh. "You didn't wear enough sunscreen."

"Raccoon eyes?"

I nod and snort.

"Har-har."

"I'm sure I look just as bad," I say, although I slathered on a lot of sunscreen. The sun's been beating directly on my face for five hours; there's not enough sunscreen in the world to counter the effect.

"Perfection, Alex," he says, which catches me off guard. With very young and very immature Conner, it's obvious he's flirting with me, but it's playful and harmless. Carefree, college Alex would be swooning stupidly. But thirty-five-year-old Alex with loads of baggage and worries is not at all interested.

With David, however, it's disconcerting. I don't want to read into it. Maybe I'm just another paying customer. Maybe he feels sorry for me because I'm here alone. Is he more attentive toward me than the rest of the group? But that word *perfection* felt like something more than a business transaction, and he used my name. I haven't been flirted with in a long time, and the attention is so appreciated, even if I don't know what to do with it. At the very least, it's a welcome distraction from all the crap that is waiting for me outside this canyon.

I look nervously away, which makes me feel so foolish because, again, I'm a thirty-five-year-old divorcée and have enough life experience to be able to distinguish between flirting and work banter. "It's probably the hat." I'm wearing one of those utilitarian UV bucket hats that are basically the opposite of cute.

There's something to be said for being with someone twenty-four hours a day for more than two days in the wild. You get to know one another in a different kind of way. It's the lack of distraction and the beauty of the surroundings. I don't remember ever talking so much to anyone before. Definitely I never talked this much to Michael in one sitting, at least, not in a very long time.

There's also the finite aspect to it. He'll be gone and out of my life soon, and any judgment will be gone with him.

Isn't there some sort of saying about it being easier to open up to a stranger than someone you know? I bet Mima has a quote somewhere in her house about that. I haven't bathed properly; I surely have grimy hair, and my clothes are gross—but I don't care. Granted, my feminine pride would love for him to find me attractive, but I'm in a giant hole in the middle of Arizona—this is as good as it's going to get for me until I'm back to the hotel.

"What do you do when you're not helping your sister?" I ask.

"I'm a pediatric nurse."

Of all the professions he could have said, that would have been my absolute last guess.

"What's with the face?" he asks with a smile.

I lift a shoulder and drop it. "If I had to guess, I'd have guessed a fire jumper or a park ranger. Maybe an alligator wrangler or something?"

He laughs loudly. "Let me take a stab at what you do."

"Have at it." He will never guess.

"You're a snooty executive at an auto-parts store."

My mouth opens and then closes. "Wh-what? H-how'd you guess that?"

"I read the forms you filled out. And place of employment said AutoRey. I can't remember your title, but I know it was something important. I remember because I thought, almost immediately without meeting you, that you'd turn around half an hour into the hike and go home crying."

"You shouldn't stereotype." I wag my finger at him.

"Says the lady who thought I was an alligator wrangler."

"Well, I'm not snooty."

"That is true," he says. "Can I ask you something?"

"Sure."

"It's absolutely none of my business, and feel free not to answer, but . . . who were you so desperately trying to call last night?"

"I wasn't trying to call anyone. I wanted to check my emails from work. My boss told me to take some time off, and I'm not sure whether that means to literally take time off or if it meant that I was fired."

"Why would you assume you're fired?"

"I screwed up a presentation. Two of them, actually."

"Wouldn't your boss tell you, straight-out, whether you were fired? Don't they have to do that?"

"Yes. No. I'm not sure. I should have clarified. I was in a daze when it happened, and I didn't handle it well."

"I thought maybe you were calling a husband or a boyfriend."

"Nope. No boyfriend, just an ex-husband."

He doesn't say anything, just puts his glasses back on his face and leaves me hanging as to how he took that information.

"Hey, wait. It's my turn now." I jog the few steps to catch up. "Are you married? Is there a girl somewhere waiting for you?"

"Nope. Engaged once but . . . nope, there's no one." Normally I wouldn't pry. It's not in me. Maybe the lack of questioning people is what's gotten me all riled up with work. But the Grand Canyon feels almost otherworldly. There's nowhere else I can go. I mean, there's so much yet to go, but we're still in the same hole. If I had an emergency right this second, what would I do? I have no cell reception. I have nothing. It's a feeling of isolation, even though I'm surrounded by people. I feel vulnerable. So I pry. "What happened? Why didn't you get married?"

"She died. Car accident." He pulls down his glasses and points at his scar.

"Oh, David." I take his hand in mine for a moment and squeeze it. "I'm so sorry. I shouldn't have asked."

"No. It's fine. It was eight years ago. A drunk driver T-boned my Jeep, rolled us over twice. She died instantly, and I was in a coma for a week. After that, I swore I wouldn't take anything for granted ever again. So many dumb arguments and things left unsaid, you know? It's not worth it."

I don't know what to say. He's right. It's not worth it. But he's been through so much, and here I am opening up old wounds.

"I know what you mean. Life's too short." We have more in common than he'll ever know.

"It sure is, Alex. It sure is." He clears his throat and adjusts his hat. "So why'd you come here of all places?"

"My sister and I talked about coming here. Well, here and a bunch of other places." I smile, but there's no humor behind it. "She died and never made it."

He looks at me with so much sadness and understanding. I shrug and continue. "Anyway, I decided to do the trip for both of us." It's sort of a lie, but the longer I'm here, the more truth there is to it. If I'm going to end up a vegetable or dead, I may as well get in these memories. My sister would have wanted me to. "So here I am."

"That sucks. I'm sorry."

"We all have a story, right?" I shrug again.

"So what's next? Home?"

I haven't gotten past Arizona. I sort of thought I'd feel better after this time alone, but I don't. I'm more confused than ever. I think it's because I feel good. I feel great, actually. I've never felt more alive. I'm not ready to go home and face what's waiting for me. I have three weeks left of paid time off.

"Honestly, I don't know. I've never had the opportunity to do whatever I wanted without having to worry about anyone or anything. You'd think deciding what to do next would be easy, but it's not."

"The world is huge. There're so many places to choose from—of course it's not easy."

"It's not just about where to go. It's *do I even want to go anywhere? Should I just go home?*" Go home and do what? Worry about my job? Worry about Bob looming over me? That's the last thing I want to do.

"Where else did you and your sister want to go?"

"Costa Rica. I'm not even sure why. I think it's because of the zip-lining photos in a book our mom gave her. It's funny—she was afraid of heights, and I can't imagine her actually going on it."

"Are you afraid of heights?"

"No. I love things like that."

"Maybe she picked it because of that. Because she knew you'd love it even if she didn't."

I think about that for a moment. It was something we dreamed of together. We lay on her hospital bed giggling and googling what we would do once we got to Puerto Rico or Nantucket. Mom got the book for her, but it was really for us. "I'd never thought about it that way." And now that I'm about to embark on a major life-changing surgery, it's ironic how apropos it is for me too. Except that instead of finding it a thing to look forward to, which was the intent of the book, I'm scared as hell that I won't ever be able to do it.

"What else is in that book?" he asks, but I'm distracted with my thoughts. "Alex?"

I shake my head side to side, as if that'll get the negative thoughts out of my head. "Uh . . . Puerto Rico, the Bahamas, specifically that island with the pigs. Galapagos and swimming with the sea lions."

"Seems to me that you know where to go next. You have at least five places you can choose from."

"Disappearing and going to all five sounds like a great plan." I'm not completely serious, but the more I say it, the better it sounds.

"Are you on the lam?"

I laugh. "You caught me. I shot a man in Reno just to watch him die."

He clasps his chest. "Johnny Cash. A woman after my own heart."

"Life's so short. You're here today, and tomorrow you can have a brain tumor and die."

"Kind of morbid, but you're right. I learned that the hard way."

I almost keep going on about my tumor, but I don't want him to feel sorry for me, and I don't want it to be something that we have to talk about. Because if there's something I know for sure, it's that once you say *brain tumor*, people have questions (and I don't have answers).

"I vote for you going to all five destinations."

"I'm going to take your vote into serious consideration," I say playfully. "I'm not going to sit around waiting for someone to have the time or the means to join me. This is the perfect time to do it!" I'm getting amped as I say it.

"Ballsy. I like it. Zip-lining and daiquiris; I might just be a little jealous."

"You should be. The more I think about it, the better it sounds."

"Well, if you do decide to go to Puerto Rico, let me know. I'll tell you all the best places to go."

"How? You've been?"

"I'm Puerto Rican. Born in Dorado."

"You are?" I look at him again.

"I am." He laughs. "Puerto Ricans are Americans."

I playfully swat his shoulder. "I know that, silly."

"My mom is from here—Flagstaff, actually. My parents met in college, and Mom moved to PR with Dad. They divorced when I was two years old, and Mom moved us back to Arizona to be closer to my grandparents. My Spanish isn't great, but I'm still Puerto Rican."

"My mom's Cuban. I've never been to Cuba, but I do speak Spanish fluently. My mom made me practice and was pretty tough about my sister and me needing to be able to communicate with my grandparents. In fact, she even made my other mom learn."

"That's pretty awesome. I need to practice mi español," he says with an accent, and I laugh.

"You haven't asked about the two-moms situation."

"Was I supposed to?"

"No." I laugh. "But most people ask or comment or at least flinch."

"That must get old. Being asked about that every time it comes up."

"Depends on how it's asked, I suppose. I'm used to it. My sister had a hard time with it and used to hide it from her friends when she was in first or second grade; I can't remember. She eventually got over it, though."

One day, Annabel came home in a terrible mood, tossing her book-bag to the side and stomping up the stairs. Eventually, my mothers learned that two little girls were saying nasty things to her about having two moms. I vividly remember being horrified by what they'd said and Annabel turning red with embarrassment at sharing it with my mothers. But my mothers stayed calm. *A bully is only as powerful as you let them be,*" Mom had said. They spoke openly about their relationship and our unorthodox family life, which to us was completely normal and full of love. Annabel seemed comforted by the talk. However, the next day, during lunch, I found the two girls and poured applesauce over their heads. It's the only time I've ever done anything like that. I had detention for an entire week, and my mothers grounded me for a month. I don't regret it, though. The girls stopped picking on Annabel, and I became her hero after that.

"Do they both go by Mom?"

"One has always been Mima, and the other one is Mom."

"That's pretty cool."

"Wasn't always cool growing up, but once I stopped caring what others thought, it made things easy."

"I can imagine."

Growing up with an unconventional family was difficult when I was young. People didn't always get it or agree with it. But my mothers are the best parents a girl can have, and when I came to terms with that, everyone else's opinion faded away. But I'm starting to think that they overcompensated for not having a male figure by raising me to be too tough and too independent. Is that even a thing? Can someone be too independent? Now, how am I supposed to just lie down and let people do everything for me while I recover from surgery? The thought of losing control, physically and mentally, is what is making me the most anxious.

"Two moms are better than one mom and an absentee dad," he says.

"I'm sorry," I say, because I don't know what else to say. We're getting into deep-conversation territory again. I start getting clammy hands again. Should I give him a soft pat on his arm, a hug, maybe? It seems cold of me, but it's not. I swear. I do care. It was just hard not to lie down under the comforter with Mima and cry myself to sleep after Annabel's death. Someone had to keep it together, and Mom was so preoccupied with everything else, she was as distracted and absent-minded as Mima.

"Shit. Sorry. I made things weird," he says, and I quickly look back at him.

"No. No. Why would you say that? It's terrible that your father checked out on you guys."

"Alex, you looked like you wanted to jump into the Colorado River, and I already know how much you hate cold water," he says with a smile. "I heard you yell last night."

How is it that a virtual stranger is able to read me so quickly? "Sometimes, I'm not good with emotional situations. It's not that I don't care," I add quickly. "I do. I want to know more. But I stink at knowing how to act. Like, if you broke down in tears right now, I'd probably jump off that cliff over there."

He laughs. "And I told you about my accident. Sheesh. I've overloaded you."

"No. It's me. I'm weird. I'm sorry."

"Don't be sorry for being you. I appreciate your honesty."

"I don't want you to think I'm insensitive, because I'm really not. Please tell me about your dad and ignore my social awkwardness."

"I'd rather hear more about this quirk."

I smile. Quirk? Being unable to shed tears is not a quirk. "Sometimes I think I'm broken," I admit. "In high school, my best friend Sylvie's dog died. She was beside herself when she told me. Thank goodness there were about six other people around us when she broke down and, unlike me, they knew how to handle the situation."

"You say it like she was a bomb about to detonate."

"That's exactly how I felt. If I tell you what I did, do you promise not to judge me?"

"I'll probably judge you," he says with a sweet smile.

I exhale. "I ran away. Literally. I ran to the bathroom and hid in the stall until school was over."

"Yikes!"

"I know!" I say matter-of-factly. "But when I went home, I spent all the money I'd saved from working part-time at the grocery store to buy a purple urn for Coco's remains. Purple is Sylvie's favorite color. I also spent the weekend with her, watching movies and eating junk food. Basically, distracting her."

"You're a woman of action."

"I guess. It's not that I don't care; I'm more of a 'why sulk?' kind of person. When has crying ever solved anything? Let's fix the problem and move on."

"But not every problem can be fixed," he says, and I can't help but think of my tumor. He's right. I'm trying to pretend I don't have a tumor. I know it's there. Three doctors have confirmed it. But I'm trying to pretend I can fix it by showing that I'm not really sick. But who am I showing?

"Well, Sylvie loves me and my emotionless black heart." Years later, I told her about it, and she said she never noticed that particular incident, but she did know how awkward I became around big emotional situations. I think what I love most about her is that she loves me for me. She knows I care and that I show it in my own weird way.

"Eh . . . I don't know you that well, but I doubt you're emotionless."

"I'm not! I don't want you to think I'm heartless." Why do I care what this virtual stranger thinks? But I do.

"I don't," he says somberly. "I bet when you do let it go, it's like a dam that won't stop."

I wonder if that's true. It's been so long since I *"let it go"* that I don't know what would happen if I did start crying all of a sudden.

"Guess what? We're here," he says. I look around, surprised. Then he turns to the rest of the group. "How's everyone feeling?"

How are we already here? I feel like today went by so fast. I'm sad it's almost over. Tomorrow we walk the final way and go home.

The next morning, everyone is up early, or rather, earlier than the other days. I'm not sure whether it's that everyone just wants to get back and sleep in an actual bed, whether it's that we're used to waking up at sunup, or the incessant crickets, chirping up an annoying storm. It was cute the first night, but now I want to find all those crickets and shut them up. All night, I tossed and turned thinking of what waited for me at home.

A tumor and unemployment.

And insurance. I do need to make sure I have medical insurance the moment I have Wi-Fi. That worry has moved up on the list of things to be concerned about.

As exciting as that seems, I don't think I'm ready for all that fun just yet. Which made me think: Why not keep going? There are so many places I want to go, and I have money and time to go. *What is holding me back?* I woke up a little excited to plan my next adventure, and for the first time in weeks, I didn't wake up with that nagging worry that has been sitting in the pit of my stomach. I feel so wonderful and full of life. I need to experience things. If I have to have surgery, isn't it worth seeing and experiencing as much as I can? I don't know what the future holds, and I don't want any regrets.

And if it turns out that the surgery goes south, well, I can say I've lived and done things I've wanted to do. *So where to next?*

I'm still the first one up this morning and, therefore, I'm on coffee duty. It's the routine around here. First one up makes the coffee. I have a small line of campers waiting for me to pour as soon as it's done brewing.

"Ready for our last day, everyone?" David hollers.

Everyone mumbles grumpily under their breath. It's too early. But I do notice that even if they're not voicing their excitement, they're all moving quicker than usual.

It's funny how everyone started with excitement, and it quickly bottomed out into exhausted grunts, yet now it's day-one attitude all over again. Everyone's excited to go home to their loved ones and their lives. Being in the wild is fun for only a few days; then it becomes lonely, I suppose.

Today is a pretty strenuous five-mile hike up the south rim through Bright Angel Trail. One of the guys begins a cadence march, and we all fall in line for about half an hour until we're too winded to speak.

It feels as if we're walking faster today, even if it's a hard hike. We'll be back to the base in no time.

Once we're there, we're supposed to hop on a school bus that will take us back to Flagstaff, where the greatest adventure of my life comes to an end.

The couple is still holding hands. I thought that by now the cutesy, lovey-dovey-ness would have ended. This is a hard hike—who wants to do it holding hands? Well, apparently, these two do! Barf! Then I giggle, mostly to myself. I'd probably be holding Michael's hand, too, but only because I'd have to drag him up this mountain. I wasted all these years not traveling, not seeing the world, and now I may never be able to do it.

Or worse, I won't even remember what I've done.

"You've been quiet today, Alex."

"Have I? I guess I'm a little sad that it's ending." What is it about this guy that causes me to say exactly what I'm feeling? Maybe it's the magic of the canyon and not David.

"Without sounding misogynistic, I have to admit, I'm impressed. You kept pace, did not complain once, and were up for most anything."

That makes me smile. If he only knew about Bob, he'd really be impressed; it's one thing to do it and it's another thing to do it with a big, huge tumor living inside your brain.

"Thank you for saying that. It means more than you know. I have to admit, I feel wonderful. Maybe it's the air here or the exertion. I don't know, but I'm so glad I came."

"What's the first thing you're gonna do when you get back to your hotel?"

"Take a long, hot shower. Then I'm booking my flight to Costa Rica."

"I'm excited for you. You're going to love it."

When we get to the trailhead, the bus is already waiting for us. We're all exhausted, since going up is always harder than going down. My thighs and calves are on fire, and the grime from the last four days is getting to me. I just want—no, need—a shower. The ride over to the tour shop is about an hour and a half, and we spend it talking and laughing and reminiscing as if we're all old pals who just overcame a yearlong ordeal. The honeymooners show us some of the photos they took and so does Greg. There are some shots of me that I didn't even know were being taken. One in particular—I'm sitting on that rock, the one where we saw the sunset. It's morning; my legs are bent up, my chin on my knees, and I'm simply looking out into the vastness. It's a silhouette because the sun is rising, so there's a shadow around me.

It's beautifully sad, mostly because I remember what I was thinking at that moment. I was thinking, *Am I ever going to see this sunset again? Am I going to remember this moment?* Anyone who saw this picture would probably think I look serene. But it's all a facade; there are a million thoughts going through my mind at that very moment. But isn't that me? A facade? I smile; I go through the motions, and I don't let anyone in to know the real me. It's an epiphany, this picture. Maybe in Costa Rica, I won't just go through the motions. Maybe it's time I'm present and open to what I'm really feeling. Maybe if someone asks, *How are you?* I'll start answering with something other than, *Fine*.

We exchange numbers and emails and send one another the photos we have. Even David participates, which makes me wonder if it's something he always does or that we are a special group.

When we arrive at the store, we turn in any rented packs, mine included. The guys all give me big bear hugs, especially Conner. "Hope you find your unicorn," he says.

"You too!" I have no doubt that he will. Once you get over the "I'm too manly to ever settle" pretense (a.k.a. scared to death of commitment), he's endearing and quite charming.

Greg also gives me a hug. His is quick but just as sweet. Like the kind your abuelo gives you after Sunday lunch, when it's time to go home. I'm going to miss Greg.

"You need a lift to your hotel?" David asks. Again, I wonder if this is the kind of service everyone gets. The guys are piling into their rental van, and the honeymooners and Greg are waiting for a Lyft. He only offered the ride to me.

"Um . . . is it on your way? I'm at the Hilton off the 44."

"Come on," he says, hiking his bag over his shoulder. I'm not sure if it's out of his way or not, since his answer was noncommittal.

"Feels weird not to have anything to carry other than this." I have a small duffel bag. Everything else I returned to the tour company. He unlocks a Subaru in the parking lot and tosses his pack in the trunk as I get into the passenger side.

"That shower you mentioned yesterday, I'm looking forward to it," he says and then realizes it sounds like he's suggesting he's going to shower with me. "Shit. I didn't mean . . . I meant, I feel gross, and I can't wait to get home to shower too. Alone."

I laugh out loud and so does he, although I notice he's a bit red around his neck and ears. I'm glad I'm not the only one who's feeling out of sorts.

"I understood what you meant. Don't sweat it."

"Would it be weird if I said I'm going to miss you? I've really enjoyed talking to you the last few days."

"Same." I ponder that pleasure for a moment. How was I so taken aback by Michael's leaving? With conversation and communication, things could have ended differently. "I should be flying back home in two days, and now I'm flying to Costa Rica. This is not me. Who've I become?"

"A spontaneous adventurer. Do you like this side of you?"

"Yes. I think I do."

"Then maybe this *is* you. Maybe the other one was stifled."

I shrug. Maybe.

When we get to the hotel, he pulls up to the front and gets out of the car and opens my door, which I love. Yeah . . . I may be trying to rough it out and be independent, but a man opening my door still makes me giddy.

"You've made this the best trip I've had, Alex. I really hope you stay in touch."

He gives me a tight hug, and I awkwardly go in to give him a kiss on the cheek, but he turns his head at the same time, and I accidentally kiss the corner of his lips.

Oh God . . . I'm such a doofus. Now I'm the one who's red.

"Oh . . . uh . . . I'm sorry . . . I."

He smiles and then softly brushes my cheek with his hand and moves down and places a soft kiss on my lips. It's slow and deliberate. And even if it's closed-lipped and we're grimy and stinky and I just made an idiot of myself . . . I can't help but smile big.

"Bye, Alex," he says.

"Thank you so much . . . for everything. Wait . . . I didn't mean for the kiss. I meant thank you for the trip and the memories and the . . ." I cover my burning face with my hands. "I'm going to stop talking now."

He grins and backs away to his car, still watching me. He waves, I wave, then he waves again . . . because we both stink at this . . . and then he's finally in his car and driving away.

But alas, this is it. He'll be back nursing children in a few days, and I'll be in Costa Rica petting a sloth. And whether we meet again or not, this is one adventure I'll never forget.

CHAPTER NINE

The first thing I do when I get into the hotel room is plug in my phone and turn it on. I have so many messages. Probably texting my best friends that I was leaving the state and going to a remote area of the country, then turning off my phone, was not the best idea. Hindsight is twenty-twenty and all that . . .

WTF! You left and you didn't tell us? What about Bob? Sylvie asks.

Why aren't you answering? Again, it's Sylvie.

The Grand Canyon? Why are you going to the Grand Canyon? Is that a euphemism for something? Margot asks.

I'm calling your mothers! It's Sylvie this time.

Oh shit. I quickly connect us all on a group call. "What the hell, Alex?" Sylvie says by way of hello.

"Did you tell my moms? Please say you didn't!" I reply.

"Not yet," Sylvie says, sounding more than just a little upset.

"How could you leave like that without telling anyone? It's so out of character, Alex. We are so worried," Margot says. "Bernie was shocked. I don't like keeping this secret. Everyone at the office is worried too!"

"I told my mothers, and I texted you both. It's not like I disappeared. Bernard told me to go on a vacation. Why would Bernie be that worried? And I do feel bad about asking you to keep a secret."

They both sigh. "Bernie was worried because I was worried," Margot says. "And because he didn't know about his father and your vacation until you'd already taken off. He doesn't agree with Bernard about hiring the agency. You should call them, Alex."

"I needed to get away and think. I don't have anything to talk to them about. I'm still on vacation."

"I'm sure he gave you the time off so that you could get Bob removed, not so you could go on a freakin' hike, Alex!" Sylvie says, her tone louder than usual.

"Actually, you're wrong. I didn't even tell him about Bob. He just said I needed a vacation."

"You couldn't find anything less strenuous than a four-day back-country hike? Is this Bob talking now? Jeez, Alex!" Sylvie says.

"I feel great, ladies. So good. Well, I'm sore and smelly, but no headaches, nothing. Not one! I was able to keep up with everyone. I've never felt this good and this alive in my life!"

"Well, that's good," Margot says.

"But you still have to be careful," Sylvie adds.

"I will."

"And you're having the surgery when?"

"When I get back."

"Which is when? I don't think you're taking this seriously, Alex."

I roll my eyes. I'm tired of hearing Sylvie say this. "While I'm feeling great, why would I have my head split open and have such a massive surgery? It makes no sense. I'm going to actually go and enjoy some vacation time, and when I get back, I'll have the damn surgery."

"Didn't they tell you it would get worse?" Margot asks. "Can you wait that long?"

"They didn't say I had to have it tomorrow. Surgery is dangerous, and I won't be able to go on vacation for God knows how long. I should've done this years ago."

"Everything's dangerous, Alex. You hiking the Grand Canyon is dangerous. Getting in a car to go to work can be dangerous. But you take precautions. You wear a seat belt, you go to the hike with a guide, you follow safety rules. You don't just say that it's dangerous and then not do it or do it carelessly," Sylvie says.

"I'm going to enjoy these next few weeks, and then I'll come home and figure things out," I say, annoyed. They don't get it. It's not their skull.

"Weeks? I thought you were coming home in a few days."

"I'm going to Costa Rica and then probably to Puerto Rico."

"What? Does this tumor affect your sense of reasoning?"

"I'm completely competent. This is something I should have done years ago. I'm mad it's taken a tumor and a failed presentation to get me on a plane and travel."

"Alex . . ."

"And I have another favor, which I feel extremely guilty for asking, but . . . please, please don't tell my mothers. A few more weeks won't hurt, and they'll worry for nothing."

"You are seriously a pain in my ass," Sylvie says. I'm not exaggerating about the guilt I feel for asking them to keep it a secret, which is bothering me because I have so many other things to worry about and guilt shouldn't be one of them, but I love them, and I know that I'm overstepping by asking this of them.

"Love you both." And then I quickly add as they start to protest, "Call you in a few days." I know they love me. I know they care, and I also know they make complete sense. But so do I, and I don't want anyone raining on my parade.

My next call is to my mothers, who, unlike my friends, are nothing but excited that I enjoyed my trip and even more excited that I decided to extend it.

"Send us photos!" Mom says.

"Sí, muchas fotos, please. I want to see you with a smile and having fun," Mima says.

"I will," I say. "And I'll call you the moment I land in Costa Rica."

"Okay, mija, we love you!" Mima says, and then Mom sends me a kiss, and we hang up.

Then I decide it's time to check my email. I'm reluctant. I don't want to get upset. Ignorance is bliss, except not really. Vacation is bliss. Ignorance is bliss unless you think you got fired, and checking your email may confirm this tragedy or keep you in the dark.

I log on to the sign-in to my email account from my phone and wait for the hundreds of messages to load. I've never been this many days without checking my email. Except there're only five new emails. Five! How is that possible? I log out and log back in and refresh and press "Send" and "Receive" but nope . . . still the same five emails. I click on the oldest one first, and it's a company-wide email congratulating Gretchen from Store 832 on her newborn son. That one was five days ago, maybe two hours after I'd arrived in Arizona.

The next one is three days ago, and it's from HR approving my vacation days.

The next one is also from three days ago with the company-wide newsletter.

Finally, there's one from Victor from just today, an hour and twelve minutes ago, to be exact:

> Hey, Alex. Hope you're having a great time. Hate to bother you on vacation but just wanted to give you the heads-up that you received a big fruit basket from Sherry and we're going to eat it before it rots. Here's a photo. —V

Sherry's one of our suppliers, and she sends an extravagant thank-you basket every year. I always look forward to it. This makes me grumpy and super irritated.

I click "Compose" and then scroll through the company directory for Vilma from HR.

> Good morning, Vilma,
>
> Hope you are well. I was wondering about the status of my medical insurance. Is there anything I need to do? Until when am I covered?
>
> Thank you,
> Alex

This is a roundabout way of finding out if my job's in jeopardy. It's definitely the cowardly thing to do. But I think the five emails in my in-box are a good indication that I'm no longer employed. I should be freaking out, but there's only so much freaking out a person can do. I'll get unemployment, my mothers will help, and I have some savings. The medical insurance issue is a real big problem, though.

After I hit "Send," I finally go and take a long, hot bath.

I want to be able to ignore the stress, but of course, I check my emails as soon as I step out of the bath. Bless Vilma's heart, she answered right away.

> Hey, Alex.
>
> I hope you're having a wonderful time. There's been no change on your insurance as far as I know. Why do you ask?
>
> If you need anything, don't hesitate to reach out.
>
> Vilma.

This gives me a huge sense of relief. I haven't been fired. Not yet, at least.

With this weight lifted off my shoulders, I sleep the rest of the day and most of the next. It's amazing how removing just one piece of stress makes such a huge difference, even if that one piece of stress was so insignificant in comparison with all the other crap I'm going through. I order room service and lounge on the bed while searching the internet for the activities I want to do while in Costa Rica. On the corner of Annabel's book, she wrote *zip-lining* with three exclamation marks. I decide on Monteverde, which is about four hours from the airport in San José.

It's the place that Annabel would have chosen had we been lying in bed together searching for places to stay. It's an ecolodge that's actually a tree house in the cloud forest reserve, right in the middle of the rain forest. It's whimsical and magical-looking and exactly the kind of place Annabel would have jumped up and down on the bed in excitement over. There's zip-lining, river rafting, hanging bridges, and a nearby sloth farm, just in case I don't get to see them in the wild. After booking the flight, I email my mothers the itinerary and barely sleep from the excitement. All night I dream of Annabel, her sweet face and crooked smile. In the dream, she doesn't zip-line, because she chickens out when she realizes how high up in the sky it is. She's about ten years old, but I'm an adult, and I'm just trying to get her up on the zip-line to live out her dream and have all the fun she can grab hold of. In the dream, there's no sense of impending death; it's just joy and laughter and dreams coming true. I don't want to wake up. I want to ask her what she wants to do next. Am I choosing the correct places? Has she changed her mind again on where she wants to go? Unfortunately, when I wake up, I feel distraught and desperate. As if I need to get to Costa Rica right now and get on that zip-line. I know that it won't bring Annabel back, nothing will, but nevertheless, I need to go on these adventures and fulfill my promise to my sister.

Whether Arizona had anything else but the Grand Canyon, I'll never know, because the next time I leave the hotel is to go to the airport to catch a plane to Costa Rica.

———

"Hi, Mima," I say as I open the balcony door of my tree house for the next week. It's really a tiny cabin on stilts that gives the impression of being in the canopy. Regardless of its size, it's breathtaking.

"Mima, tell Mom to get on the call; I want to show you this place." A moment later, two pairs of loving eyes are looking into the camera.

"Mira, it's a tree house." I show them the view, then turn around and show them the inside of the cabin, which is a beautifully varnished dark wood. The walls are mostly floor-to-ceiling windows overlooking the rain forest; the high A-frame roof matches the wood from the floor, and there's a small kitchenette on one corner and a door that leads to a bathroom that has a shower, toilet, and sink all inches apart. I wasn't lying when I said it was tiny.

"Ay, Dios mío!" Mima says and does the sign of the cross. "Are you all alone in the middle of the jungle?"

I roll my eyes and go back to the balcony and turn my phone to my right, then my left. There are rows of identical cabins next to me. "And there's a huge lobby that's more luxurious than the one in Arizona and a pool that's actually a natural hot spring. It's a five-star resort. You don't need to worry."

"A very small one," Mom says, since the tour took all of two minutes, and turning around and walking into the room is pretty much all there is of the room.

"But it's cool, right?"

"Very," Mom says.

"You look exhausted, mija," Mima says.

"It was a really long flight—more than twelve hours including a layover." At some point, I regretted my decision. That all changed as soon as I arrived at the resort and saw the Arenal Volcano right from the ginormous tiki hut–style lobby. Whereas the Grand Canyon was grand, for lack of a better word—breathtaking and otherworldly—this is raw nature. Trees, mist, sounds of exotic birds, even the smell is different. It's humid and fresh, almost sweet.

"Why didn't you go somewhere closer? Costa Rica seems rather random, doesn't it?"

I don't like to mention Annabel to my moms; it's always a sad conversation. "I found that book that you guys gave Annabel. The travel one." My moms' smiles soften and, just like it always does, that sadness returns. "I just thought it would be nice to go to those places we talked about, ya know?" We avoid talking about Annabel at all costs. Grief really is a personal journey, and I wish we would have talked more about her, but I know it's too much for my mothers to bear.

"That's nice, Alex," Mom says.

"I wish Annabel could've gone with you. A sister trip," Mima says, and I think a tear will slide down her face, but it doesn't. "I think it's very nice of you to do that. She'd be proud." That's the most I've heard Mima speak about Annabel in years.

"I miss her so much. I've been thinking about her a lot lately," I admit. I'm cautious, though, not knowing how much I can or can't say before they fall apart. "I dreamed of her the other day. It felt so real, like she was right there, laughing and excited about something. Do you ever see her?"

"All the time," Mom says. "Those are always good dreams too."

"They hurt because they come to an end when you have to wake up. But I find they're comforting," Mima adds.

"Yes. Comforting. Exactly," I say distractedly, because I'm thinking of Annabel's face when she looked up at the zip-line and decided not to climb up.

"I'm glad, honey. You never talk about her."

"Neither do you two."

"Because it's so painful, and we don't want to open that wound for you," Mima says, and I'm utterly shocked.

"For me?" It comes out in a high pitch. "I didn't talk about her for you! I didn't want to cause either of you any pain. It took you so long to start getting out of the house and feeling better . . ."

There's silence as we all realize how foolish we've been. "We need to change that," Mom says. "Annabel deserves to be talked about and remembered."

"Maybe we can do something special in her honor when you get back? What do you think?" Mima asks.

"I'd love that."

"I'd love that too," Mom says with a smile, and she turns to look at Mima with so much love, it hurts. Mima looks back at her, and I feel like an intruder for a moment.

But in true on-brand style, the moment there's a little bit of uncomfortable emotion being displayed, I change the subject.

"Anyway, I just wanted to show you the room."

"It still looks like you're in the middle of nowhere, honey. Even for a resort, it seems remote," Mom says.

"Don't worry. I'm sure when it stops raining, things will look brighter." I say that to them but also hope it'll stay this way. I like the gloominess of it. It's what I expected it to look like.

"I hope you're not planning on doing anything reckless while you're there. I was not a fan of the hiking trip," Mima says. "If you hadn't gone alone, maybe—"

"I went with a guide, and it was a group tour. I was not alone. I sent you the photos."

"Speaking of the photos, who is that young man with the hat and beard who's in so many of them?"

Was he in so many photos?

"That's David. He was the guide."

"Is that all he was?" Mom prods.

"We're friends. He's a good guy. Maybe we'll cross paths again one day."

"Well, be careful out there and when meeting strange men, okay, mija?"

"Don't worry, Mima."

"And don't do anything reckless," Mom says.

"Define reckless? I did pick Costa Rica because of the jungle. I wanted to zip-line, river raft, see a sloth."

"Aside from the sloth, I don't like the other things," Mima says.

"It'll be fine," I say with a roll of my eyes and subject change.

"Are you sure you're okay?" They've asked me this many times. "You know there are many jobs out there. It's AutoRey's loss."

"I know."

"And maybe spending all your savings on a trip isn't the best use of your money," Mom says.

"You're probably right, but I feel good. I needed a break, ya know?"

I know they don't *"know."* They don't get it, but it's because I haven't told them the entire reason.

"I understand, honey. It feels like you've been getting one blow after another. I wish we could make it all go away for you," Mom says. And they don't even know about the tumor. I've never lied to them before. Although is this a lie? If I go back home and get another opinion and decide that monitoring this thing is the way to go, would not telling them about this now really be the problem? It's a moral dilemma I don't want to think about.

"So how are you guys?"

"We're good, mija. Missing you, of course. We got used to you being home with us, and now it's so quiet."

"Enjoy the quiet. I'll be back soon enough. I love you both so much," I say, and I actually get a little choked up. I am their entire world. This is one of the reasons I never wanted kids. Putting so much of yourself into someone else and then losing them—I could not survive that kind of heartbreak. Maybe I'm selfish that way.

"Be careful and take good care of yourself. Don't worry about us—we're fine," Mima says.

I always worry about them.

"Bye," I say one last time and hang up.

I quickly unpack and, without bothering to take a shower, head down to the lobby for a quick dinner. Because the lobby doesn't have walls, I can feel the moist heat coming in from the outside. Since this is an all-inclusive resort, I head to the buffet, where I stuff my plate with everything I recognize. I'm not in the mood to experiment tonight. I take a pasta salad, a burger, fries, and finish it up with ice cream. On my way back to my room, I pass by the concierge and grab the brochures of things I want to do, which is everything. I'd like to go on a hike to the volcano, definitely do zip-lining; and some of the best white-water rafting is in Costa Rica.

I want to book something tonight, but as soon as I finish showering and sit on the bed to figure out what I want to do the next day, I fall asleep.

I wake up abruptly, almost falling off the bed. There is a loud-ass noise coming from outside. The only way I can describe it is like the world's loudest burp. Except it repeats itself over and over, and then suddenly there are hundreds of these deep belching sounds. "What in the hell?"

I look at the bedside clock, and it's only 6:14 in the morning. I open the curtains, and there's only trees; there's not a group of world belching champions on my balcony. I chance opening the door to the balcony, and the sound is even louder and more obnoxious, so I slam the door shut. "What the hell is going on?"

I plop back into bed and put a pillow over my head. It does nothing to stifle the noise. Frustratedly, I stomp into the bathroom and decide to get ready for the day. It's not as if I'm going to be able to get any sleep with all that racket. In a pair of leggings, an old Pink Floyd T-shirt, and sneakers, I head out to breakfast, hopefully someone will be able to tell me what is happening outside. Maybe there's construction going on in the hotel? Weird-sounding construction. Nonetheless, it would account for the noise. From the lobby and then the dining room, you can't hear the sound as intensely. I pour myself coffee, assemble a bowl of fruit, and sit at a table. When a server comes by to pick up my empty bowl, I ask, "Excuse me?"

"Buenos días, señora."

Thank God I speak Spanish. I ask her what is that unpleasant sound coming from outside my room. "Le pudiera preguntar que es el ruido tan desagradable que oigo desde mi habitación?"

She laughs. "Probablemente son los monos aulladores. O también puede ser los cicadas."

Cicadas, I know. Even though her pronunciation is different in Spanish, it's easily translatable. However, I have no idea what the other thing is. I know mono is monkey, but . . . I furrow my brow, and when she realizes I have no idea what she said, she repeats slowly, "Howler monkey or cicadas," in a heavy accent.

"Howler monkeys!"

"Sí," she says.

"Oh. Okay. Gracias."

She nods and walks out. I've never heard a howler monkey before. I take out my phone, google it, hear a YouTube video, and yep—freaking loud monkeys jumping all over the jungle—howling. Loudly.

I did want to experience the rain forest. Well, this is the freakin' sound of the forest. I sigh and then giggle. "Not funny, Annabel. Not funny." I look up to the heavens with a big smile on my face and can picture Annabel laughing at me from above. Of course I'd pick a resort surrounded by howling howler monkeys. I sit for a while longer, enjoying my coffee and wondering whether my earbuds will drown out the sound tonight. I can almost hear Annabel's infectious laugh.

Since I'm already up, I go straight to the concierge to see what is available for the day and to book the zip line.

Again, I wrongly fantasized this trip. I envisioned the glory of the Grand Canyon to be one thing, but once I was there, it was something completely different. Same with zip-lining. Maybe I didn't think it through, but it never occurred to me how I'd have to get to the top of the tree in order to propel to the next tree. Obviously, I knew there was not going to be an escalator or an elevator; I'm not that naive. But I never expected that I would need to go on a hike. It's not a long hike, but it's a hike over muddy terrain; then I have to climb up a big tower. This is more exhausting than I expected. I did the canyon without getting winded, yet this climb causes me to stop and catch my breath a few times. Annabel would never have gone up here, which just reinforces how this trip wasn't for her. It was for us. She picked this spot because she knew I'd love it.

The guide and the other people on the tour wait for me with slight annoyance. Once I get to the top, I'm strapped in, and I try to avoid looking down, because—holy shit! I'm high up. Like—way, way too high. Does the Costa Rican government have an OSHA-equivalent organization? Are these metal ropes that go from tree to tree safe? Did they pass inspection? Is there any inspection?

Why the hell did I decide to do this? On paper, it looked fun. In reality, I'm freaking out. I'm about to be pushed off a platform that is in the canopy of the rain forest. Suddenly I'm scared shitless.

"Wait, wait, wai—" I say, but it's too late; the guide either didn't hear me or didn't care because I'm off, the wind blowing through my hair and the adrenaline pumping through my veins. I feel like Hercules. It doesn't just jet forward—because of the wind, it also swings side to side. It's like the world's worst roller coaster. Except worse because there're fifteen more of these to go. Which means more trekking. More climbing. And more soaring.

After the third one, I open my eyes, and the height, although still scary, isn't as daunting anymore. I see a toucan at one point, numerous parrots and other birds. I hear a loud burp and look down, and the noisemakers themselves are swinging back and forth from tree to tree. Around the eighth line, we stop at a gorgeous spot, where a small rustic picnic is set up. We're provided water; there's fresh Tamarindo, pineapple juice, and coconut water. There's a ton of fresh fruit, some of which I've never even seen, and there's also meat empanadas and plantain chips. The zip-lining hasn't been my favorite, but lunch is pretty perfect. The last thing I want to do with a full, satisfied belly is climb up a tree to be tossed back seven more times. But I don't have a choice; I can't very well stay in the middle of the rain forest. So, reluctantly and on the verge of actual real tears, I follow the guide up another damn tree.

This is the worst idea ever.

"Hola, señora," the greeter at the hotel says as the tour bus drives away and I walk back to my resort. Unlike the tour in the Grand Canyon, this is not an excursion that inspired friendship or even conversation. This was me, alone, zipping—quite literally—on a thick cable all alone. There were other people on the excursion, but I didn't so much as get their names.

"Hola." I smile back.

"Did you have a nice time?" he asks with a deep accent.

"Sí, gracias," I say, not really wanting to tell him that I did not have a nice time.

"Did you know that Costa Rica is where zip-lining was invented? People come from all over the world to experience the rush and beauty of it."

"Wow. I can see why," I say, feigning surprise. I knew that, because it's on all the brochures, plus the tour guide told us a dozen times. But I don't want to hurt his national pride by telling him it was—blah.

"Good, good. Lunch buffet is still open," he says, and I smile and walk into the lobby. Why hadn't I noticed the heat in the lobby yesterday? There are some enormous rattan-looking fans over the sky-high tiki ceiling of the lobby.

Gorgeous as they may be, they don't work. I almost yell: *You need AC. You need insulation. You need walls!*

Clearly, I'm cranky. After the long flight, bad night, and worse morning excursion, I'm exhausted.

Relief fills me when I walk into my room and don't hear the howler monkeys. I take a shower, which feels heavenly. The zip-lining was exhilarating, even if grueling and scary. My heart felt like it would come out of my chest, especially on the first line. The things I saw and experienced . . . they weren't "eh." They were magnificent. I guess it's my own fault for not researching things enough. If I'd gone into it knowing how strenuous a walk and climb it would be, I'd probably have had a different experience. But now that I'm in my cool, air-conditioned room, wearing my comfortable sweatpants and T-shirt sans the restriction of an underwire bra—I don't regret doing it. I lie down for a few minutes. It's not even three in the afternoon; maybe I can go to the spa later or take a late swim in the pool, I think, as I doze off to sleep.

Maybe the monkeys howled, maybe the cicadas cicada'd. I don't know, because I slept like the dead. I wake up because my head is throbbing. It's a continuous thump-thump-thump that I not only feel but I can hear. *Shit, it's Bob. He woke up.*

From the way the light comes in from the small slits around the curtains, I know I've slept through the night and probably even the morning. I look over to the clock and open my eyes wide when I see that it's two in the afternoon.

I've slept for almost twenty hours!

Rubbing my face with the palm of my hand and using maximum effort, I get up. I don't remember the last time I slept so much.

I feel my phone vibrating. It's David. The corners of my lips immediately curl up, even though my head's still hurting.

How's the jungle? he texts.

Moist, I reply. Eww . . . I hate that word, but it's a perfect description.

He sends a laughing emoji.

How's Arizona?

Dry.

We really are in opposite climates.
Any special plans today? he asks.

I was going to go to a sloth sanctuary.

I'm jealous.
You should be. I laugh as I type.

Was this an Alex wish or an Annabel wish?

Mutual. We're both animal lovers. Well, she was.

Enjoy, Alex.

Glad you texted.

Me too, he says. There's no reason whatsoever for him to ever contact me again. We could have very well been two people who shared an experience and never saw each other again. Part of the problem with divorce is that feeling that you'll never connect with someone the way you connected with your ex. And, even as a rational woman who knows I don't have to have a man, I want someone to share my life with. Not that David will be that man—but having that first post-divorce flirt gives me that little something I needed.

What a weird feeling to have—hope. One text from one man shouldn't make me feel hopeful. Nonetheless, it does. Not so much because we're going to start this big, epic long-distance romance. No, it's just that, if I'm being honest here, I don't know what is going to happen past Costa Rica. With Bob looming, I can't see past what I'm doing in the moment. There's nothing that I'm looking forward to.

But now, this small little thing, even if it's only friendship, means there's something on the horizon. Something to look forward to. But even with the distraction that came from the short texting session, the thoughts of the tumor start overshadowing everything. I'd been feeling so well. I take two Advil and a shower.

By the time I go down to the restaurant, I'm better. People get headaches all the time, and they're not tumors. Or maybe the Advil kicked in. Regardless, I have a lovely meal. After dinner, I sit by the pool on a lounge chair. I am really enjoying being alone. I've never traveled alone and, until my divorce, having a meal at a restaurant alone was rare. It takes some practice—what to do with my hands? Where do I look? I felt awkward at first, but now it's nice, and my mind doesn't even wander. I'm in the present, and it's comforting. The heat from the natural spring rises, and there's so much foliage around the area that it doesn't feel like I'm in a resort. It feels like I'm in a hidden pond in the middle of the jungle. It's hauntingly beautiful and almost mystical, as if a dragon is going to come out of the pool at any moment.

"Do you mind if we sit here?" a woman asks, pointing to the only other empty lounge chairs.

"Be my guest," I say, and she takes one seat, and the other woman with her takes the other.

"May we ask you something?" The women look to be late twenties. Sisters, maybe?

"Sure." I sit up a little as they make themselves comfortable on the lounge chairs.

"Which part of the resort are you in?"

I eye them suspiciously.

The one sitting next to her laughs. They're both gorgeous, even though they look like opposites. One is tall and curvaceous while the other is short and lean. The one laughing, has the most perfect white teeth that contrast beautifully against her dark, cinnamon-colored skin. The other one is slightly darker, but her hair is in a wild shade of lavender that immediately makes me like her. No one with the boldness to dye their hair lavender can be anything but fabulous. "Donna, you don't even know her. You make everything so weird. Excuse my cousin. I'm Heather, and she's Donna. We're going crazy with the noise coming into our room. It's not too bad down here, though. We're contemplating sleeping out here at this point, unless there's a side of this resort that is less noisy."

"Thus, my question," Donna adds, she's the one with the lavender hair. She removes her phone from a selfie stick and then disconnects the ring light that's also attached.

I laugh loudly. "I'm Alex, and I'm right over there." I point to where my room is, more or less. "And it sounds like the howler monkeys are in bed with me. I think that's why the rates were so cheap."

"Oh no . . ." Donna exhales and lies down. "We're on the other side, which means the noise is everywhere."

"Except here," I say, not having noticed earlier.

"The receptionist said that it's mating season, and they offered us noise-canceling headphones and/or ear stoppers," Heather says. And I plan to find them both before I go to bed later.

"Worst vacation ever!" Donna whines, which causes me to laugh. "I can't wait to vlog this later."

"Where you ladies from? Are you bloggers?" I ask, which would explain all the phone attachments.

"We're from Atlanta. We have a blog called The Traveling Gals. Look us up and subscribe. We go on trips and vlog about it."

"Wow, that's cool. What a fun job."

"Yeah, when we had regular views and a steady stream of subscribers and likes, but lately things have gotten a bit stale," Heather says. "But enough about us—where you from?"

"Miami."

"We try not to read reviews before we book a trip so we can have a fresh, unbiased opinion, but I'm regretting it now," Donna says and opens up her phone and searches our hotel. "And yep, I definitely should have checked those reviews."

"There're reviews? About the noise?" I ask. "I just thought the price was great. The pictures were even better."

She turns her cell phone to me, and there're one- and two-star reviews all about the noise.

"Of all the things . . . howler monkeys!" I say out loud, and it causes a little bubble of laughter to come out of my chest, and then suddenly I'm laughing so hard, I can't contain myself. The situation is so absurd that they start laughing until tears come out of their eyes and our cheeks hurt.

"Donna's boyfriend cheated on her after three years, and mine refuses to commit. We weren't scheduled to go anywhere this month, but we thought we needed a peaceful getaway. And we got monkeys! Monkeys! We have the worst luck!" Heather starts to laugh so hard, she snorts.

"Farting monkeys!" Donna chortles.

When the laughter has started to subside, and I wipe the tears from my face, Donna asks, "And you? What's your story?"

"Donna, jeez. I'm sorry; she's very intrusive."

"No, it's fine," I say with a final chuckle. Uh . . . so why am I here? "I had a shitty week at work. No, not at work. At life."

"So you came to Costa Rica to relax," Heather says matter-of-factly.

"It's a long story. My sister had dreams of traveling the world, but she died before she was able to go anywhere. I had this time off and the aforementioned shitty week, so I decided to go on her trip."

"I'm sorry about your sister," they both say with a head tilt and sorrowful eyes.

"It's okay. It was a long time ago." It's my go-to line, because obviously it's not okay and it feels like it was yesterday, but I'm not going to burden these women with all my sorrows.

"Still sucks," Donna says.

I smile. "Yep, still sucks."

"So you're doing your sister's bucket list," Heather says.

"I hate that term *bucket list*. It implies that someone's dying or old." Which is actually close to the truth.

"And you're neither," Heather says. But she's wrong. I may be dying. Stupid Bob. And just like that—with strangers, in a loud rain forest, after laughing more than I have laughed in a very long time—tears start falling out of my eyes. Over and over. Uncontrollable. These poor strangers.

But in a second, without hesitation, these complete strangers are on the lounge chair holding me. I secretly wish it were Sylvie and Margot, but I welcome them just the same.

"Oh my God, are you okay?"

"I know I say dumb things; I'm so sorry," Donna says.

"No, no," I sob. "It's not you. It's, it's Bob. He—it . . . he's killing me."

"Oh!" They stop and look around. "You don't need to put up with his shit, girl. Did he hurt you? Is he here? There're places you can go . . ."

I wipe my face with the back of my hand. "No, no. Bob's not a man."

"Well, women can be vicious too."

I laugh-cry. "No, no." I hold out my hand. I need a second to get over the consuming sobbing. They move back a smidgen so I can get myself together. "Bob is what I named my brain tumor. I have a brain tumor." I wipe my nose with the back of my hand. "I think I've never said that out loud."

The way they look at me—sadness, pity, uncertainty—thinking Bob was my abusive boyfriend was probably better.

"I'm not dying. It's not cancer," I say as I use the tip of my shirt to wipe my eyes and runny nose. Gross, I know. But . . . it's that kind of evening.

"Okayyyy? So that's good?"

"It's complicated. I'm terrified of having this surgery." It's the first time I say those words out loud. "I don't want to end up in a long, dragged-out death. My sister was in and out of hospitals for years, and I saw her wither away and how it took a toll on my parents. I don't want that. Or what if I have the surgery and lose my memories or end up unable to walk?"

"Damn," Heather says.

"Exactly!" I say.

"I think we need drinks," Donna says, standing up. "Wait, you can drink with this Bob thing, right?"

I laugh-hiccup; a little bit of snot runs down my nose, and I just wipe it clean. These women must think I'm gross, but they'll surely give a tumor-stricken gal a pass, right? "I can."

I was avoiding it, but screw it. I need a drink.

Donna gives me a thumbs-up and goes to the bar.

"You probably wanted some alone time, huh? We totally interfered, didn't we?"

I was enjoying my time alone, but I don't tell them because I'm also enjoying the company of these ladies. "I don't know what I wanted, to be honest. But I think maybe you two were exactly what I needed. I'm sorry I put a damper on things."

"Oh, girl, twenty minutes ago, I was sobbing over Patrick and Donna was covering her ears at the sound of the monkeys. Things can't possibly get damper-er than they were in our room."

I laugh just as Donna comes back with three margaritas. "To shitty vacations!"

"That's a shitty toast." I laugh. "How about, to making shitty vacations better."

"And making new friends," Heather adds, and we lift our plastic margarita glasses and drink. And then we drink two more rounds. Turns out that the women are hysterical—even without the margaritas.

"Tell me more about your blog," I say.

"We love traveling, so four years ago, we started filming it. People thought we were hysterical, and we just started getting followers and some sponsors. So we quit our jobs as tellers at a bank and made it into our job."

"That's amazing. Do you just document yourselves or do you give tips and reviews?"

"A little of both."

"I love that," I say, and I can totally see why they'd have followers. They're funny and relatable, and I bet they're an open book on their vlog. "Do you have plans for tomorrow?"

"We were thinking of sitting by the pool all day with fruity drinks," Donna says.

"Let me translate that for you, Alex: she was thinking about crying for two hours in the morning, getting rip-roaring drunk by the pool and feeling horrible by three, and then crying into the toilet."

Donna gives Heather the middle finger.

"I'm mourning; give me some slack. It was a long relationship that ended up terrible. You, on the other hand, are here with me instead of confronting the real problem."

Heather rolls her eyes and says, "I do not have a problem."

"You know you do. It's time to break up with Patrick. He's not going to propose, and if he does, it's only out of a sense of obligation, since you're giving him an ultimatum."

"I am not!"

"Oh really?" Donna says and turns to me. "She told him she was coming here with me to think. Which is code for: while I'm gone, you better come up with a ring and a good-as-hell proposal or I'm out."

I look at Heather, and she tilts her head just ever so slightly. "Oh, honey, don't marry some guy who doesn't want to marry you. Trust me."

"Your ex-husband didn't want to marry you?" Heather asks.

"I thought he did. We were friends in grade school, then dated throughout high school and then college, and then we got married. No big fanfare. Not a lot of surprises."

"He just felt that it was the next logical step. That's a failure waiting to happen. You need passion, not just love," Donna says, and that hits me in the solar plexus. Did he just feel it was the next logical step? Did he ever love me? Not just love me like you love someone you've known your entire life, but love me like a man loves his wife? Hell, did I love him that way? Would I fly to Costa Rica and cry into my margarita over Michael? Would I ever have? Did I ever have passion? This reminds me of how I felt when I saw the way the honeymooners kept holding hands and running off to make out. It felt odd to me, but I think maybe I'm the odd one.

"Well, as fun as that sounds, you ladies want to go pet some sloths with me tomorrow?"

"Yes!" They both cheer, forgetting their men troubles. Because . . . who doesn't want to pet a sloth? "We were going to get around to doing that this week, but we just got here yesterday. We also want to go zip-lining. Maybe we can do that the day after—what do you say?"

"Did that yesterday. Definitely not doing it again. Make sure you hydrate, wear hiking shoes, and read the brochure carefully."

"Really?"

"Oh yeah!" I say and burst out laughing as I tell them about my ordeal. At some point when we've drank so much the monkeys stop bothering us and we're the only ones still out by the pool, we part ways and plan to meet tomorrow for the sloth tour. "I bet it'll be great content for your vlog."

"That's what we're hoping!"

That evening, I look them up and watch a bunch of their videos. They're all over the place. I don't know if they're supposed to be reviewing, recommending, or just entertaining their viewers. I think they need a bit more direction and definitely need some branding, but their content is, as I suspected, hysterical.

———

Hi. Checking in. How are you feeling? Sylvie texts as I'm brushing my teeth the next morning. I probably shouldn't have drunk as much as I did, but I had a great time. In your midthirties, it's not easy to make new friends, but spending time with those two women last night was exactly what I needed.

I'm good. And I send her a photo of me with toothpaste all over my mouth.

You're playful this morning.

I'm going to see sloths with my two new friends.

I think I may be jealous.

Of the sloths or the two new friends?

Both.

You're irreplaceable. You know where all the bodies are buried.
I really do miss you, though.

I miss you too, she says and adds two heart emojis.

As I finish getting dressed, my phone chimes with an incoming text. It's a photo of Heather and Donna behind a huge stack of pancakes.

I laugh, and my stomach rumbles. I quickly text, On my way!

They're sitting at a table by a big panoramic window. "Good morning! How'd you guys sleep?" I sit down.

Donna says, through big bites of food, "The great thing about margaritas—they muffle the sound of howler monkey."

I crack up. I think when you're younger, you try to impress everyone. You're constantly on your best behavior because you don't even know yourself. As you get older and you come to terms with who you are and that there's no need to make apologies for your actions, it's easy to be silly. I wish I had Donna's cool confidence. She's silly but also open and honest—I can tell from just a few hours of knowing her. Heather, on the other hand, is the voice of reason. She's more reserved. She's almost like Donna's handler.

I love how Donna is bold and honest with her feelings and needs. She doesn't beat around the bush; she just blurts things out. I love that she stuffs her mouth with two pancakes, that she cried so unabashedly at the mere utterance of her ex-boyfriend's name. But mostly, I love how unapologetic she is.

And I didn't even feel like running away at her tears.

That's a first.

I did not feel an ounce of awkwardness.

She makes me miss Sylvie so much. Sylvie's seen me crying, she's seen me scared, she's seen me worried. She knows me so well, and she doesn't make me feel weird about it or judge me. She knows that if I'm at the point of tears, things must be really bad. I've been taking my relationships with Sylvie and Margot for granted. I should have come on this trip with them. I should have told them how scared I really am about this surgery. They're not mind readers, and they would have understood.

"How'd you sleep?" Heather asks.

"I popped in those earplugs from the reception area and slept wonderfully," I say, but I think I fell so deeply asleep last night when we finally said our good nights that I don't think I would have heard anything.

"Yeah, we did too," Heather says and then slides a plate toward me. "Please, take some food."

"I'm so freaking excited to pet sloths!" Donna says. "Hurry up and eat, girl."

"Me too!" I chime in.

"I'm not too thrilled about the hour ride on a crappy van on crappy roads, though," Heather says. "We need to find something exciting to post tonight. We need something exciting and new to drive shares."

Without even putting too much thought into it, I suggest, "Instead of just posting for the sake of posting, why don't you rate your experiences at the hotel, with the tour guide . . . like a live Yelp review. When my sister was planning her trip, she didn't just read a book—she looked at what other people did in those places and what they said about the experiences. She looked at reviews like she was looking for a good restaurant, and I'm not talking just about privately owned businesses like hotels. She looked up reviews of national parks and mountains and beaches."

"Are there Yelp reviews of beaches?"

"Yes, girl. There are people who review everything, but it's one thing to read a review. It's another to see it, and that's what I think would make your blog stand out."

"Interesting," Donna says. "That's something to consider. You have any other ideas up your sleeve?"

"I do, but I want to think them through. Did I mention I work in marketing?"

"No! Oh, maybe you can help us. We don't have too much money, but we have almost three hundred and fifty thousand followers on YouTube. We need help monetizing that."

"I'm a little rusty on the creative side, but I'll definitely think about it."

We continue to eat and end up right on time to catch the tour van to the sloth sanctuary. This was on Annabel's list, and it's something I'd put on a list if I were making one. Donna and Heather aren't as excited about this one as I am, but they keep saying it's going to be great content and therefore they came along enthusiastically, even though we are not too happy about the lack of AC on our bus.

"See, this is something you could vlog about," I whisper. "If you're up for an adventure, be prepared to sweat your ass off."

They laugh, and Donna uses the pamphlet to fan herself, which doesn't do any good.

By the time we pay the admission into the park, I'm drenched in sweat. I feel a headache about to make an unwelcome appearance. I pull the top of my shirt away from my body and fan it a bit, as if that would ever make a lick of difference. "Wow, it was hot in there!" I say, referring to the van.

"It wasn't that bad," Donna says. "Not for a Floridian. Shouldn't you be used to the heat and humidity?"

I should, and normally, I am. But I'm beat, and we haven't even walked into the place. Heather and Donna are younger than I am, and they're dressed in casual summery dresses. I stupidly wore jeans and a T-shirt. And this sloth farm is even higher up in the mountains than our resort. I struggle to keep up with them throughout the day. When we are offered a sloth to hold, I take it gently, pet it, and coo into its face, careful with the ginormous claw-fingers. Heather takes a million photos of me. I do the same for them, and then we do some together. We walk around some more and see the other animals and learn about the fauna and flora of the Costa Rican rain forest and the many kinds of birds.

In the middle of one of the shows with some gorgeous toucans flying regally over us, I excuse myself and go to a kiosk and buy a Coke. Maybe the caffeine will do me good.

When that doesn't help, I go to the bathroom and splash water on my face.

"Are you okay?" Heather asks when the women find me sitting in front of a big fan. I look like a menopausal lady having a heat stroke.

"It's just so hot here," I say.

"Maybe some lunch in the AC will help," Donna suggests, which I wholeheartedly agree with. I don't want to ruin their day, but I'm ready to go back to the room. This is the second time I've felt under the weather since arriving in Costa Rica, and I'm getting more and more concerned about Bob.

I order another soda and a grilled cheese, because it's the only thing I recognize, and I'm still not in the mood to explore.

"Did you see the baby one? Oh God, I want to take it home," Heather says, looking through her photos.

"Patrick would definitely never propose if you brought one home," Donna says, and Heather smirks.

"He doesn't like animals?" Not that she'd bring a sloth home.

"He's allergic to pretty much everything. I can't imagine a sloth would be any different."

"Oh, that stinks."

"I know. I'm such an animal lover, and I'll never be able to have pets," she complains.

"A fish?" I suggest.

"That's what I said!" Donna says enthusiastically.

"That is not a proper pet."

We finish eating, and then we look through the map. We've been here for half a day, and there're still acres and acres of park to cover.

"Can I tell you a secret?" Donna says, leaning close to both of us. "I would kill for a margarita by the pool right now."

We laugh. "I would be in jail for murder right next to you." We both look at Heather, and then I quickly backpedal. "But I'm good here too. Whatever you guys want to do, I'm game."

"Let me go to the gift shop first, and then we can go. I'm pretty beat."

"Thank God—I thought it was me. Glad to hear this heat is hell on you too."

Thirty minutes later, we're sitting in the back of a taxi, holding a huge life-size stuffed sloth. I'm not sure whether this is supposed to help or hurt Heather's chances of Patrick proposing, but it's a pretty cute souvenir.

I wonder how she's going to fly home with it.

———

When we get back to the hotel, we agree to take an hour rest, then meet up at the pool. Four hours later, I'm walking out of my room feeling well rested. "That was a four-hour one hour," Donna says with a silly snort when she sees me approach. She's lounging on a blue float in the pool.

"Sorry, sorry. I overslept."

"No worries. You're on vacation. Why don't you jump in? It's the perfect temperature," Donna suggests. "The springs are supposed to have healing properties."

I pull off the swim cover-up I'm wearing. I'm in a black one-piece. Most women are in tiny bikinis, including Donna and Heather. Heather is petite, with not an inch of fat on her physique. Her bikini sags a bit on her flat behind, and there are bones that stick out from her hips. I don't own bones like those. All my bones are well protected by a layer of fat. Donna, on the other hand, is a big girl. She must be close to six feet with thick thighs, a plump butt, and voluptuous breasts, and even though her belly doesn't bulge, it definitely jiggles. She is gorgeous. In fact, she fills out her small bikini better than the rail-thin women lying around the pool with bones protruding from their skin. She cheers for me to jump in. It takes me a few minutes, but eventually I'm completely submerged, and she's right—it is the perfect temperature.

Heather brings us tropical drinks. I swirl the straw around a few times while we chat and laugh.

"I wish I had more family," I tell them. "I'm not close to any of my cousins. I have a few back in Cuba who I've never met, and Mom is an only child, so I have no one from that side."

"That's a bummer. Cousins can be like best friends."

"Well, I do have a couple of those, and they're the best. Sylvie and Margot. I've known Sylvie forever, and Margot is the wife of my boss. They're the only other people who know about Bob, you know?"

"I'm glad you have a support system at home and people you can confide in."

"I do. I made them keep it a secret, and I'm feeling crappy about doing that to them, especially Margot, who's keeping it from her own husband."

They both look at me in a way that confirms I'm a shitty friend. I exhale loudly. Good friends don't let crappy behavior slide. Their silence is confirmation enough.

"I'm sure it'll all work out," Heather says when the silence is too heavy.

"We have reservations at the steak house upstairs tonight; you want to join us?" Donna asks.

I would love to, but I'm feeling so tired still. "I think I'm going to order room service and call it an early night."

"If you're sure?" Heather asks.

"Yeah. I'm sure, but thank you."

They are only here for four days, and tomorrow is their last full day. I want to be energized enough to hang out with them tomorrow.

"We should head out and get ready, Heather," Donna says as she hops out of the pool and dries off. Heather follows. "If you change your mind or want to grab a nightcap, call us."

"I will. Have fun tomorrow zip-lining. Dinner after?"

"Absolutely."

"Hydrate and take hiking shoes!" I yell after them, and they laugh.

When I get to the room, I toss my bathing suit aside, dry off, and slide into the hotel robe. I sprawl out on my bed and send Sylvie and Margot a text: I miss you both. I'm sorry I've been such a bad friend. I'll make it up to you. I promise. And then I add a heart emoji.

You're not a bad friend, Margot replies.

Sylvie quickly replies, Well, you haven't been the best. I know you're going through a lot, but I wish you'd let us in instead of pushing us out.

She's absolutely right. I'm close to Margot, but Sylvie is the closest thing I have to a sister since Annabel's death. I want to talk to her. I need to make things right with her; I know I haven't been a good friend to her lately. I dial her number.

"Hey," I say, and my voice immediately cracks.

"Hey back at ya," she says tenderly.

"I'm sorry."

"For?" she asks. She knows why, but Sylvie, being Sylvie, wants me to say all the words.

"For being a bad friend."

"You're not a bad friend."

"For taking you for granted. For asking you to lie for me." Tears are flowing down my face. "I'm so scared, Sylvie. What if I don't wake up from the surgery? Or worse, I wake up and I don't remember who I am. Who Annabel was. Or my headaches get worse, or I go blind or paralyzed or—"

"Alex, honey, stop. It's absolutely normal to feel all those things. But you're letting your fear overshadow the positive what-ifs. What if you wake up, the surgery is a success, and you stop getting headaches?"

I inhale and then exhale. Why can't my mind see the positive side of this? I'm not generally a negative person.

"Annabel didn't wake up. Mima still has bad days, and I'm afraid she'll fall into a major depression again. Mom's still trying to act as if everything's okay. How can I possibly tell them that I have a brain tumor?"

"First, Annabel's situation was completely different."

"I know." Because I do, but also, it feels so similar too.

"And your moms are stronger than you give them credit for. They had some rough years, as anyone who lost a child would, but I don't think Mima's as fragile as you think. Give them some credit. And give Margot and me some credit. We know you better than you think, and we're going to be there for you even if you push us away. It'll be easier if you don't, but . . ."

I snort and wipe my noise with the back of my hand.

"And it's okay to fall apart once in a while. And it's okay to inconvenience people, and it's okay to feel your feelings. The people who love you will still love you. When Mom died, I cried for weeks and weeks, and you stayed with me at my house, cooked, and slept with me. You called me every hour from work to check in on me and sent Margot when you couldn't be there. You've seen me at my worst, and you just took charge and let me fall apart. If you think I'm not going to do the same thing for you, then that tumor of yours is screwing with your common sense too."

"I feel like the worst person for making Margot keep a secret from her husband."

"You give yourself a lot of credit, Alex," she says with a snort. "Margot is a grown-ass woman. No one can make her do anything. If she kept it a secret, that's on her. You didn't make her do anything. But it was messed up to put her in that position."

"I knowwwww . . ." And then I start sobbing louder. "I'm such a jerk."

"You're not a jerk. You're reacting like someone who's scared. And I'm not mad at you; I just want to shake you into admitting that you're worried and scared, because you need to process those emotions."

"Well, I am scared and I am worried." I say those words again, and it's weirdly liberating to voice that out loud. It's as if I'm giving a part of those emotions over to someone else to deal with. "Thank you for putting up with me, Sylvie."

"Finish up that vacation and come home and get things done so you can start the process of moving on."

"I will. I just have one more place I need to go, and then I'll fly home."

"One more place?" Sylvie asks.

"Yeah, I'm going to Puerto Rico. I have to see something that Annabel had on her list, and then I promise I'll go home."

"So this *is* about your sister?"

"Sort of. I keep thinking of her. I know this is going to sound weird, but I feel like she's cheering me on to go to these places and have some fun. Like her wish list was written for me—they're things I would enjoy more than she would have."

"I like that."

"I do too. I feel connected to her."

"And you feel okay?"

"I felt wonderful in Arizona. I've gotten two headaches while I've been here, but they've gone away with Advil and some rest. Sometimes a headache is just a headache, though I can't help but think it's not just a headache."

"Promise me that if you start feeling worse or the headaches become more frequent, you'll come home."

"I promise."

"Okay. Good. I'm glad you finally came to your senses."

"So am I, Sylvie. So am I." I feel some relief having the overdue conversation with her. We've been friends for so long, I never want her to think I'm taking our friendship for granted. I'm sure I'd be overbearing and worried out of my mind if she were the one who was sick. Plus, I needed her to know I wasn't going through some sort of midlife crisis. Going to these places was intentional, and there's a purpose for it, even if I'm sort of finding those purposes as I go along. But a major weight is lifted off my shoulders when we hang up.

There're three texts in our group chat from Margot. **Hello? Where'd everyone go? Why isn't anyone writing back?** And she adds a crying-face emoji.

I chuckle and call her instead of texting. "Hi!" Margot says in that sweet and perky tone.

"Hey, you. Sorry about the text. I was speaking with Sylvie."

"Everything okay?" she asks, her voice a little less excited now.

"No, things are not okay, because I'm a jerk. I shouldn't have asked you to keep Bob a secret. Bernie's your husband, and it was wrong of me to put you in that position."

"It's fine, Alex."

"It's actually not fine, but thank you for being sweet about it. And thank you for putting up with me. I know I've been a big flake lately."

"You have a brain tumor and you're scared. I understand."

"Pfft! Well, I wish you would have told me that sooner. I just figured it out myself."

She chuckles.

"I'll be home next week. If you want to tell Bernie, it's fine. I'd like to tell my mothers myself, though."

"I'll let you tell him yourself."

"Thank you, Margot. And by the way, I think I didn't get fired. I still have insurance, and HR seemed at a loss when I inquired."

"I knew it. They love you. They wouldn't do something like that so callously."

"See you next week and, if I don't say it enough, thank you for your friendship, Margot. It's very important to me."

"Ohhh, sweetie, you're gonna make me cry."

I smile, and then we say our goodbyes and hang up.

As I'm about to step into the shower feeling both emotionally drained and lighter and able to take deeper breaths, another text comes in. This one is from Mom. Mima probably assisted. It's a string of emojis that makes no sense because they are not good with texting. But I get the gist of it, and I send them a few photos of the sloths and me.

Then, for the heck of it, since I'm feeling all the feels at the moment, I decide to send David a photo of me kneeling down and trying to feed a sloth. There are better photos of the sloths, but this one is the best of me. I'm not dumb! I send it with a question: Why did the sloth cross the road?

When I finish showering and slide into bed, I see that I have a reply from David.

Cute photo. Both the woman and the sloth. More the woman. I smile. You left me hanging . . . why did the sloth cross the road?

No one knows. He's not there yet.

LOL. That was the best worst joke of all time.

I'm sure I have more in my arsenal, but I'm exhausted.

And I have to get back to work. Good night, Alex.

'Night, David.

Rest comes easily that night.

———

The next day, I put on my bathing suit—a one-piece—more functional than cute. Because I spent my teenage years trying not to make waves during my sister's illness and her death, I never went through the "dressing up and loving to shop" phase of my life. While other girls were worried about makeup and bikinis, I was trying to get good grades and making sure Mima didn't have anything to worry about. Plus, Mima would have been that person who would have taken me to go shopping and shown me everything to do with makeup and cute outfits.

I don't have a memory before Annabel's death where Mima did not have bright red lipstick. She always took care of her appearance, never leaving the house without her hair perfectly styled. She was light and quirky just like Annabel. Mom, on the other hand, usually had her head in a book and a ponytail on her head. After Annabel's death, Mima never wore colorful clothes or makeup again. It was grays and blacks—a perpetual feeling of mourning clouded her. Until right this moment, I had never analyzed this fact. I was just "in the moment" trying to survive, and I never really stopped to examine how much I had lost after Annabel's death.

There's an aqua-colored sarong with yellow hibiscus flowers on it in the gift shop that reminds me of a bathing suit Mima used to own.

Going to the beach on Sundays with sandwiches and soda and just hanging out all day was something we did all the time when I was young. Annabel and I would make sandcastles, bury Mom in the sand, and wade in the ocean until the sun started to set. I miss that time with my mothers. Later today, I'll buy it for her. It's time she stopped wearing muted colors. It's time she went to the beach. It's time we all went to the beach. As for Mom, I knew what I'd buy her the moment I saw it. It's a CD of the sounds of the rain forest. She sleeps with a noise machine on, but I wonder if her noise machine has the lovely sounds of howler monkeys and cicadas.

With my Kindle that's already loaded with the newest women's fiction book, I head to the pool, ready to relax.

I pass a shop at the lobby, and there's mannequin after mannequin with cute little bikinis. I might have more meat on my bones than Heather, but I'm in great shape. Why don't I ever wear bikinis or sexy clothes? I guess Michael never seemed to notice, so I never made the effort. But isn't this the moment to have a little fun and do the things I wouldn't ordinarily do? Even if I don't do it often, I want to feel sexy and desirable just like any other woman. I hear Annabel's voice cheering me on to go into the shop and browse.

Annabel and Mima would have been in this shop for most of the trip, and they would have bought big straw hats and fabulous-looking sarongs. They would've rolled their eyes at my one-piece Speedo with the functionality of a well-made swimsuit but the appeal of a muumuu. There's one swimsuit in particular that catches my attention. It's a one-piece, but it's very high on the sides and has a cutout in the middle. It's black. Mostly, it's sexy in a subdued way. I can't picture myself wearing it. But Annabel's smiling down at me and giving me the encouragement to buy it and wear it proudly. Why not. I pay for it and then use the changing room to change into it. "You would have picked the blue bikini with the bows," I whisper to Annabel, because even though this is more appealing than what I wore coming in, it's not what Annabel would have chosen for herself. "But I like this for me. Thanks, sis." I look at myself in the mirror, twirling in a circle, and am pleasantly surprised at how good it looks on me. I throw my Speedo in my bag and put on the cover-up and head to the pool.

That was wild! Donna texts me later that afternoon when I'm halfway into my book. We're going to head to the pool. Join us and we'll tell you all about it.

I'm already here, I reply, and she sends me a thumbs-up emoji.

As I'm waiting for them, I get a text.

What did the tortoise say when she was dating the sloth? It's David. I smile. What?

Let's take it sloooooow.

Good one! I laugh as I type.

I wish I could take you on a proper date, David says, and I feel the heat crawling up my neck and into my cheeks. God, I'm a thirtysomething woman with an ex-husband. Why am I acting like such a fool?

That would be nice, I reply. Maybe if I'm ever in Arizona or you're in Miami.

I'd like that, he says. Have a great rest of the day.

You too.

In many ways, this is a first for me. I met Michael so young, and we married without having dated other people. This flirting is new to me. I don't even remember ever flirting with Michael. And these butterflies in my stomach . . . wow, it makes me feel like I can fly.

"Well, someone looks cheery," Heather says as she plops her big Lilly Pulitzer bag on the chaise next to mine. I see Donna at the bar filming something.

I put my phone down because I cannot multitask flirting and talking. "It's a guy I met last week. David. He texted me."

"A guy? We've been telling you all our secrets for the last forty-eight hours, and you failed to mention that there was a guy."

I laugh. "I told you both more than I've told anyone," I say, meaning Bob.

"Okay, yes, but this is juicy, exciting news!" Heather says just as Donna arrives juggling three Imperial beers in her hands. We each take one, and she sits on the edge of my chaise. "What juicy, exciting news?"

I tip back the beer and mumble a "thanks," and then I tell them about David. "Not much to tell. He was the tour guide last week. I didn't even know he was interested until the last day."

The truth is, it scares me. I've never been with anyone other than Michael. It feels like too great of a leap. But a great kiss and maybe a roll in the hay would be a wonderful memory to hold on to if my surgery went south. What if I'm left a mess, and this was my last chance at a fling?

"So tell me about zip-lining."

"It was freakin' awesome!" Heather says. "But before we get into that, can we please talk about that swimsuit, girl? It is h-a-w-t!"

"You think? I just bought it in the shop inside. I don't normally wear these kinds of suits." I pull up the strap and adjust the bottom. I feel exposed, physically and emotionally.

"Good purchase!" Heather says with a cheeky wink.

"Own it, girl! Stop fidgeting," Donna singsongs. I don't like the focus to be on me, and by messing with the straps and looking generally awkward, I'm unintentionally causing the focus to be on me and this silly bathing suit. I may be uncomfortable, but no one needs to know that.

"So . . . zip-lining?" I change the subject back to them and sit up straight and act confident. "It was awesome, you said? I'm glad you enjoyed it."

"How was it awesome, Donna? You had to be pushed off the first ledge, and you cursed loudly for about twenty minutes," Heather says.

"That is true, but then it was the coolest thing I've ever done."

"It really was," Heather agrees. "It was exhausting, though; you were right."

"I'd do it again, that's for sure," Donna says, drinking her beer.

"You remind me so much of my friend Sylvie," I say to Donna. "You say exactly what you're thinking without any filter."

"And that's a good thing?" Heather says, and Donna playfully shoves her shoulder.

"It is such a good thing. That's what I love most about her. Her honesty."

"Well, she is honest and also very loyal," Heather says with a sincere smile, and Donna throws her a cheeky air kiss.

"I'm glad I met you both. Otherwise, I think I would have been a bit lonely here."

"Awww, we're so glad we met you too, Alex," Heather says.

"Group hug!" Donna exclaims, and we all lean awkwardly toward each other from the chaise and, with beers in our hands, hug.

"I don't have a lot of friends," Donna admits when she lets go. In fact, I think there may be tears in her eyes. "I'm not a girls' girl, if that makes sense."

"You sleep with all the girls' boyfriends, that's why," Heather tells her, and because it's obviously a joke, I laugh.

Donna looks up to the sky as if she's thinking about it, and then she says, "Yeah. Shit. That's probably why."

I toss my head back and burst into laughter again.

"Damn, I really have got to stop doing that!" I am not certain whether she's being serious or not. She continues as if she's just had an alcohol-induced epiphany (it happens). "In my defense, the guys aren't very forthright about their relationship status."

"Yeah, but you don't really ask," Heather says.

"Is it my job to ask?" Donna asks, facing me.

"I don't know. Maybe?" I shrug. "You're asking the wrong person. I'm divorced and only have two real friends, and at work I'm the only female in my position, so I can relate to not being a girls' girl."

"You?" Donna says, surprised. "You're a riot, plus you might be the coolest woman I've ever met. You're so brave! I had to drag Heather to come with me. I couldn't travel alone."

"Me, cool? No way. I'm a tomboy, a loner, who works way too much."

"No. You are an independent woman who's comfortable in her own skin. That's a hard thing to pull off. Trust me," Heather says.

I had never thought of myself that way. Not at all. "I'm usually overthinking something and haven't really stopped to think about my surroundings or how I may look or what people think, if I'm being honest."

"Well, whatever you're doing, it's working!"

I think that over.

"You know, when I was growing up, most of my friends were boys. Not that I didn't want to be friends with girls, it's just that it was easier with the guys. I was on the basketball team. I ran cross country. I wasn't interested in cheerleading or dance, so I didn't have a lot in common with other girls. My sister was the only one who understood that and didn't think it was weird that I didn't like Barbies or shopping, even if she was all about Barbies and shopping. She just got me, you know?"

"No one knows you like your sibling," Donna says. "Heather's not my sister, but as an only child, I feel like she's my sis by default, and she knows the good, bad, and the ugly."

"Ditto," Heather says.

"Most of the guys are married now and have their families and their own lives, so I've only kept in touch with Sylvie—she's definitely my default sister. Margot has become a friend in the last few years, but other than that, I was in a bubble while I was married."

That reminds me of one of those little sayings that my mom gave me: "It's not about the number of people around you but the quality of the people around you." I have quality people.

"Who'd you tell all your secrets to when you were younger? You can't do that with a guy. Well, not really."

I think about this, and I don't have an answer. Actually, I do, and I don't like the answer. After Annabel died, I felt alone. I couldn't talk with my mothers because they were so deep into their own loss. But Michael was there. He was that person. Luckily, I don't need an answer because I'm saved by a server who brings more drinks.

Two hours later, I plop down on the bed the moment I walk into my room. The question hasn't left my head. I don't know why I'm dwelling on it. *Who'd you tell all your secrets to?*

It was Michael. Michael was my sounding board. The one who helped me off the ledge when I was having a hard time with chemistry, or couldn't make a three-point shot, or didn't know how to manage violin lessons and the track meet. He was the person who I'd let see me cry or get frustrated. He always saw me at my worst—like when my sister's death made my mothers seem to forget they had another child. I don't hold it against them, not at all. I felt the same way for a long time too. Mom picked herself up and started to join the land of the living faster than Mima did, and I did my best to do my best. I was the star of every sport, I got straight As, I never gave them a single moment of problems.

Around the same time, his parents were going through a divorce, and we leaned on each other for support. We talked about life and love and the future. We relied on each other. We did things to take burdens off our parents. Well, I did it to take the burden off my mothers, and he did it because his parents were embroiled in a horrible divorce and they sort of forgot about him too, so I'd make sure he was always taken care of. I made lunch for both of us and packed it in a red polka dot lunch box. I reminded him he had a test coming up and that we had to have our college applications in by a certain date. We were each other's chosen family, and now I realize, marriage was just the logical next step. It wasn't undying love and passion. It was affection and the need to have a person by my side. Unfortunately, he realized the faultiness of our relationship before I did and went about leaving me in a screwed-up way. In time, I think I can forgive him. We both deserve a real marriage based on something more than just comfort and familiarity.

———

Heather and Donna are leaving today. In big floppy hats, tans, and bright sundresses, they drag their luggage through the lobby where I'm meeting them to say our goodbyes. I have to admit, being surrounded by them has made me realize how much Margot's and Sylvie's friendship means and how important the power of friendship with other women can be.

I turn to the two women trekking my way, recording selfies. I don't know how they don't fall with their phones, their luggage, sunglasses, and hats. "See you all on our next adventure!" Heather says, and then they put down their phones and turn their attention to me.

"I can't believe we just met!" Donna says. "I feel like we've known each other forever."

"I feel the same way," I say.

"We're going to miss you so much!" Heather says as we hug. I'm crying. Two times, I've cried with these women. There's something about being able to express your emotions to total strangers. I don't know why it's easier, but it just is. I sniffle. "Call me and tell me all about the proposal," I say to Heather.

"And you better keep us posted on your health! And when you're better, let's talk about The Traveling Gals. We love your vision, and we'd love to have you as part of the team!"

"Really?"

"Of course! We love you!"

That makes me sob loudly. "I love you too!" I made new friends and am getting my creative mojo back. It's ridiculous, really. But I feel that I was meant to meet these women. People say they'll keep in touch, but they never do. I will make an effort to stay connected with them because it's not every day you find someone you connect with. Counting David, I've already made three meaningful relationships on this two-week trip, which automatically makes it worthwhile.

CHAPTER TEN

After a three-and-a-half-hour flight from San José, Costa Rica, I'm finally in San José, Puerto Rico. My mothers could not be more excited. Mima actually suggested I take a flight into Havana and meet some long-distance relatives, but this trip is supposed to be fun.

Although I'm sure Cuba is beautiful, it's also impoverished and full of political strife. It's a place I'll visit when I want to engage and learn, not escape and relax. So I'm in Puerto Rico, probably the country with the most similarity to my culture and heritage.

I send David a text. What do you call two Puerto Rican guys playing basketball? I slide my phone into my pocket because I know he's working and won't be able to check his phone until later.

It's only been a week since I last saw him. *How can you miss someone you barely know?*

On another, happy note: I'm thrilled to be in a place that is closer to sea level. My headache is gone. Maybe it wasn't just Bob wreaking havoc. I read that where I was staying had a pretty high altitude, and that could be part of the tiredness and headaches. I'm no doctor . . . I don't actually know. What I do know is that right this second, I'm feeling great as I step out of Luis Muñoz Marin Airport in San Juan. After the week here, I intend to go back home, feeling a little more centered, more able to process my emotions, and ready to face the operation.

Costa Rica, although sunny and humid, had a perpetual overcast. It felt hazy, as if it would rain at any moment—thus the rain forest.

Here, the sky is cornflower blue, and there are modern buildings and familiar chain stores around. It feels very much like some parts of Miami, especially the climate, which I very much welcome. Even the Spanish-speaking cabdrivers and street vendors feel like home.

When I booked the flight, I also rented a Jeep and a room in a small hotel in Fajardo, which is about an hour from the airport. Staying in the capital didn't appeal to me. I want to explore the east side of the island.

Easily, I find the rental area at the airport and put my Spanish skills to good use as I fill out the paperwork; then I'm given the keys to a bright yellow soft-top Jeep.

I've already downloaded a map of the island and input the address of my hotel, and so I head out. I'm excited to get to the hotel, get settled in, and enjoy a nice lunch with a tropical drink. The area around the airport is crowded, and I just don't feel comfortable stopping here to eat.

Unfortunately, that Miami similarity ends the moment I'm ten minutes out of the city. Though the beauty of the island still surrounds me, the poverty has become more prevalent as I drive. The streets have potholes, and there's still a lot of damage from Hurricane Maria after so many years. Children run around, some without shoes, chasing an unhappy rooster. There are people grilling in the front of their homes, which seem to have major structural damage. I wonder how Annabel would have felt about this. She surely didn't consider the poverty when she was planning the places she'd want to visit. Hell, I didn't think of it myself.

I have to make an effort to manually shift as I move up a mountain and circle down and around, over and over. I can already tell that the hour stated on Google Maps is only in theory. In reality, this is going to take a lot longer, and my stomach begins to rumble. I reach into my open purse with one hand, trying to see if I have anything in there. I think I grabbed some of those airplane pretzels. There's always something hidden in my purse. I know . . . gross . . . don't judge me. In moments of emergencies like right now, it's great.

Alas, there's nothing but a red-and-white mint from a restaurant somewhere. *Damn it.* Well, the map says I'm only twenty minutes away. The towns alternate between poor to higher end, then back to poor, then there will be a brand-new shopping mall equivalent to any one that I've seen in the States, except that it'll be between two old bodegas.

My phone rings, and I press the speaker button with one hand; it's David. "Hey, you," he says. "Did you make it safely?"

"Yeah. Trying to find the hotel."

"Okay, good. So what do you call two Puerto Rican guys playing basketball?"

"Juan on Juan. Get it?" I crack myself up.

He laughs into the phone. "You are too much, Alex. Have fun! Gotta run back to work." And he disconnects. But then my mother calls.

"Hi, Mima."

"Did you land safely, mija?"

"Yes, but I can't talk. I'm driving, and I'm trying to find the hotel, and . . . Shit, I missed the exit. Can I call you back?"

"Yes, be careful. Love you."

"Love you too," I say and toss the phone aside. No one is coming from the opposite side of the narrow road, so I decide to do a U-turn. Except spots fill my eyes, and my vision tunnels, and just as I'm turning, I lose sight of the road for a second as a splitting headache hits me hard and fast, right behind my eyes. I slam on the brakes viciously because I don't want to fall off the road, but I'm momentarily blinded. It feels like when you've been in a dark room for too long, and suddenly the sun's in your face, and then a sledgehammer hits you on the head—you know . . . just like that.

"Arghhh," I say as a car passes by me at full speed and honks the horn and curses at me in Spanish. "Coño!" I yelp and inch closer to the side of the road and then brake. My heart is pounding as hard as my head.

I crank the AC of the car as high as it goes and open the bottle of water I took from the airplane and gulp it down. I sit in my car for what could be five minutes or an hour, my head resting against the back of the seat. I take a deep breath. Then another. The headache is still there, but I can see again. I grab my phone and see how far I am. Five minutes. I'm right there. Just one left turn to the hotel. I can do this. I have to do this. I can't live on the side of a road in Fajardo forever. With a deep, shaky breath and another gulp of water, I grip the steering wheel hard and press the accelerator slowly. The five minutes is closer to ten, but when I see the name of the inn in front of me, I almost cry in relief.

This isn't high altitude. This isn't the weather or a hangover. This is Bob, of that I am sure. But why now? It's a slow-growing tumor—I read it. Hell, the doctor said it. He told me I'd have some time. I'm nervous now. I'm not at home, I'm alone, and I almost crashed. I wonder if Annabel ever had these moments of complete defeat.

I barely remember checking in, though I do remember the woman in the front desk asking me if I was okay. I think I nodded and asked if there was room service available, and she said, "Sí," which gave me such wonderful relief because I'm in no state to sit in a restaurant right now. With shaky hands, not just from the headache but from the scare down the road, I grab a banana from a basket by the front desk and head to my room.

After the tree-house adventure in Costa Rica, I opted for a conventional room in a familiar chain of hotels.

First things first, I press the button for room service on my phone, and a woman answers in Spanish. I don't know what is on the menu, but I know what I want. "Hola, tienen hamburguesas?" A cheeseburger and fries would be perfect right now, because I need comfort food. Tomorrow I'll explore.

"Sí, señora. Algo más?"

Do I want anything else? "Una Coca-Cola, por favor."

"Okay, Señora Martinez," she says. I suppose by the fact that she knows my name and doesn't ask for my room number, she knows where I'm at. "Trenta a cuarenta minutos."

"Okay, gracias."

Damn thirty to forty minutes. I hope I make it. I'm so hungry, I feel faint. I eat the banana and then decide to unpack and take a shower. That should kill time, right?

It doesn't.

You know when you have to go to the bathroom and the closer you get to your house, the more you have to go? Well, it's the opposite with food. As time ticks on, my hunger becomes nausea, and the thought of eating a burger makes me sick to my stomach.

There's an incoming text from David: Knock-knock.

I smile. I like this game we've been playing. Who's there?

HIPAA.

HIPAA who?

I can't tell you, he says. Nurse joke, he types next.

I need to find an auto-parts marketing-personnel joke to compete with that.

He sends me two laughing emojis. Did you make it safely to the hotel?

Define safely, I almost say. Yep. Just waiting for room service.

Great. Have a wonderful time.

Thanks, David.

I take the opportunity to call Mima. "Alex, hello." She sounds agitated.

"Hi, sorry I couldn't talk earlier. I was lost."

"Alex? You've gotten a few calls from a Dr. Devi. He says he's been trying to reach you. He didn't say why."

Damn it. Mima's my emergency contact. Of course he'd call. "Oh, it's fine. I'll call him when I get home."

"Who's Dr. Devi?"

"The neurologist I went to for my migraine." Not a lie.

"And why is he calling?"

"You're my emergency contact."

"I understand that, but why is he calling at all? Is there something wrong?"

"Probably just following up. Who knows?" I don't blatantly deny that there's something wrong. It's not really a lie, right? An omission. Anyway, I'm saved by a knock at the door. "Oh, it's room service. I have to go. My lunch is here, and I'm starving. I'll call you tomorrow. Love you."

She hesitates for a moment as I walk to the door. "Okay, we'll talk tomorrow. Te quiero." But it sounds like a loaded phrase. *"We'll talk."* She has things to say. Or rather, questions to ask.

"Love you, Mima."

"Love you, mija."

I hate lying to them. I just can't tell them anything until I know what to tell them. That nausea I had a few minutes ago leaves my body the moment I smell the thick steak fries that accompany my fat, juicy burger. I eat the fries first and fast and then gulp down the Coke. I gulp it so fast that it burns going down my esophagus.

With a full stomach, even though I didn't touch the burger, I close my eyes, trying to think of anything but the headache, but just like it's been since I was diagnosed with this tumor, all I can think about is my sister.

Annabel was tired for weeks, falling asleep in school, not wanting to go to soccer practice and generally lethargic. My mothers took her to her pediatrician a few times, and the doctor told them that Annabel needed to start going to sleep earlier. However, when she started getting bruises and rashes, the doctor ran some tests, and my mothers started becoming really concerned. Mom kept trying to get Annabel to go outside and ride her bike, but Annabel mostly wanted to sleep. Mima kept making different kinds of "potajes" and other Cuban remedies that she said would give her the energy she needed.

Then it was the day of the oncologist appointment; the energy in the house was palpable even though my mothers were making it seem as if they were okay. Fake smiles and awkward conversations took place, but no actual explanation as to what an oncologist was. At that time, neither Annabel nor I knew what that meant. I found myself with an inexplicable pain in the pit of my stomach as I waited for them to get home.

Eventually, they returned. Annabel was mostly tired but in cheery spirits. No one said much, and Mima started making dinner like she would any other day, except it wasn't any other day. It was the day they got the worst news of their lives. "Hello? Can someone tell me what's going on?" I asked my mothers, who looked at each other back and forth as if no one wanted to say the words. Eventually, the words were said—*"Leukemia." "Cancer." "The doctors are optimistic." "Chemo." "Radiation." "Caught it early."* Those are the words I remember hearing over and over.

Then it was a whirlwind of doctor appointments, and eventually she was pulled out of school when her immune system was too compromised to be around so many other kids. But being young and busy with school, I wasn't as aware of how serious the diagnosis was until Annabel stayed in the hospital weeks at a time, frail and too weak to get up. I caught my mothers crying and sometimes arguing when they thought I couldn't hear. I made sure to get out of everyone's way so that all the focus could be on my sister's recovery. If I was hungry, I'd open a package of ramen noodle soup or make some scrambled eggs. I didn't participate in extracurricular activities that would cause my mothers to have to divide their time between my sister and me, and I got straight As, so as to not cause any more stress on anyone. It was a surreal time and not something I think about often. I was there, but also, I was too young to ask the questions that I now wish I had asked.

Mostly, I wonder if Annabel knew she was going to die. Was I any comfort to her during that time? I wish I could talk to her again. Give her a hug . . . I doze off with these thoughts swirling in my mind.

The next day, I wake up rejuvenated and feeling much better. My headache doesn't feel like an entire marching band is lined up inside. It's dulled down to one drummer practicing the cymbals.

In a pair of Nike shorts, matching tank top, and sneakers, I set off to explore the area. Fajardo is mostly a beach town, which I plan to fully enjoy tomorrow. Today, I just linger around the pueblo. It reminds me a lot of Key West with its lime-green, teal-blue, hot-pink storefronts. I buy a few souvenirs for my mothers—knickknacks made of ceramic with sayings in Spanish, similar to Mima's T.J.Maxx ones. For lunch, I decide on a hole-in-the-wall restaurant that has a lot of stars on Yelp. There are four tables, and all four are taken. Luckily, there's a small bar area, and the hostess offers me a stool and hands me a menu.

Gracias, Mima, for making me learn fluent Spanish.

The food is divine. It reminds me a lot of my grandmother's cooking. Instead of arroz con gandules, Abuela would make arroz con frijoles. And instead of mofongo, she used to make fufu. Otherwise, the flavors and the spices are very similar, and so is the inflection of language. I didn't get to experience this in Costa Rica because I was mostly in the resort, and when I left the resort, I went with an English-speaking guide recommended by the hotel. The Spanish in Costa Rica is similar to the Spanish I know, but there were little nuances that I didn't understand. It wasn't difficult to figure out, of course, but it's not the Spanish I'm used to. Here, however, it's almost like being at home.

The Puerto Rican *R* is almost nonexistent, unlike the Cuban *R* that rolls off the tongue like two people salsa dancing. Otherwise, the words, the speed, and tone are almost the same.

Time to get acclimated to the island and get my adventure on. With a full belly and a few bags of trinkets and gifts, I decide to go back to the hotel and take a quick nap before I go out again in the evening.

———

A banging sound startles me. I jolt out of bed, dazed. *Where am I?* I look around the dark room, not recognizing anything. I shuffle to the window and slide open the blackout curtains and squint. The bright light hurts my eyes, and I recoil. Through squinted eyes, I see the beach in the distance, and I'm transported back to reality.

I'm in Puerto Rico.

I was going to take a nap.

The knock comes again, but this time louder.

What day is it?

I hurry to the door, unlock the bolt, and stupidly open it without asking who it is.

"Ay, Dios mío. Gracias a Dios estas viva!"

Of course I'm alive—why would she think I'm dead? "Mima?" I'm baffled. Is this a dream? I yawn and wipe my eyes with the backs of my hands. "What are you doing here? How'd you know where I was?"

She walks in and closes the door behind her. "You told me the name of the hotel you were staying at, and I had to bribe someone to give me your room number. I know about the tumor, and I don't know if I want to hug you or hit you."

"Uh . . . what? How?" I'm still in that dazed state. "Where's Mom?"

"There was only one seat left on the plane, and I took it," she says. "Sylvie and Margot told us. But before you get mad, it wasn't easy getting it out of them."

"What day is it?" I'm so confused.

"Wednesday."

"Wednesday!" I say groggily. "What happened to Tuesday?" I say that mostly to myself.

I step around her and then grab my phone. It's 10:22 a.m. Shit, fourteen missed calls and a bunch of texts.

"Give me a minute." I grab some clothes and head to the bathroom. I quickly brush my teeth, change clothes, and tame my hair.

Mima's here.

In my room.

She knows about the tumor and is probably worried out of her mind. *Shit.* It hits me. I don't know if I'm ready for this conversation, but she's here, and there's no possible place for me to hide. I really should've come up with a plan on how to break the news.

I splash water on my face when the room spins round and round for a moment. I've now been feeling ill for almost three days, and I know it has something to do with Bob. Luckily, Mima is looking out of my balcony and doesn't notice. "Have you had breakfast?" I ask her.

She looks over her shoulder and then walks back inside, closing the sliding door. "No, and I don't want any. I can't eat right now." *Here we go.*

"Sit," I say, pointing to the bed. "You need to eat something. I'll order room service. You're probably tired from the flight and—"

"Stop!" she says abruptly. "I don't need food, and I'm not tired. Stop trying to avoid this conversation."

I almost call her by her full name and tell her to calm down, but when has telling anyone to calm down actually worked?

"I'm not avoiding it. I'm worried about you. I didn't tell you for this exact reason."

"What reason is that, Alex?" Her accent gets heavier when she's upset, and her arms fling around wider.

"That you get so worried that you make yourself sick . . . or worse."

She lets out a big breath, and her shoulders sag. She pats the space beside her on the bed, and I reluctantly take a seat. I don't want to have a heart-to-heart.

"Annabel—" she begins, but my throat closes up and tears well in my eyes. I shake my head side to side.

"No," I say over that lump. "I don't want to talk about this. I'm sorry I didn't tell you about the tumor."

"That's the problem—we don't ever want to talk about anything. It's my fault, mi amor. I messed up. I got so depressed when your sister died that I abandoned you," she says, and her voice cracks and tears start flowing from her eyes.

"No! Don't say that. You didn't abandon me. You're a great mom."

"But I was so deep in my depression, you've always felt the need to protect *me* when I'm the mom. I should be protecting you. Damn it, Alex, you couldn't even tell me you needed surgery. You ran away instead of facing it because facing it meant I'd have to know."

"You're reading too much into it. I came on this trip because I just wanted to do some of the things that I've never done. What if the surgery goes wrong, and I'm never able to hike or zip-line? Now I can say I've done it."

"I don't think that's true. Maybe you think that's why you left, or maybe that's part of the reason. I think you were scared of telling me. I'm not an invalid, Alex. I can handle it. I can help and support you. You're my daughter, mi amor." She turns and takes me into her arms. We're not a touchy-feely family, never have been, so this is surprising. Maybe that's why I feel comfortable working at a mostly-male office. Men don't expect you to tell them how you feel. It's a wonderful place to repress your emotions. "There's no one in this world more important to me than you. No one. I'd give anything for that tumor to be in my head so you wouldn't have to go through this. Do you understand?"

I'm crying now with big, loud, shaking sobs.

"Annabel's death is a pain I wouldn't wish on anyone, and I'd be lying if I said it still doesn't hurt deeply. But that doesn't mean that it overshadows how much I love you or how important it is to me that you let me in. Good or bad—I want to know, and I want to be there for you."

"I'm sorry, Mima," I say between sobs. "I should've told you. I should've told both of you. I was scared. Scared of hurting you. Scared of how you'd react. And I'm also scared that I'll die like Annabel did."

"Ay, no, Alex. Do not say that." She closes her eyes, and I can see under her breath she's whispering a Hail Mary. I roll my eyes. "You have to think positive. You cannot think that the surgery will be a failure because then it will be a failure. And I'll tell you right now, I'll probably worry and cry, but I'm not going to break. I didn't break with Annabel. I was there until the bitter end. You have to trust me with that. You can't worry about me. This is about you and the journey ahead."

I nod.

"So, tell me, mija. What's going on exactly?"

"I have a cerebral meningioma. It's a benign tumor that's right here." I point to the top of my head, which is where it's located. She massages the area as if she'd have a way of feeling it. "The doctors don't know how long I've had it. Could be years, but now it's big enough that it's pushing on nerves, and it's what's giving me headaches."

"It's benign? How sure are they about that?"

"Pretty sure. I don't think they would know for certain until they remove it and biopsy, but by the scans, they've said it's benign. It'll keep on growing and making me miserable, so I have to have it removed."

She looks at me as if she'd never suspected otherwise. "And the surgery?"

"It's intense. They make a small incision and remove the tumor. There's a lot of possible side effects to the surgery."

"Like what?"

"I can go blind, I can lose my memory, I can have permanent issues walking or severe headaches for the rest of my life. So yeah, I'm scared out of my mind."

I can see her swallow. I've worried her, obviously. It's a serious procedure, and there's a reason I want to get to live life a little before I go under the knife. This may be the last time.

"I'm scared, too, but we're going to get through this together."

"But Annabel didn't live, and we did all the things the doctor said to do."

"I know." Her voice falters a bit. "Sometimes God has other plans, but you still have to make the effort, because we don't know what is in store for us. Living with headaches and whatever else is not something I want for you, and it's not something you should want for yourself."

"It's not."

"Then you have the surgery, and we'll help you through the recovery. One day at a time. That's all we can do, honey. One day at a time." I'm seeing all these long-term possibilities. I'm already past the surgery and, in my mind's eye, dealing with memory loss. I am getting way too ahead of myself. She's right. "What about your insurance?"

"I have to figure things out with Bernard. It doesn't seem like I was fired, but now that I'm going to need a lot of time off, that may change. On top of all that, I met these women on the trip, Heather and Donna, who have this fabulous blog and asked for my help with marketing. It never occurred to me not to work at AutoRey. But the thought of helping these women and possibly doing some freelance work where I get to use my creativity makes me so excited. Being the liaison between a marketing firm that will be doing all the work while I do the administrative tasks isn't something I really want to do. Am I crazy?"

"You're not crazy, Alex. You are one of the most creative people I know. You only stay at AutoRey because you love the people there and you have a need to please everyone. You don't do things for yourself. Ever. But you're going through this major scare, and it's normal to see life through a different lens. You don't want to squander a single moment. Working in a job that you don't love doesn't feel worth it. I get it. You may not have ever realized that if it wasn't for this diagnosis."

"I should thank this tumor for giving me the wake-up call I needed?"

"Not quite," she says with a smirk. "I don't want you to worry about work right now. Meanwhile, you stay with us. You don't need to worry about work or money or anything. You have insurance, and that's the most important thing. Just focus on recovering."

"That's easier said than done if I end up without a job or insurance."

"We will figure out the insurance thing. If we have to get a mortgage on the house, we'll do it. There's insurance you can pay for, and we can help you. It will work out. As for work . . . eh." She shrugs.

"What is that supposed to mean?"

"You have a job that you just said you don't love. Worst-case scenario, you get a different job. Best-case scenario, you stay at AutoRey or you start doing that work for your friends you just mentioned. You have other things to worry about, and work should not be one of them."

"One day at a time," I say.

"Exactly. Like it or not, Alex, your life's going to change. You're going to have to stop working and recover, and once that's done and you're better, then you can figure out what you're going to do about work."

"You make it sound so easy."

"It's not easy, but it's something you have to do. What's the alternative?"

I guess there isn't any. "I can work part-time and while I—"

"Maybe, but what if you don't feel well after or you're tired or whatever . . . you're going to do a half-assed job just to please your boss, who's not going to be pleased because you've done a half-assed job. Meanwhile, you're going to be stressed over that half-assed job."

Damn it. She's right. "I'll think about it."

"And how are you feeling now?"

"I'm okay."

She glares at me.

"I'm tired," I say truthfully. I've gotten so used to saying I'm okay and I'm fine that it comes out naturally. "I have a headache that comes and goes, but it's mostly the fatigue that's become an issue now."

"And when is your surgery scheduled?"

"I haven't scheduled it yet. I didn't think it was an emergency. I was going to do it as soon as I got home, but I'm worried that the headaches are coming more frequently and I'm so tired suddenly."

She stands up and runs her palm over her face and then looks up to the ceiling. "Esta niña me va a volver loca!"

"I'm not trying to drive you crazy. I sincerely was feeling fine, and I wanted to do this one last thing for Annabel and for me."

"Stop saying things like that! It makes it seem like you're not going to survive. Like this will be your last vacation." She reaches into her cavernous purse and takes out her cell phone. "I'm going to call your mom and let her know I'm here and what's going on. Then I'll arrange for flights out of here ASAP. Meanwhile, I want you to call that surgeon and make plans for surgery."

I grab her forearm. "Wait. Wait. No."

"Alex."

"Mima! Stop. I'll call the surgeon. I'll make the appointment, but I'd like to do one last thing while I'm here. It's something that Annabel wanted to do too. I want you to join me, please."

"But your health . . ."

"Look at me, Mima. Do I look sickly? I'm tired, but I can walk and go out. It's one more day, and then I'm all yours."

I'm still holding her arm, and she's not answering. She's thinking. I can see the wheels turning.

"Ugh. Okay. Okay. But I'm booking the flight for tomorrow, and that is it."

"Deal."

Then she turns and starts making calls.

An hour later, we're lying in bed; people have been called and plans have been made.

"So what did you have planned, mija? What is it that you needed to do?"

"I had reservations to go to the bioluminescence. It's in a canoe." Mima is not a big fan of nature or the ocean. She came to the United States on a raft and has nothing but bad memories of that week. Even when we'd go to the beach, she'd stay sunbathing on the sand.

"And that is?"

I get up and walk over to my suitcase and take out Annabel's book. I show it to her as I lie back down. She looks at it lovingly, petting the cover as if she were trying to grab on to the past. "Wow, it's been so long since I've seen this. How many times did you and Annabel argue about the places you'd visit?" She gets comfortable on the bed, and I do the same, and we go page by page for what feels like an hour. I tell her funny stories and conversations I had with my sister—the places she marked and unmarked and why she wanted to visit one place and not another. When we get to the page that says *Puerto Rico*, Mima sees the blurb on the side, *Things to Do*, and the handwritten star under *bioluminescence*.

"It's a large concentration of plankton that basically glows in the dark. It's supposed to look magical."

My mother exhales heavily and nods.

"We have to be there at seven tonight, and we take canoes into the bay. I know you're not big on canoeing, but it'll be fun. We can order room service or go down to the hotel restaurant for dinner before."

"Anything for my girls," she says. "And then tomorrow, we catch the evening flight back to Miami."

"And on Friday I have my pre-op labs, and the surgery is scheduled the week after that on the fifteenth."

"Okay, good," she says bravely, but I know she's just as scared as I am. But neither of us says it.

—————

"You're not going to fall," I say, trying not to laugh. I'm sitting behind her, and I'm doing all the rowing while she sits like a statue. Is she even breathing? "Try and relax."

She mumbles a bunch of curse words in Spanish.

"Que?" I ask louder, and my movement rocks the canoe just a hair, and she squeals and grabs the sides.

"Ay, Dios mío!" she says, and I see her doing the sign of the cross.

"This is not going to be fun if you don't relax. Are your eyes even open?"

"Sí."

I don't believe her. "Let me see." I inch a little, and the entire canoe rocks.

"No! No! Do not move. My eyes are open. I promise!" And she slowly moves her head to the side so I can see her eyes. I chuckle.

Together with four other couples and a guide, we paddle to a lagoon-like area, the guide explaining the reason why the plankton glows and how there're few places in the world where this happens.

"Mima, look up," I whisper. It's quiet, except for the sounds of coqui, the small but loud frogs nearby; a few birds; and one of the couples chatting softly.

"Wow, I don't think I've ever seen the moon so bright and big." I reach my paddle upward as if I could touch it. It's low and breathtaking—that light is all we have right now, and it doesn't feel dark.

"No. No. No. I am not moving."

I laugh and then continue to paddle. It's so tranquil, and the air smells so clean and refreshing. I think this is exactly what I needed. I take in a deep breath, the warmth of the tropical air filling my lungs. I hold it in and then exhale.

"This reminds me of growing up in Havana," she says. "There's something about the ocean breeze and the smell of marine life and saltiness from the water." I guess she is taking it all in, notwithstanding her fear. I like that. It makes me proud.

"So beautiful, isn't it—oh! Wow! Look!" Suddenly we're glowing, and it's absolutely amazing. I've never seen anything like it. It's more intense than I thought it would be. The sea is alive underneath us; ebbing and flowing light emanates upward, and as the water flows from the movement of the canoes, the light is distorted in the most unusual way.

I run my fingers through the water, and my hands glow, too, until all the water washes away. I can tell my mother is starting to unwind as she moves ever so softly, trying to put her hand into the water also.

"Annabel would have loved this," she says. Annabel loved everything magical and beautiful. She loved stories of unicorns and dragons and loved to smell flowers and look at rainbows. "It looks like we're surrounded by little fairies."

"It really does," I say, mesmerized by the absolute brightness of the water. A glow stick has less wattage than this water. "And look up. There are so many stars out now."

She looks up and then turns her head back to look at me. "Gracias, mi vida," she says, and her eyes have unshed tears in them. "I would have gone my entire life without seeing this if you hadn't pushed me."

I reach forward carefully, take her hand in mine, and squeeze. "Te quiero."

"Te quiero también," she says. "How I wish that your sister could've made this trip with you."

I look around at the ethereal vista surrounding us. "I think she's here with us."

She looks around, too, and nods. "Yeah, I think you're right."

PART THREE

I'VE GOT NINETY-NINE PROBLEMS, AND
NINETY OF THEM ARE SCENARIOS I'VE
MADE UP IN MY HEAD

CHAPTER ELEVEN

As I'm walking out of the terminal, I see Mom waiting by the gate.

She looks distraught, although I spoke with her yesterday and again before the flight departed from Puerto Rico.

"I'd like to remind you that I have a tumor and therefore you cannot be mad at me." Unfortunately, my weak physical state lacks the humorous punch I was going for. She does not even smile.

"She didn't have a great flight," Mima says, and Mom's anger seems to fade away a bit. "She's very tired."

I am. I'm exhausted in a way that I know has nothing to do with lack of sleep. My head's pounding too.

"I am so mad that I want to yell," Mom says and takes me into a big hug.

"I already told you, I didn't want you to worry."

"I'm a parent—worrying is what I do. It doesn't mean I want you to keep things from me. From us." She pulls out a notebook as we walk to the parking garage. "I've spent the last two days researching meningiomas, and I spoke with Dr. Devi."

I stop and turn to the two of them. "What? How'd—"

Mom waves me off and takes the rolling luggage from my hand. "Remember, he had called asking for you. I kept the number. But that's not important; what is important is that he wouldn't give me any information about you but was very helpful in discussing what a meningioma is. I had to speak in hypotheticals."

"HIPAA? Is that not still a thing?"

She waves me off and continues explaining all the details of a meningioma, ignoring me completely. Everything she says are things I already knew and things I told Mima, but I don't say this because she clearly needs to vent and seem helpful somehow. We arrive at the car, and Mom helps me stuff my luggage in her sedan. Mima tries to give me the front passenger seat, which I've never, ever done while sitting in their car. I will not allow them to treat me like an invalid. I slide into the back seat in protest, which causes my mother to mumble a bunch of Spanish things under her breath as she sits in the front.

"The way you are feeling is indicative of it growing," Mom begins again. "Usually these growths are slow, and maybe you've had it for years, but it is making you feel worse every day."

"I'm really sorry I didn't tell you. I know you don't understand, but in a messed-up way, I was trying to protect you."

"You don't need to protect us," Mima says again. She said that a lot in Puerto Rico. "We're your mothers. Our job is to protect you and care for you, not vice versa."

"How are you feeling right now?" Mom asks.

"I have a headache, and I'm tired."

My phone rings at that moment, and I hold my finger up and answer. "Hi," David says.

"Hi," I say back.

"How's Puerto Rico?"

"I actually just arrived back in Miami. I wasn't feeling great and cut my trip short."

"Oh, sorry to hear that. Anything concerning?"

Ha! Yes! I want to yell, but my moms are listening intently to the conversation. "I'm okay. Can I call you later?"

"Sure."

"Thanks. Bye, David." And I hang up.

"David, huh?" Mima says. "I like him."

"You don't know him," I reply.

"I know he makes you smile. I've already seen some of the photos of the two of you, and he has kind eyes. Me gusta él," Mima says.

"All true," I say, feeling little butterflies in my belly as I think of David. I hope that I see him again, even though I'm stupid and keep pushing him away when he clearly doesn't want to be pushed away. But he lives in Arizona, and I live in Miami. I also come with baggage. A lot of it. "I need to focus on Bob, not my love life."

"Bob? Who the hell is Bob?" Mom asks.

"My tumor. That's its name."

"I don't understand most of the stuff that comes out of your mouth sometimes, but I agree. You need to focus on healing," Mom says just as we park at home.

"The surgery isn't going to be easy. It's a big surgery with real risks, and I'll need to stay with you for a bit. I might need some help too."

"Well, of course. You didn't have to tell us that. We are going to take care of you whether you live with us or somewhere else. We're your parents," Mima says as if I'm crazy for even having uttered such obvious words.

"That's why you ran away? You're scared of the risks from surgery?" Mom says, which surprises me.

"Stepping away from the situation to think and make calm decisions is not running away."

"Except that you do this often," Mima says as she puts a comforting hand over mine and Mom steps behind me and holds me.

"Oh really? When?" I'm annoyed with this narrative.

"Well, let's see," Mima starts. "Most recently is your divorce. You act like it all came out of nowhere, but you have to know that things weren't great for a while between you two."

"No, actually, I didn't know that. I'm coming to figure that out now, but I didn't until literally this trip. How did you two know? Michael and I didn't argue."

"*Because* you and Michael didn't argue," Mom says as if it's the most obvious explanation ever. "People argue. You can't just agree on everything every time. You were both just going through the motions. I'm sure you loved each other, but it seemed . . ."

"Boring," Mima adds. "It wasn't our place to say anything, but you guys seemed more like roommates than lovers."

I almost gag.

"Oh, and how about Jimmy?"

"Jimmy? Clarita's son?" I ask. Clarita is a friend of Mima's.

"Yeah, Jimmy. I'm your mom; I know everything. I know that you stopped running at West Park after years and years of going there because you didn't want to hurt Jimmy's feelings."

Oh my God, how the heck do they know these things?

"How did Jimmy even know that's where I ran?" I ask accusatorily.

Mima shrugs, but there's a devilish smirk on her face. Jimmy's a lawyer. He's extremely handsome, and Mima tried to play matchmaker. One day, four months after my divorce, Jimmy *happened* to also be jogging at West Park at six forty-five in the morning. *What a coincidence.* At first it was fine, but then a week later, he asked me out. I wasn't ready to start dating, so I did the logical thing . . . I changed parks and haven't seen him since.

"You literally ran away from him," Mom says.

I roll my eyes. "Okay, fine. I get it. I don't like confrontation."

"You're not a pushover, sweetie. When you need to argue, you can be scary. It's not about confrontation. It's about avoiding the truth so you don't get hurt or so you don't hurt someone else you love. You're a people pleaser, and that's a wonderful quality, but sometimes you need to be a little selfish. You're no good to anyone if you're falling apart yourself."

Interesting.

"We're scared too, honey. You are our whole life. But not having the surgery doesn't seem to be an option, right?"

"I know."

"Tell us about the risks."

"I can lose my memories and my motor functions. Those are the two biggest risks, but there are other things that can go wrong. The recovery is long, and I'll need physical, occupational, and speech therapy afterward."

"You could also get hit by a car," Mima says. David and his fiancée. So many things can happen just by living your life. "There're so many unknowns and what-ifs, but there're also so many reasons to live and to have a good quality of life. You're young, otherwise healthy, so why are you dwelling on the worst-case scenario? Do you want to spend the rest of your life in pain?"

"Of course not." I sniffle and then wipe my eyes. We walk inside together. "I am so sorry for keeping this from you, and I love you both so much."

"We love you too, honey."

I receive a text from Sylvie as I'm walking to my room. How mad at us are you?

Not mad at all, I say and add a kissing-face emoji. I shouldn't have kept it from my moms or asked you to keep it from them.

She replies with a heart.

Next it's time to call Bernard. Like it or not, it's time to face the music with all aspects of my life—work being the priority.

I'm nervous. I don't know what he's going to say. We haven't spoken in almost three weeks. When he told me to go on vacation, he may have meant for me to leave and come back in a week. He may have meant for me to go and not come back at all. I now realize that my head was not on straight that day that I walked out of the office. It's as if I had information overload and, rather than processing it, my system crashed.

"Hiya, Alex," Bernard says after just one ring. "We miss you. Are you back? I have so much to catch you up on."

Immediately, I feel a huge sense of relief. It's not only about my job; it's also about the Rey family. I love them. They've become an extension of my own family, and thinking that I was so disposable was adding to the stress. "Hi, Bernard. I miss you all too."

"Have lots to fill you in on. I had your emails routed to Bernie. I wanted you to enjoy your trip without having to worry. I knew you'd be checking your emails instead of resting."

Ahh, that explains the lack of emails!

I love Bernard. He really does know me well.

"That was sweet of you. I really appreciate it, and I can't wait to hear about everything, but something's happened, and I was hoping we could talk. Maybe today or tomorrow? I can meet you at the office."

"I'm in Virginia scoping out a few new stores. Can we chat now? Your tone worries me."

He sounds genuinely concerned. "This conversation is better in person, but it can't really wait, so I'm going to have to just spit it out over the phone." I take a deep breath, and then on the exhale I blurt out, "I have to have surgery. Brain surgery, actually." I breathe and then continue a little slower. "The doctor is telling me I'll need to be out for six weeks or so."

I know my voice is trembling, and the fear in my voice is easily readable, but what choice do I have? I have to come clean. I can't hide brain surgery.

"Alex . . ." It comes out soft and gentle. "You're scaring this old man." I hear a door open and close and fumbling around. "You know you can have as much time as you need, but that's not important right now. Are you okay? What exactly is going on?"

"I'm sorry—I know it's a lot of information."

"No. No. I just—I need to take a seat. Start from the beginning. Why do you need surgery?"

We spend almost forty-five minutes on the phone. Mostly, he's asking questions about my health, about the diagnosis, and about doctors. He's not Bernard Rey, my boss, right now; he is Bernard Rey, my friend. He's barely addressing work. "Alex, I'm disappointed in you. You should have come to me. Why didn't you tell me? Did you really think I wouldn't have understood?"

"I don't know. I didn't even really believe it myself, I guess. I think I was hoping that it would all just be a misdiagnosis. I didn't feel that bad, really. Well, until I felt really bad."

"You know you're like a daughter to me, right? You take all the time you need. You have long-term and short-term disability. You're insured. I don't want you to put a single thought into work or job security or money. Anything you need, Alex. Anything."

I'm crying now. How could I have misjudged the situation so immensely? "I have something else I need to tell you, Bernard. Oh my God, I think this is even harder to say than the tumor itself."

"Not funny."

"Sorry. Sorry. Bernard, it's not just that I'll need time to recover. I think you were right; I've lost my passion, and these last weeks and all that's happened have made me realize that it may be time for me to move on once I recover."

"Alex . . ."

"I will not leave you hanging, I promise. I can work as a consultant until you're able to find someone else or if you want me to help bring Victor up to date. I could really use the insurance coverage as long as possible."

"I want you to do whatever makes you happy, Alex. I won't lie and say you're not going to be missed, but I understand. Boy, do I. There're days I want to quit and go work exclusively under a car—get my hands dirty—but that was never an option for me. I'd never fault you for doing what you need to do. I'd like to take your offer to help train Victor, and I'd like your input on the new firm's ideas. It would be immensely helpful, even if it's on a part-time basis. That way you can stay on the insurance and make some income while you recover. I don't want to pressure you, but it would help both of us. What do you say?"

"Yes! I say yes and thank you so much."

"Of course. You're family, Alex. You'll always have a job here."

"Can you have my emails routed back to me, please? I'd really like to catch up and help until I have surgery next week. See how I can get Victor up to speed on everything."

"Alex, are you sure? You don't have to. I want your priority to be your health."

"I'm sure. I need to work. I need to think of something other than this tumor."

"Okay. We'll really miss you around here, kiddo." He exhales. "Jeez, you took ten years off me just now. Does Bernie know?"

"No. I'll speak with him next."

"Okay," he says. "And, Alex, you know me; you know our family. We are tight, and you are one of us. You must know that. Keep us up to date, not for work purposes but because we love you."

Again . . . the tears.

"O-okay, Ber-n-ard. Th-thank you."

"Bye, dear."

"Bye."

Next, I call Bernie, and I get a very similar earful from him, but also, I hear him give Margot an earful for keeping this from him. By the time I'm done with all the phone calls and planning, I lie down for a nap, feeling a massive weight lifted off my shoulders.

Turns out that confronting things is actually a lot easier than running away from them.

CHAPTER TWELVE

It's the day of the surgery. I'm nervous. So nervous, in fact, that my hands shake while I sign the final paperwork. Mima is holding her rosary tightly. Mom is trying to be strong, but I can see her strength waver when she speaks and her voice trembles. Sylvie, Margot and Bernie, Nora, Bernard and his wife are here too. They're all hanging out in the surgical waiting room, surely causing a ruckus. Donna and Heather sent me texts this morning wishing me a quick recovery. The excitement of all the plans I have for The Traveling Gals and being able to wrap up my AutoRey work on my own terms is keeping me from falling into depression. Too many major life events and changes in too short of a time. Regardless, my heart is full, even if I am freaking out.

And then it's time to say goodbye. I get kisses and hugs, and then I'm wheeled to the operating room, where I close my eyes and pray to God. Funny how my mind goes straight to the rock where I saw the sunrise at the Grand Canyon. As I think of all the colors and the serenity I felt, I begin to calm. Even if the surgery doesn't go as planned, there's no way I'll ever forget that spot. It's my happy place.

You can't forget your happy place.

A bright light shines on my face from overhead. The room smells like disinfectant products. There's a bunch of people in gowns around me, all doing different things. I'm slid over to a small, hard table—the operating table, I assume—and then I'm asked to count backward from ten. "Ten, nine, eight, sev—"

———

Everything hurts, especially my head. This is not like any headache I've ever had. This is excruciating, and it burns and hurts at the same time. It's pounding so hard, I can actually hear the thump-thump-thump. There're also sporadic beeps. Beep. Beep. Beep.

I swallow, and it feels like little razor blades against the back of my mouth, which is drier than the Sahara.

What a terrible dream. I try and open my eyes, but I can't. I tell myself, *Alex, open your eyes!* Nothing. I try to move my arms, and I can't. I don't think I'm tied down, but maybe I am.

Alex Martinez, open your eyes and move! Move. Move. Wiggle your fingers. Move your head. Blink. It's like I'm stuck in my body, and my brain is misfiring the commands. I want to yell, but I can't seem to command my brain to do that. I'm scared and in pain and the damn beep doesn't stop.

Help! Someone help!

Then . . . darkness.

———

The next time I wake up, there are voices around me, along with that annoying beep that doesn't seem to go away. The words are muddled, but by the inflection and the tone, I feel anxiety build. The beeping gets louder and faster, and the voices start becoming louder too. I want to tell whoever is talking so incessantly to be quiet. *Turn off the beep!* I have a headache, and I'm trying to sleep, but the words don't come out of my mouth. I try and yell, but it's as if I'm stuck inside my own body without a way of getting out. The anxiety builds and builds, and the beeps quicken, and then a peace washes over me and I'm asleep again.

———

Familiar voices are whispering by my ear. The beep lulls in the background, calmly, like the voices. It's in Spanish. Someone, or some people, is speaking Spanish. I know those words. "Padre nuestro que estás en el cielo . . ." It's a prayer, a prayer I've heard hundreds if not thousands of times. It's Mima's voice. She's praying the Our Father. No, she's reciting a rosary; I can hear the beads in her hands. Why is she doing the rosary? Why doesn't she just come sit by me and speak to me? I haven't heard her do that in a long time. After Annabel died, she would kneel by her bed, eyes closed, head down, and pray the rosary for hours and hours. That was so long ago. *Mima, why are you praying? Is it Annabel? Mima?* I try to say, but no words are coming out of my mouth no matter how hard I try.

Am I dead?

The beep starts to quicken again, but this time I feel something squeeze my hand. Not something. Someone. "Alex, sweetheart, it's Mom. Do you hear me? Wake up, honey. Please wake up. Alex?"

I can hear you. I'm trying to wake up. Don't you worry, Mom! I'm fine.

"Mija, can you hear us? Ay, Dios mío, she's not waking up." I can hear the terror in my mother's voice and the sniffles from both of them.

I'm okay. Really, I'm just tired. Don't worry.

"This is not uncommon," I hear an unfamiliar voice say. "It's been two days. The doctor has asked to wean her off the pain meds—that should get her up. Alex, this is Nurse Williams—can you hear me?" I can feel her touching my face, my eyes. "Come on, Alex. Wake up for your mothers."

I'm trying!

Nothing happens.

"Give her time," the unfamiliar voice says. I'm not as sleepy anymore. I'm tired, and my head throbs, but I have a desperation to open my eyes that is eating at me. I need to wake up. *Wake up! What the hell, brain? Get up. Move.* I yell at myself to move.

"Oh, look! Her fingers. She moved," I hear Mom squeal. "Did you see that? Alex. Alex."

I thrash my head side to side, but I can't open my damn eyes.

"It's okay, honey. Calm down. We're here." I feel Mima's comforting palm rubbing my cheeks and then down my arm as she coos. "It's okay. When you're ready, we're here."

The effort, however, overtakes me, and I'm back in the hopeless darkness.

——

I don't know if it's ten minutes later or two days later, since time means nothing right now, but at some point, I open my eyes. I feel instant relief. I move my head, trying to get my bearings.

I had surgery.

Bob is gone, I hope.

My head hurts like a bitch. *Ow.* I cough, and it hurts. *Ow.* My throat feels like I swallowed sand. It must be sometime in the middle of the night.

Shouldn't there be lights? I reach around the bed slowly and then cough again.

"Alex?" Is that Sylvie? "Alex? You're awake! It's me, honey." I hear a noise and then a speaker coming from somewhere else. "She's awake," Sylvie says to the intercom, I think.

"T-turn on th-the . . ." I cough again, and she puts a straw in my mouth.

"Slow. Just a sip," she says, and I do as she instructs.

I clear my throat. "Turn on the light," I croak out. "I can't see a thing."

"Alex?" she says, worry clear and thick in her shaky voice. "The light is on. It's ten in the morning."

I hear fumbling. "Looks like Sleeping Beauty's up." This time, it's a man's voice.

"I—I . . ." My friend is stammering, and her voice is quivering, and I know what is happening. This isn't the same kind of darkness as being in a dark room. I rub my eyes.

"I think she can't see." Sylvie says the words I'm thinking.

"Alex," the man says, and he's holding my lid up. "Look at the light and follow it."

"Turn it on," I say, panic in my voice, and I know, without him actually saying it, that the light is on.

"I'll be right back. I need to page the surgeon." The man's voice—a doctor? A nurse?—it's no longer cheery and friendly, and his tone makes my heart race. I'm no longer Sleeping Beauty. I'm the blind patient. That stupid beep starts to quicken.

"I can't see. Sylvie!" I reach out weakly to her, and I feel her hands take mine, and she entwines them with mine, which are shaking like a leaf. "Sylvie! Sylvie! Please do something." Complete and utter fear overtakes me. I can't live in pitch-black for the rest of my life. It's claustrophobic. I feel around until I feel a dip on my bed, and then my best friend is lying next to me and holding me.

"Listen to me. Take a breath. We knew this was a possibility. We were prepared for this. It's not permanent."

"No, I was prepared for amnesia, not blindness." Although I do remember reading how eye issues usually subside shortly after surgery as the inflammation decreases. Unfortunately, I also read that it could also be permanent.

"It's going to take some time," she says, trying to sound comforting. But it's not comforting, not even a little. "How do you feel otherwise?"

"I don't know. My head hurts a lot," I say, having overlooked the pain when I realized I couldn't see. A moment later, there's the man's voice again.

"Alex, we've ordered an MRI."

"Who's talking?" I ask.

"Sorry. I'm Dr. Fisher, the attending doctor."

"She's had so many scans," Sylvie says.

"I have? What day is it?" I don't remember anything but being wheeled into surgery. Certainly, I don't remember having any scans.

"Friday."

"Ohhh . . ." My surgery was Tuesday. I lost days, a lot of them.

"It's probably fine. Just inflammation. But we need to make sure there's nothing else going on. Let me check the rest of her body," he says.

I reach my trembling hand forward. What I'm reaching for, I have no idea, but my friend takes my hand. I know it's Sylvie's hand instinctually.

"I paged Dr. Chen, and he's up to date on the situation."

"The situation?" Blindness is a situation?

He doesn't answer. "Alex, sit up, please." I try to do as he says even though I can't see a thing. Not having the ability to see anything is the most uncomfortable and unusual feeling. But I can't sit up correctly. I feel like I'm lopsided. There's an eerie silence, and I'm not being touched. It's as if Sylvie and the doctor are having a silent conversation.

"Alex, please sit up."

"I am."

"Both legs forward, please."

I furrow my brow and feel blindly around the bed. My left leg is here, and my right leg is—

"Can you feel this?" he asks.

I start panicking. "Feel what?"

There's more silence.

"Feel what!" I say in terror, and my friend squeezes my hand.

"Alex, he's examining your right leg. You're not feeling anything he's doing?" I can hear her concern.

"You're touching me? Oh my God! I can't feel anything, and I can't see. Sylvie!" I yell in complete panic.

"Take a deep breath, Alex," the doctor says, and Sylvie just holds on to me. I jump slightly when I feel the cold stethoscope against the opening of the hospital gown on my back. I didn't even realize he'd changed from examining my leg to my back. He moves to my front. "Take a deep breath and hold it. Exhale." He repeats this a few times. Then I feel other instruments and his hands touching me. "Are you dizzy?"

"No. I don't think so."

"Lie down." And I feel Sylvie and the doctor help me to a flat position. My leg is lifted, and then someone is pushing my knee back toward my chest, bending at the knee and then the other. "Any tingling? Anything?"

"Nope, nothing," I say. He's holding my right leg, and I can tell because my knee is on my chest, and I feel the movement of the bed as he's moving my leg around. "I can walk, right? I feel my legs. I'm feeling everything you're doing," I say, panicked. He does something. "Oh, I felt that!"

"I'm checking your plantar response. I ran my tool down the sole of your foot."

I sigh in relief. "Well, I felt it, so that's good."

Again with the pregnant pause. "The correct response is for your toes to curl downward. But they didn't move."

"But I felt it!"

"And that's . . . something. But we need them to curl downward. Like when I do this, I need your leg to move forward."

"Do what?"

"I'm checking your patellar reflex. The little hammer on your knee," he explains.

"I'm paralyzed? Is that what that means?" I'm fisting the sheets with my hands at my sides.

"There's no reason to think that just yet. When these tests are skewed, it merely means that there is a disruption of the signal from the ligament or nerve to the brain, and the fact that you had a major surgery on that specific part of your brain, which is now swollen and recovering, could be the cause of this temporary disruption."

"Disruption." I say it under my breath. What a stupid word. I get disrupted at work while I'm trying to focus. Commercials disrupt me when I'm watching TV. Those are annoying nuisances. Not being able to walk is not a disruption. It's a goddamn tragedy! I swallow down the fear and try to sit back up. "If I could just try. I bet if I just got up and walked—" My body would know what to do. I've walked since I was one year old. "One leg in front of the other. Easy peasy."

But the doctor, and I think Sylvie, gently hold me back down.

"I don't want you getting up just yet, Alex. Why don't you start by trying to swing your legs over and just rest them there."

"My head," I say and cup my head. All this is giving me a headache. Or maybe I already had a headache, and the bad news just exacerbated it.

"You're going to have some pain—that's normal."

"Normal? I'm blind and paralyzed and I have a headache. All this is not normal!" I yell at the poor doctor who is not at all at fault.

"It is not normal for other people, Alex. You're right. But for someone who just had a massive tumor removed from their head, it's normal. I'm not sure if the surgeon explained to you after the surgery, but the mass was larger than expected, and it was making its way into the crevices of your skull. The surgery was more complicated than expected. Successful in that we believe all of the tumor was removed and radiation will not be needed, but complicated nonetheless."

"He didn't tell me that."

"She was in a daze when he came and spoke with the family," Sylvie clarifies. "He did tell us that, though."

The pain just starts to intensify, which causes me to get nauseous. I don't want to sit up anymore. I just want to sleep. "Argh," I moan and push my thumb against my forehead. "It hurts."

"If I give you something for the pain, we can't stand you up," he says. "Do you think you can wait just a little?"

I nod. "I'll wait a little."

"Alex." A voice comes from what I can just assume is the door. I know that voice. It's Dr. Chen.

"I can't see," I say in a panic. "And my head. It hurts so much. I can't walk."

I hear whispers, and I can't make them out. "Okay."

He is doing something—I can tell just because I can feel him near me. "What are you doing? What's happening?"

I hear Sylvie crying, and my anxiety is just getting worse and worse. "What? What is it?"

"You don't feel that?" the doctor asks.

I look around—or rather, I try. "Feel what?" I ask.

"I'm pressing my pen against your thigh."

Instinctively, I put my palm against my thigh, and I don't feel it.

"I went up to the pelvis," the other doctor says to Chen. "There's sensation up past the lumbar vertebrae."

"What went up to the pelvis?"

Sylvie, God bless her, takes my hand and narrates what is happening. "The doctor pressed a tool of some sort up your leg all the way to your thigh, and he's going over all of this with Dr. Chen now," she whispers.

"Oh God." I try to stand, but I'm quickly pushed back down. "No!" I yell. "I want to stand. I need to see! Sylvie? Where are my moms?" I want my mothers. I'm thirty-five, but I want my mothers, and I want them to make it all better.

"They went home to shower and change. They'll be back soon, sweetie."

"My head," I moan and yell. "Ow. My head." I'm gently pushed into a flat position. I hear the doctors talking as Sylvie caresses my forehead, and then the world becomes fuzzy again. The pain washes out of my body slowly, and the covers are laid over me. It feels nice, like I'm floating in a pillow of warmth where there's no pain. Soon, I'm asleep.

———

The next time I wake up, my head is on fire, I can't see, and . . . I press a finger to my right thigh to see if there's any changes and nope, nothing. I can't feel my leg. I groan loudly.

"Ay, mija. How are you feeling?" Mima asks, her hand now on my face, cupping it, caressing it.

"My head hurts," I groan.

"I'm going to let the nurse know you're awake," Mom says.

"Mi amor, are you up for a call?"

"No," I quickly answer crabbily. It's not my mother's fault that my life has fallen apart.

"Okay," she says patiently. She smooths out my hair with her palm and doesn't say anything else. She knows me. They both do, and they know when I need space and quiet.

"Mami?" I say after some time. I haven't called my mom Mami since I was a little girl, but it just comes out of my mouth. "I know they did another scan, but I'm afraid to know the results. You know, don't you? Something went wrong with the surgery, didn't it?"

"Ay, mi amor. Don't be scared." I can hear her sniffle. "I don't know the results yet. We've been waiting. But remember that we talked about this, and we knew these were possibilities. The post-op swelling can cause these exact symptoms. We knew this."

"Stop saying that. I know it was a possibility. Sylvie said the same thing. But those were worst-case scenarios. Deep down, we didn't think I would be the one experiencing all of it. I didn't expect it. I should have just left the tumor where it was. If it killed me, so be it. This is worse, Mima. I can't see. Do you understand? You're not even a shadow. It's just black, like if my eyes were closed!" And I break down in sobs. Sobs so loud, I don't hear Mom walk in, but I know she's there when I have two soothing pairs of hands trying to comfort me, even though my moms are crying too. This is what I didn't want. But I also realize that they're stronger than I give them credit for. They'll be fine so long as I'm trying to fight my way out of this. But it's so damn hard to be strong when I feel like an invalid.

I welcome the comfort for the first time. Normally, I balk at it and push it away, but right now it's all I have. I cry for a long time, and I can hear my mothers trying to stifle their own sobs. "It's okay," I tell them because I appreciate their being strong for me, but I also understand they're hurting. "I know you're upset too. You don't have to hide it from me."

"Good afternoon." I hear Dr. Chen's familiar voice. I think he's dragging something with him because I hear wheels rolling on the linoleum floor. Then some clicks and clacks on a keyboard and mouse. "The results of the MRI and of the CT scan are in," he says, and then he's quiet.

I swear to God, years from now, when I look back at this moment, I'll retell it as if there were dead silence in the room for four hours. That's how long and heavy the pause is as he reads the novel that must be my results.

"What? What!" I yell in frustration. "Just say it already!"

"He's reading, honey," Mom says, and I try to calm down, but it's so hard.

"I'm sorry. I can't see, so I don't know what's going on." If they only knew what your mind imagines when you can't see. In my mind's eye, the never-ending silence, in my addled brain, is Dr. Chen giving my mothers the terrible news. *I'll never walk or see again.* "Please don't leave me in the dark." Literally and figuratively.

"There's a lot of swelling, more than expected. We really won't know exactly what is happening, neurologically, until that swelling dissipates. But there's no reason to believe this isn't temporary. I've already called for OT and PT, and I want that to start immediately. What we don't want is for your muscles to atrophy or for you to lose muscle mass. The treatment will augment your ability to start walking again once the inflammation goes down."

"And how long will that be?" I ask, already knowing the answer: *I don't know.*

"Hard to say. Let's give it about three weeks and we can reevaluate."

"Three weeks!"

"Give or take. I suspect you'll start feeling some tingling on your leg and maybe a little improvement on the vision sooner than that, but it may not just come back all at once. I don't want to keep exposing you to scans if we can't see anything through the inflammation. Better to wait."

"Good news, then," Mima says with fake enthusiasm. I know her. She's not even an optimistic person generally. There's no way she's smiling and thinking happy thoughts right now with the news we've just received.

There's a knock coming from the door just as the doctor says, "I'll be back tomorrow morning." I feel him squeeze my shoulder like he did that fateful day when he gave me the bad news about Bob.

There's another knock. "Come in," Mom says.

"Hey, champ." My ears perk up. Oh no. No. No. No. "You wouldn't take my calls," he says. I can hear his footsteps, his gait long and confident, as he walks across the room. "So I had no choice but to swing by."

"David? What are you doing here?" I pat the space around my bandaged head, as if that somehow will make me more presentable. I know some hair was shaved off, but most of it is covered by gauze, and the rest of my hair is just a rats' nest. I may not be super girlie, but I don't want the man I kissed to see me like this. I bring the covers up higher. If I could toss them over my head, I would. Oh God, and my breath. When was the last time I brushed my teeth? I hide my mouth under the sheets.

"Oh, are you David?" Mima asks. "I recognize you from the photos."

"Yes," he says. "And you must be Alex's mothers; it's so nice to finally meet you both." There's some exchange of pleasantries as Mom and Mima introduce themselves.

"You shouldn't have come," I say and flip to my side, away from all the visitors. It takes a lot of effort, and I have to physically lift my right leg with my hands to get it to move. But I really don't want him to see me right now.

"Yeah? Why's that, Alex?" he asks, and I feel a dip on the bed from behind me.

"I don't want company."

"Then you shoulda taken my calls and told me so." He smooths some hair away from my face, and I can't help but love the feel of his big, calloused hand. I vaguely remember Mom asking me if I was up for phone calls, and I said no. Ugh. I should've answered.

"She's stubborn, but she's worth it," Mom says.

"Glad you came. She could use the cheering up," Mima says, and I roll my eyes. "We're going to grab some dinner, and we'll give you both some privacy."

I groan and try and lift the covers over my head, but he stops me. "Hey," he says. "I don't remember you being so grumpy."

"Yeah, well, you don't really know me."

"I think I know you pretty well, actually." He stands up, and for a split second, I think he's going to leave, but instead he just comes to the other side of the bed, and I feel his breath close to my face. I rub my eyes and blink repeatedly, but it's the same as when they're closed. There's nothing, just a void. "Talk to me, Alex. Look at me."

"You didn't hear? I can't look at you. I'm blind now."

"I heard you can't see, but no one told me you were blind. I didn't take you for being melodramatic."

"Not being able to see and being blind are the same thing."

"Maybe. But according to Sylvie, who is very nice but also very scary, whether or not you're blind is something to be determined in a few weeks. Right now, this is just a temporary consequence of a major surgery."

"How'd you get in touch with Sylvie?"

"I kept calling you, and finally she answered your phone and told me everything, and then we exchanged numbers, and she's kept me up to date. I was able to take some time off work, so I came."

"You took time off for me?"

"Who better?"

My lips start to tremble. Shit, I'm going to cry. I feel arms around me, and they feel good and comforting. I want to be enveloped in the arms, and I want this nightmare to go away. I'm the worst feminist ever!

"So a meningioma, huh?"

"Sexy, right?"

"We talked for four days nonstop, and you didn't tell me about the tumor. You should've told me."

"It's not something that you bring up in casual conversation."

"We didn't have casual conversation and you know that. We had a connection. A pretty deep one, I thought. How shallow do you think I am?" There's an edge to his voice, but he's still holding me.

"I don't think you're shallow. I just—I don't know, David. I've never done this before."

"Done what, exactly?"

"Had a fling? An affair? I don't know what to call what I feel." I wouldn't normally let myself sound so vulnerable, but I guess when

220

you're in the hospital and feel like you're on death's door, there's no need to beat around the bush. "David, I used to be married to the only man I ever slept with, and I wasn't sure what the protocol was for tumor disclosures."

I can feel his chest vibrate. "The only protocol is honesty, Alex."

"I'm sorry, David."

"You're forgiven," he says and kisses my temple. "I like you, Alex. Life's not perfect, but you're brave, funny, independent, and I'm not going to let a little tumor stop me from seeing you."

"It was actually a big tumor, which is not even the problem at the moment. There's also blindness and walking. Why would you want to deal with all that? Oh, and I quit my job."

"Well, you've been very busy." I hear him laugh. "Didn't I just tell you that I like you? I don't give up on people I like. Friends or people who I want to be more than friends with. So I'm not going anywhere."

"You don't even live in the same state. We have so many things working against us."

"You are really good at running away from reality, huh? Anything else you want to tell me to convince me to leave? Because nothing you've said is making me want to go."

I squeeze him tighter and then mumble a sob into his chest, which smells so good. "I wish I could see your face."

"I thought you didn't cry."

"Apparently this tumor came with tears."

He chuckles.

"I'm learning to be more open, and I feel like I can be myself with you, which is very disconcerting, if I'm being honest."

"Glad to hear it."

"I really like you too, David."

"Good."

I smile, and then I feel him stand. "Come on, sit up."

"I don't want to."

"Blah, blah, blah." He pulls me from under my armpits into a sitting position, and I let him. It's something that I'm going to have to do more often because I can't do it myself.

"I look terrible."

"You're blind; how would you know?"

I smirk.

"Too soon?" he asks, and then I actually smile.

"When do you have to go?"

"Tomorrow. Unfortunately, I couldn't get more time off."

"You're so sweet, David."

"I try." I can sense a smirk. "Can you feel this?"

"No. What are you doing?"

"I'm rubbing your calf muscles," he says, and again I let him. He takes my arms and twists them and rubs my biceps.

"What are you doing? I can feel my arms, you know."

"I know, but you're going to start overcompensating for your lower body by using your upper body more. You're going to be sore. You feel what I'm doing? You should do that every day. I'm going to send your moms and Sylvie some exercises they can do with you. Your PT will mostly focus on your legs, and your moms can help you with your upper body."

"Oh, okay. Thanks." He does this for a while, and I can feel the tension leaving my shoulders. "Ahhh . . . this is nice."

He chuckles.

Unfortunately, there's a chime followed by the hospital speaker indicating that visiting hours are about to end, so David shifts me around and helps me back down. "Try and sit up as much as you can during the day. Don't be prone in bed all day."

"Having a nurse around sure is handy."

I don't have to have sight to know he's smiling. Once I'm all tucked in, he says, "I'm going to take off. It's late, and I have to check in to my hotel. I'll come by again tomorrow."

"Yoo-hoo!" I hear from the door.

"It's Margot and Sylvie; can we come in? We only have a few minutes before they kick us out. Oh—"

"Whoa, who's this?" That's Sylvie.

"David."

"Oh, David. We thought you'd be getting in tomorrow. We were hoping to doll you up a little before he arrived," Margot says, presumably to me.

"You knew he was coming?"

"Yeah. He's been calling every day."

"Nice to meet you all." I hear shuffling and introductions going around. Then I feel David's lips on my forehead. "See you tomorrow, Alex."

"Thanks for everything, David."

And then I hear feet moving away.

"Well, that was nice," Margot says, but I've turned over (with a lot of difficulty) and pulled the covers over my head.

"Oh, Alex . . . it's okay," Margot says and then hugs me.

"I can't see, and I'm frustrated and sad and tired. I don't even know who is in the room right now. It's just black." I start to sob into my pillow.

"I'm here." It's Sylvie.

"And me." It's Margot. "And there're balloons and flowers from the office and one huge arrangement of roses from Bernard. Bernie wanted to come visit, but I didn't think you wanted visitors quite yet."

"I don't. Please just go. I have a headache. Please."

I feel the bed dip behind me, and just by the feel of her hand against my skin, I know it's Mima. "Qué pasa?"

"What's wrong? Seriously?"

"You were fine a little bit ago."

"I wasn't fine. Nothing about this is fine."

"You actually cry a lot for someone who doesn't cry," Sylvie says, and I feel a dip on the bed behind me.

I give her the finger, and she laughs.

"You're frustrated and scared, but you're not alone," Mima says. "This, too, shall pass."

"And if it doesn't?"

"Then we'll figure it out," Mom says from somewhere else in the room.

"You're not alone," Margot says. "We're all here for you."

"You should know that Donna and Heather have been calling, too, and they sent you a card and a bottle of tequila," Mom says.

I wipe my nose with the back of my hand and smile. "Really?"

"Yep," Mima says and gives me a kiss by my temple.

"Visiting hours are over, ladies," I hear from the door.

I'm peppered in kisses. "Get some rest, mi amor. Mañana I'm getting you out of this bed, like it or not."

Then I don't hear anyone anymore.

I wish they had all stayed.

CHAPTER THIRTEEN

The next morning, a nurse, who I may just hate, comes inside my room and loudly and with a singsong voice says, "Good morning, sunshine." My circadian rhythm is all screwed up, but I'm assuming it's early by the noise coming from the halls as new nurses change shifts. I'm tired. Exhausted. Cranky. I groan and move the covers high above my head.

"Oh no. No. No. Time to get up, Alex. You have a busy, busy day."

"I'm exhausted. You guys woke me up every hour, and I have to pee."

"This isn't a hotel, darlin'. Don't want you gettin' too comfortable here. The goal is to get you fixed and outta here."

"Fixed? Is this even possible?"

"Only if you think it's possible. Don't give up on me just yet."

"I'm not giving up. I just can't see. I can't possibly do PT without eyesight."

"Sure you can." She pulls the covers from my head. "You can hear, right? You can feel? That's all you need."

"What's your name, by the way?"

"Nurse Morris, but you can call me Peggy."

"Peggy, I have a feeling you're going to be a pain in my butt."

She chuckles. "You, my dear, are a great judge of character."

A few minutes later, Peggy is helping me out of bed and into a wheelchair. Then I'm wheeled to the bathroom as she gives me very clear instructions so that I can move, wobbly and awkwardly, onto the toilet seat. I had a catheter in since the surgery (fun!), but it was removed last night (even funner!), so it's now on me to use the facilities all on my own.

"I can't do it!" I whine. "I can't even see." I feel tears coming out of my eyes.

"Of course you can do it. You don't need to see to pee," she says, and I can feel her strong forearms slide under my armpits and steer me the right way. "Use whatcha got, Alex. You can put weight on your left leg." The thing is . . . it's not that it's painful so much as difficult. My instinct is to stand up and take a step. I tell my brain to do just that. Except my leg doesn't cooperate. It's a floppy dead limb that dangles, and I have to use the weight on my other leg together with my upper-body strength to go from the wheelchair to the toilet seat.

I'm sobbing now. Is this going to be my life? I can't remember the headaches being all that painful now. Maybe I shouldn't have had the surgery. "Are you going to sit and cry or are you going to use the bath-room? I ain't got all day."

"It's not that easy!" I yell. I know I'm being difficult, but this is difficult.

"No one said it would be," she says, and then somehow, between the complaining and the crying, my ass is on the toilet seat, and it feels like the world's greatest accomplishment. I don't even care that she's surely watching me, that the door may be open . . . I just had this tiny wonderful victory and that's all that matters right now. "It's gonna hurt this first time because of the Foley, but you gotta try. Let it flow."

"I don't need a cheering squad, Peggy," I say, but she doesn't leave or stop talking. In fact, she completely ignores me and turns on the faucet because she says the sound of water makes some people want to go. The sensation to go is there—in fact, I have to go so badly, it's actually painful, but nothing happens. "Oh God, is my pee broken too?"

"No, I told you it would be hard. Focus and relax your muscles, otherwise the doctor will want to put the Foley back in, and let me tell you, sweetie . . . it's not pleasant to have that put in."

"You're not helping, Peggy."

She chuckles. "I'm going to change your bed linens and give you some privacy. Do not attempt to get up on your own, you hear?"

"I won't."

"Okay, I'll be back in a minute."

Maybe I do need a cheering squad. When Annabel was eight years old, she went through a reality-cheerleading-show phase. It was so annoying. She would clap and toss her arms up in fists or do splits all over the house. "C-e-r-e-a-l! Eat your cereal! Woo-hoo!" I would roll my eyes and groan at the early-morning peppiness. But right now, I would love to hear a peeing cheer, and I smile thinking that my sister would undoubtedly be standing next to me cheering me on, and I'd be rolling my eyes and possibly cursing at her. I actually laugh out loud.

"Everything all right in there?" Peggy hollers from the other room.

"Yes. All good," I reply back and take breaths and try and relax as the pressure in my bladder mounts. Eventually, a tiny tinkle comes out. It's painful at first, like a really heavy sensation in the lower part of my belly, but once it starts flowing, it is the best relief. "Ahhhh . . ." I sigh, and she laughs.

When I'm done, I reach until I feel the toilet paper. Victory number two: finding toilet paper.

Unfortunately, however, there's no victory number three anytime soon, because getting back into the wheelchair and subsequently to the bed is probably the single hardest thing I've ever had to do. Which means that after the one simple task of waking up and using the restroom, my head is pounding like a lumberjack.

I remember when I sat down on that cliff in the middle of the canyon to look at the sunrise. I was worried that I'd forget. The thing that had made me the most apprehensive about the surgery was the memory loss. How interesting that blindness almost feels like the antonym of amnesia. Since I cannot see, I have to completely rely on my memory. I can imagine the way Nurse Peggy looks even if I've never seen her. I know what Mima is wearing when she hugs me, even if I can't see her. I can vividly recall the sweet smell of the humid rain forest in Costa Rica. All I have are my memories and my imagination.

I rub my eyes as if that'll somehow make the blackness disappear. I've heard that some blind people can still see shadows, but I cannot see shadows. God, I'm not a praying woman, but if you can hear me—if you're thinking of giving me back only one thing, my ability to walk or my ability to see—please let me see again.

I know Mima has been praying the rosary and lighting candles on my behalf; every Catholic saint has been activated and is on the case. But I need to talk to God myself right now.

Except God doesn't hear me, because my eyes are open, though I can feel the tears sliding down my face into darkness.

———

"I think she's given up," Mima says.

"Her sight's not better. Hell, her headaches are worse than before the surgery." That's Mom.

"All of this is caused by swelling, just like with any surgery," Dr. Chen says. "Nothing that she's experiencing is abnormal. I understand it's difficult, but I still believe that she should make a full recovery."

"Believe? That's not giving me the hope I need," Mom says, her words breaking.

"I don't think she's given up. I think she's frustrated," Dr. Chen adds. "I'm going to get a psych consult, just in case."

"Psych?"

"Just to help with the depression."

Mima sniffles, and I move my pinkie, then my thumb, until I'm awake enough to reach my arm forward and feel for a hand. It's Mom. I can just tell.

"Oh, honey," Mom says. "You're up."

"Don't cry," I croak, trying to wake up. I'm drowsy.

"We're not crying," Mima says.

"Yes, you are," I say.

"How are you feeling, Alex?"

"Tired."

"Anything else? It's Dr. Chen, by the way." I can feel him pressing against my chest with his stethoscope and poking my legs, and I yelp.

There is a collective silence in the room.

"Do that again!" I feel a pinprick on my calf area.

"You felt that? How about this?"

I nod and shake my head as he probes different places. It feels like pins and needles, whereas I felt nothing yesterday.

"This is good. We expect a little more with time. I need you to give it your all at therapy, Alex."

I nod and hear my mothers say goodbye to the doctor.

"Can one of you help me sit up?" I say.

"Of course," Mom says, and I feel her take my hands. "Sit up first, and then I'll help you shift your legs over."

"Ow!" I squeal. "You're not very good at being a nurse."

"Never said I was a nurse," she says.

"Vamos, work yourself into a sitting position," Mima says from nearby, one mom on each side. I'm sick of *"vamos."* It's become her favorite word since I've been in this hospital. It means *let's go*, and every time she says *vamos*, I want to yell at her to let me sleep. It's too hard. But eventually, with a lot of core strength, I'm able to sit up. "Okay, now we'll help you with your feet."

"I'm tired," I say breathlessly. It takes so much effort just to sit up. "Let's wait for the nurse. It's too hard."

"Nope. Vamos," Mima says, and I groan. It's that word again. Mom helps me move my legs, which are like limp noodles, and Mima pulls me up. It's humiliating and demoralizing to be moved about in the darkness by your mothers, and tears slide down my face. I know they see them, but they don't say anything.

"Good," Mom says. "Almost there."

It's a struggle—mostly a mental one but a struggle nonetheless—and by the time my legs are just hanging by the side, I'm out of breath. My mothers then tuck some pillows behind me to make me comfortable.

My phone rings from somewhere in the room. "Hello," Mima says; then there's a moment of silence as the other person talks. "Oh, David, guess what! She felt something just now. Yes . . . around her legs. I know, it's wonderful. And we sat her up, and we're going to do some of those exercises you emailed. Oh, yes, sure, one sec." And then the phone is placed in my hand. "It's David, honey."

How long was I asleep? I think I woke up, went to the bathroom again, complained about pain, and was given medicine, so mostly it's been sleep and loss of time. I vaguely remember David coming in and saying goodbye. He had to go back to work and promised to call and visit soon. Oh, I wish I had been more conscious. He gave me a very sweet kiss on the lips. I mumbled something that I hope was also sweet but can't currently remember, and then I went back to sleep.

"David?"

"How're you doing, Alex?"

"I'm not sure. Drowsy. Anxious," I admit. "Are you back home?"

"Yep. Caught the red-eye and went straight to work."

"Oh no. You must be exhausted."

"A little, but I wanted to call before my head hit the pillow and I passed out."

"I appreciate your coming to visit."

"No need to thank me. Keep fighting, Alex, and you'll get through this."

"Always so positive," I say.

I can feel him smile. It's amazing how you feel reactions. Or maybe I'm making it up, but in my mind's eye, he's smiling, and I'm sticking to that. "Talk soon, Alex."

"Later, David." I place the phone on the bed. "I feel so helpless not being able to see or walk. Just sitting here and having you guys take care of me."

"We're your moms—that's what moms do."

"But I can't see. I can't walk. I can't do anything, and everyone is worrying about me, and I just want to give up!"

"We can be your eyes. We'll be your legs. You can do a lot on your own, and the rest we'll do for you. But you have to just accept that we're going to help you, and you have to stop feeling guilty or worried or whatever the hell else you're feeling." Mima is practically yelling at me in frustration.

I exhale and slump forward. "I've been thinking . . . I can't remember Annabel being mad that she was sick or even sad. She was either happy or just tired and frail. How could she have been so strong? I wish I had that. I'm so scared and frustrated that it's hard to see the light at the end of the tunnel."

"Honey, you were so young too. You just don't remember. Annabel was just as frustrated as you are right now. She had good days, and she had bad days. I remember one particular day, we were going home after an especially tough round of chemo, and she asked us, point-blank, if we knew when she was going to die. She wanted a date. We weren't prepared to answer that for so many reasons, and we were so shocked by her question, because we weren't sure how much she understood. She knew what was happening, honey, and I think she had come to terms with it. She tried to fight as much as she could, but her little body just couldn't fight anymore. She was scared, and she tried to be tough for us all, but she knew, Alex. She knew."

My eyes water, but it gives me a bit of comfort, in a macabre way, that my sister wasn't just living in this fantasy world where everything was rosy and death came out of nowhere. She was a fighter and she was fierce and she did all that she could to survive. She'd be proud that I'm doing the same thing.

"And she welcomed our help. Not just because she needed it but because we needed it too," Mima says. I never thought of it that way. They need to help because they are my mothers and they can't just sit back and watch from afar. They couldn't physically remove the tumor, but they can help me recover.

Relief begins to wash away years of worry, and I just let my moms be moms.

"Don't worry about everyone else. Everyone has a choice. If they didn't want to worry and dote on you, they wouldn't. That includes us."

I'm not making anyone be with me. I would do the same. I just hate being a burden.

"You have OT in an hour. Why don't you tell us more about your trip and about David? We like him, by the way."

We spend the next hour talking while they massage my arms, like David showed them. I tell them all about my trip, and about Donna and Heather, and of course more about David. At some point, Mom leaves and returns with some food, since I mentioned I was craving a Cuban sandwich from my favorite Cuban restaurant.

"We have a problem," I say.

"What is it?" Mom asks.

"I have to go to the bathroom. Call a nurse."

I hear one of them press the button to the nurse station. It's become a familiar beep. I can now tell the difference between one beep and another.

"Let's try going together," Mom says and I can hear her rolling the wheelchair over. "You have a bit more feeling in your leg, and we're here."

"I don't know . . . what if I fall?"

"How many times did you let your sister fall?"

"Never!" I say indignantly.

"Exactly. You're not going to fall, but if you do, we'll help you up."

"Okay," I say, unfamiliar with all this power I'm relinquishing by accepting everyone's help.

I reach forward, and Mima takes my hand. I know it's Mima by her lush and moisturized skin. I think Mom is guiding the wheelchair. "Okay, now like the nurse showed you. Use this board and slide yourself over." I can feel the board placed between the bed and the chair, and now that I can feel a little more, I start scooting over, inch by inch, while trying to hold on to my bladder. "Uno, dos, y tres," Mima counts, and then, with their combined mom-strength, I'm on the wheelchair.

"Easy," Mom says.

"Not at all. Hurry and push me, or I won't make it."

Mom wheels me into the bathroom and maneuvers the chair, and Mima takes my hands, and it's a united effort, but among the three of us, I'm on the toilet seat sort of, kind of the way I've now done a few times with Nurse Peggy.

"We did it!" Mima says, and I chuckle. I'm in the bathroom unable to see or walk and both my mothers are inside cheering me on. How could I ever have doubted them? They're strong and fiercely protective and they're, well . . . my people.

Barely a year ago, I was heartbroken over Michael, "my person," but here, in a hospital bathroom as I pee, I'm realizing that he wasn't my person even when I thought he was. He didn't know me completely. In his defense, I didn't show him who I was. I was hiding behind fears, people-pleasing, and my past. But my mothers, they know me—the real me. Even if I were still married right this moment, I think I'd want my support system to remain Mom and Mima.

"Thank you," I say. "Both of you. Thank you."

"You can't thank your mothers for helping you in a time like this. It's just what moms do, honey," Mom says.

———

But, like with everything in life, things don't always turn out the way you hope, and the next two weeks are a bitch. There's no other word to describe it. It's a special kind of hell where I try my darndest to improve, then fall into a desperate depression for a few days when I don't see any improvement.

Every day, my mothers are here with me, in shifts. Mom does the day shift, and Mima does the evening shift; she even finagled herself special permission to stay well past visiting hours. I've heard the nurses talking, and I don't think they like Mima very much, which makes me giggle. She's always bossing them around or asking for something, even though she brings them a big box of fresh pastelitos, croquetas, and cafecito every day.

"I brought you your pajamas from home, mi amor," she says one day when she gets there. I may not be able to see, but I can hear her determination. "I cannot see you in that blue thing one more moment. And I brought nail polish to do your nails."

With all the stuff going on around me, my appearance is not very high on my list of priorities. I hear movement and shuffling around.

"What are you doing?" I ask.

"I went to T.J.Maxx this morning, and I brought a few things to make this room feel more like home. Those things make a difference, you know? I also brought your great-grandmother's wooden crucifix."

"The enormous one you have on the wall by the family room?"

"Yes." Her *yes* sounds more like a *jes*.

"Mima, that's huge; where are you putting it?"

"Right by the armoire in front of you—that way you remember to say a little prayer every night and every morning."

I don't remind her that I can't see and therefore that a huge cross will not serve its purpose—I don't want to hurt her feelings or make her sad. Plus, I did grow up Catholic, and it does give me some comfort that it's there. At the very least, it's a familiar piece of home.

"And what did you buy from T.J.Maxx?"

"A few things you'll love. Relax." She pats my head, and I continue to feel her wandering around the room, "decorating."

"Tomorrow, they're going to take off that bandage, and then Peggy promised to help me wash your hair."

I reach to the back of my head, and I can feel a rats' nest and the bandage that's wrapped around the front of my head like a headband. There's also a patch that is shaved and then another part that's full of dried blood and gunk. Washing my hair sounds like heaven.

"I can't wait for that."

"Good. And I was thinking that after you get up and dressed, you can sit on the chair, not the bed, and you can show me how to find those YouTube videos of your friends."

Even though I know she's using all the diversion tactics she has in her arsenal, watching Heather and Donna's misadventures gives me something to look forward to.

And that's what we do. I show her, from memory (which is frustrating as hell), what she needs to press on her phone to get to YouTube and then to The Traveling Gals' page. I listen to, while she watches, video after video of my new friends traveling all over the world, and by the time Mima is ready to leave, I have a big smile on my face. The site and their videos are a mess—which became easier to tell the harder it got to steer Mima through the site. There's no branding or structure that I remember, and I think they've mostly been lucky that they've been as successful as they've been. It's a testament to their personalities. I know I can help them. I don't know exactly how, but brainstorming it gets my creative juices flowing, and that's something that has not flowed for a long, long time.

———

Some mornings, I get up feeling a renewed sense of hope and try my best, and other days I feel hopeless. And even though last night ended on a positive note, this morning, I do not wake up on the peak. I'm at the valley, low and dejected. I'm supposed to continue PT and OT and all the Ts from home as of the end of the week. On paper, I'm fine. All the blood tests and medical exams have been coming back normal, and as the swelling has reduced, I can actually limp now, since the feeling in that leg is back. The doctors can now see from the scans that Bob the Blob was completely and successfully removed. They do not see any sign of him in my body.

I should be thrilled with the news.

Yet I'm still limping or worse, because my leg tends to fall asleep and then I'm completely incapable of using it, and I'm still blind.

"Vamos! Levantate," Mima yells at me one afternoon when she gets to the hospital and I'm still in bed. I know that Mom already told her I didn't get out of bed. It's Sunday; there's no therapy, and I'm tired and frustrated.

"I don't want to get up."

"I care that you cannot give up. I care that you get better. But whether or not you want to get up, that I do not care about."

I start to sob. It feels so hopeless. Yesterday, I worked on how to get dressed by myself, with the OT. My mind boggles at the fact that I'm having to relearn how to do mundane everyday-life things, under this "new normal." I don't want to learn how to dress myself in blindness with limited mobility, because I don't want to be blind and I don't want to have limited mobility.

"It's not fair. This was supposed to happen to someone else. This was supposed to be rare." I know I sound like a whiny brat, but it's my mom I'm talking to, not some stranger, and I need to vent.

"I know, honey. I wish it was someone else and not you. But it is you, and these are the cards you've been dealt. I didn't let Annabel give up, and I'm sure as hell not letting you give up. So get your cute little butt up and out of bed, ahora mismo."

I groan.

"Vamos. I want to see you get dressed, and then we're going to go for a little stroll around the hall."

"I'm tired."

"You're depressed," she corrects me. "I know how it feels to just want to lay in bed and sleep. It took all the strength I had to get up and take a shower, and you know why I did?" she asks, and I shake my head. "Because of you, that's why. I know I messed up, and there's not a day that goes by that I don't feel guilt and regret and hope that you'll forgive me for being such a crappy mom—"

"You weren't a crappy mom."

"Not always, but for a while I was. I know I let you down after Annabel died, but I swear to you, honey, the things I did manage to do, the getting up to shower, the having lunch . . . I did it for you. You were what motivated me when I had no motivation. And now, if you don't want to get up for you, then get up for me. Please. Vamos. Up." She cups my face with her hands and wipes away my tears with her thumbs. Then she kisses my forehead. "Vamos, Alex. Get up." And she takes my hands in hers. I don't fight her; I sit up, and with all the effort I don't feel like I have left, I eventually get up and get dressed. I groan and curse a few times when my socks fall down and I can't find them and Mima doesn't help. But eventually I'm finished, and I'm proud of myself and my mom.

This is the fiery woman I remember growing up with. She's been gone for so long, I had forgotten how wonderfully terrifying she can be when she puts her mind to it.

———

"Good afternoon, Ms. Martinez, I'm Dr. Torres. I understand you've missed a few therapy sessions." This is a new voice. It's the next morning. Even though the day ended a little better than it began, I'm still feeling down. "If all goes well, you'll be discharged in a couple of days, and Dr. Chen and the therapists are concerned. I've been called in for a consult."

My back is turned away from the voice. I cannot stop crying. I want to stop crying, but I just can't. It's like all the frustration and agony and pain I've ever suffered have been unleashed.

"It's normal to feel depressed after such a major operation," he continues. "I've reviewed your chart, and I'd like to start you on an antidepressant. As another part of the plan, I'm also recommending therapy. There's also support groups that I think you'd find helpful. Talking about it—"

"I don't want to talk. I just want to walk and see again. Listening to other people's depressing stories won't help. I have my own depressing story. I don't need someone else's."

"You'd be surprised. People don't go to support groups just to listen to other people's sob stories. They go because empathizing with others who are going through the same thing is helpful to one's recovery. I bet if you went, you'd find it helpful."

"I'm not going to turn down the meds, but I don't think a support group or therapy or talking it out are going to do anything but make it worse. In fact, part of the crying is because I'm crying." When did I become this weak person who just cries all day? It's so frustrating.

"Everyone cries. Ms. Martinez, people need to talk about their emotions—whether you talk to someone you love or a stranger. Sometimes it's easier when it's a stranger, but the fact that you think you're not the kind of person who can show emotion makes me even more certain that you need therapy." I hear him type something. "My information will be in your discharge papers. I'd like to follow up with you in my office in a month. Meds without therapy will not help as much as doing them simultaneously. I highly recommend you attend. At the very least, it won't hurt, right?"

I don't answer him, because I think it will hurt. I think the more I talk, the more I cry. I just want to see again. How hard is that to understand?

———

I've been home for a week. Mom walks in just as I'm finishing breakfast that Mima served me. I don't need to see in order to eat. "What's that smell?"

"Oh, just some bougainvillea I trimmed," Mom says, and then she gets closer, and I see a shade of purple or pink or something other than darkness.

"Oh my God!" I yelp and reach forward and grab whatever she's holding that has a tinge of color that I can actually see.

"Ow!" I yelp the moment my fingers come into contact with a thorn.

"Be careful, Alex!"

"Mom, I can see this. It's purple."

"Oh my God! Yes! It's a bunch of bougainvillea I clipped and I'm going to try and propagate."

"What's all the yelling?" Mima asks, and I can see a fuzzy figure walk into the room.

"I can see."

"Ay, gracias a Dios!" Mima thanks God. "Why are you bleeding?" She takes my hand in hers while Mom presses a paper towel to it.

"She grabbed the flowers, and they had thorns."

"I'm fine. It's fine." I take my hands away and stand. I still can't fully walk, but I'm much better. I grab both my mothers and hug them. "Annabel and her wild bougainvillea, of all things. Of course I'd be able to see them."

I can't see anything but figures and blobs, as if someone rubbed Vaseline in my eyes, but it's something, and it beats darkness.

This might not be much, but for me it's the little, tiny bit of hope that I needed. Everyone is now in a group chat—Sylvie, Margot, David, Heather, Donna, and Bernie. It's just easier to have that one text group to update everyone. I tell them all the good news.

I learned how to dictate messages on my phone, thanks to Sylvie, who set it up for me. The phone even reads them back to me. Thank God for technology. My messages could possibly be full of typos—I remember how dictating text always comes up all wonky—but I can tell my friends got the gist of it when everyone is excited for the progress.

———

I do wish I had something else to keep me distracted. Without AutoRey, I don't have much to do these days, even if I were fully recovered. I've listened to most of Donna and Heather's blogs already, but I decide to finish them. Not only are they hilariously entertaining, but I get so many ideas every time I listen. I have at least a dozen voice notes on my phone with things I want to talk to them about. Goodness, if Annabel were alive, we could have done a blog just like this. It would have been hilarious and informative and just as entertaining. Alex and Annabel Travel Abroad. The Sister Traveling Channel. I have no doubt we would have been just as close as Heather and Donna.

When I met them, I didn't realize exactly how well traveled they were. They've gone to so many places and filmed themselves. Because of their personalities, the videos became a hit for no reason other than the girls are a riot. But I have an angle. Everything in marketing needs an angle. A niche.

I open the email app and start drafting an email with my idea.

Ladies,

Thank you for keeping me entertained during the last month. I needed a laugh—your videos never disappoint. I've been researching, and there are a lot of traveling bloggers, more than I could even attempt to count. The reason The Traveling Gals has so many subscribers is because you're funny and quirky, but you don't have a product to sell or even a reason why people would follow up—other than your personalities, of course. Let's give people reasons to look you up. Let's focus on traveling single. People do it all the time, but it would be great to have a place to find resources for the best restaurants if you're dining alone or tour companies if you're solo or safest places a single woman can stay in certain cities. That should be your niche.

I keep throwing ideas at them and possible sponsorships, and I can't wait to hear their thoughts. I think it should be called Party of One.

"Wooo-hooo!" I yell out and toss my hands up.

———

To say that my life got tied up with a nice little bow and things just went back to normal would be a complete lie. When you have surgery, they tell you all the things that could go wrong; then they tell you that the probability of those things actually happening is slim to none. Obviously with certain procedures, like brain surgery, those percentages are higher. But the need to have the surgery outweighs those possible repercussions, so you move forward and you do the thing, thinking you're not going to be the person who wins the side-effect lottery.

I may never see again at 100 percent, and I may never walk again at 100 percent, but I learned that when life gives me lemons, I have family and friends willing to make lemonade for me. I thought I had to do it all alone. I thought being vulnerable made you weak, but I was wrong. Asking for help, sticking around when things get hard, and being authentic, that makes you strong. It turns out that I didn't have a person all to myself. I have quality people.

EPILOGUE

I'd like to tell you that I recovered completely and that everything was great when I went back to work five months after my surgery, doing freelance marketing for Heather and Donna and a few other small companies that I'm helping. But that is a lie.

It's been a year since my surgery, and I'm still in therapy, I still get sad every now and again, and I sometimes need a cane. It's a cool-ass cane that David sent me, however. We call it a walking stick, but it's a cane, with an elaborate handle, that he carved himself. I underestimated his whittling abilities, and it's beautiful.

I'm grateful every day that I can walk and even go on jogs (when my leg is cooperating, of course). The headaches are gone, so that's something good. I went from profound visual impairment to moderate. The peripheral vision from my left eye is almost all the way back, but my right eye is still unreliable. But I went from darkness, to shadows, to color. So I have hope. I still can't drive, but I can go on my jogs, I can take the bus, I can FaceTime with David, and I am working every day on getting Party of One sponsorships and ad deals, and so far it's been a great success.

And one of the best things that's happened is that I'm blogging my own Party of One trip as a special feature for the site. It's going to focus on traveling as a single person and as someone who needs a bit of accommodation. I'm going back to Arizona. I'm going to my happy place. I'm not scared or embarrassed at having to ask for help anymore, and there's no better tour guide than David.

How convenient, right?

So he's meeting me in Arizona.

During the last year, he's visited me two more times, and we talk every day. I'm sort of in love with him, even if we've barely kissed.

When I arrive in Arizona, the first thing I notice is that his apartment is mostly packed up. There are boxes everywhere. Granted, I've never visited his apartment, but I wouldn't think he's a man who lives out of boxes. But because he knows that I'm scared of commitment and I tend to run, he tells me nonchalantly, "I took a job in Miami."

"You what?"

"Before you say anything, this has nothing to do with you. The pay is great. It's a promotion, and I'm tired of this dry heat. I need humidity and even more heat."

I laugh, because that's such bullshit. I know he's moving there for me, but he's so cautious of scaring me that he's taking baby steps. Little does he know that I don't need baby steps for him. "Oh, is that so? And where exactly are you going to live?"

"If you must know, there's some housing by the hospital that I have applied for, so I'm just waiting on that to be approved, and then I'm going down." He gives me a big kiss. "And also, just in case you want to not live with your mothers one night or two or for a few months, you're welcome to stay with me."

I really, really love my mountain man.

"Anyway, we're not here to look at my apartment or talk about my successful career. We're here to go on a hike."

"We certainly are," I say with excitement.

"Put on your hiking clothes and let's get moving."

"I have to warn you, I'm not as agile as I was the last time."

"We'll take it slow."

I nod, but I'm a bit worried. I switch out my heavy wooden cane to two lightweight hiking sticks. We hop into his car, and he drives and chats about his sister and the move to Miami.

I was in such a bad place last year when I was here. I didn't know it at the time, but I was an emotional mess, and even though I thought I felt fine, I was far from it.

"You okay?" He parks the car and helps me out as we walk toward the trail.

A year ago, I would have smiled, said "I'm fine," and followed him. But I've evolved. "I'm nervous, David. I can't see very well still. What if my leg falls asleep on me?"

He zips up my jacket and fixes my hat and then cups my face in his hands. "Trust me. You're gonna be fine. We're not doing the entire four days. We're just going to one spot, and we'll be back up here tomorrow. We'll go slow, okay?"

I take a deep breath, exhale, take his hand, and we walk into the canyon together.

So here I am a year later, sitting on my rock with my new man. I never told him this was the place I wanted to go back to. This was my place of hope. This was my happy place. I never said those words to him.

"How did you know?"

"How could I not?" He touches my heart, and I put my hand over his. This place takes my breath away. It's where I heard my heartbeat for the first time. I look out and wait for the sunset in silence. Unfortunately, because my eyesight is still healing, I can't see the hues that I saw last year, but I remember them as if I were seeing them in real time. I imagine them, and I'm right there again at that same spot but in very different circumstances.

This time, I'm truly happy.

ACKNOWLEDGMENTS

I really wanted to challenge myself with this one. Wrapping up complicated storylines and plots with a cute romance is always my go-to. But what relationship is more complicated than a mother-daughter relationship? It's the most beautiful, dynamic, and difficult one there is. I'm blessed to have the best mom, and I'm lucky I haven't had the struggles that Alex has faced. That isn't to say I haven't wanted to yell and scream at my mom on many occasions (and vice versa). So the first person I want (and need) to acknowledge is my own mom. Thank you for being unapologetically you. I love you.

With that being said, I have to thank my husband, because he's the one who holds everything together while I'm busy working and in a bad mood because I can't figure out how to resolve a plot point. Just talking it out with you always helps me fix the problem. Also—thank you for being the roach squasher in the house. I, like Alex, draw the feminist line in the sand when it comes to cockroaches. I love you! And my kids and the rest of my immediate family, thank you for being so patient and understanding when I'm on a deadline. One day you'll understand (I hope).

Sarah Younger, my friend, my agent, and my sounding board. Truly, from the bottom of my heart, thank you. Love you. #LadiesWriteNight: Tif, Annie, Rachel, and April, how far we've come. Love you all! Gigi, my cousin, thank you so much for championing TAP and for all your help. Love you!

Finally, Chris and Krista from Lake Union—my dream team! There's nothing more an author needs than someone just "getting it," and you both just get it and that is so appreciated! And thank you so much for making the editing process so easy. I hope to have many, many more chances to work together!

And finally, to my readers, I know how invaluable your time is, and just for the fact that you took the time to read my book, *I thank you*! My heart is full of gratitude.

ABOUT THE AUTHOR

Photo © 2021 CorporateHeadshotsUSA.com

Jeanette Escudero worked as an attorney before picking up a pen at thirty years old to write something other than legal briefs. Being published fulfilled a dream and gave her an outlet for her imaginative, romantic side. Jeanette is the author of *The Apology Project*. Writing as Sidney Halston, she is the *USA Today* bestselling author of the Panic series, the Worth the Fight series, the Iron Clad Security novels, and the Seeing Red duet. In addition to writing and reading, Jeanette has a passion for travel and adventure. She and her family have been to the Galápagos Islands and have hiked Yellowstone, Shenandoah's mountains, and the Great Smoky Mountains. Born in Miami, Florida, to Cuban parents, she currently lives in South Florida with her husband and her three children, in whom she's instilled a love of nature and an appreciation for the planet. For more information, visit www.jeanetteescudero.com.